RAVES FOR
JAMES PATTERSON

"Patterson knows where our deepest fears are buried...there's no stopping his imagination." —*New York Times Book Review*

"James Patterson writes his thrillers as if he were building roller coasters." —Associated Press

"No one gets this big without natural storytelling talent—which is what James Patterson has, in spades."
—Lee Child, #1 *New York Times* bestselling author of the Jack Reacher series

"James Patterson knows how to sell thrills and suspense in clear, unwavering prose." —*People*

"Patterson boils a scene down to a single, telling detail, the element that defines a character or moves a plot along. It's what fires off the movie projector in the reader's mind."
—Michael Connelly

"James Patterson is the boss. End of."
—Ian Rankin, *New York Times* bestselling author of the Inspector Rebus series

Raised by Wolves

For a complete list of books, visit JamesPatterson.com.

Raised by Wolves

JAMES PATTERSON

AND EMILY RAYMOND

Little, Brown and Company
New York Boston London

Little, Brown and Company
Hachette Book Group
1290 Avenue of the Americas, New York, NY 10104
littlebrown.com

First Edition: November 2024

Little, Brown and Company is a division of Hachette Book Group, Inc. The Little, Brown name and logo are trademarks of Hachette Book Group, Inc.

The publisher is not responsible for websites (or their content) that are not owned by the publisher.

The Hachette Speakers Bureau provides a wide range of authors for speaking events. To find out more, go to hachettespeakersbureau.com or email HachetteSpeakers@hbgusa.com.

Little, Brown and Company books may be purchased in bulk for business, educational, or promotional use. For information, please contact your local bookseller or the Hachette Book Group Special Markets Department at special.markets@hbgusa.com.

ISBNs: 9781538767016 (trade paperback), 9781538767030 (hardcover library), 9781538770351 (large print), 9781538767023 (ebook)

LCCN: 2024935721

Printed in the United States of America

CW

10 9 8 7 6 5 4 3 2 1

People love telling stories. Sad ones, scary ones, funny ones—stories too good to be true or too awful to be believed.

But we aren't the only animals with tales to tell. Bees wiggle their striped little butts to tell the story of how to get from one flower to another. Hippos rumble the story of their territory.

And wolves sing the story of their pack.

Telling our stories is a way of saving our lives.

—Kai

PROLOGUE

Dispatch: 911, what is the location of the emergency?

Caller: I'm at the Grizzly Grocery. I think they're getting robbed!

Dispatch: Are you inside the store?

Caller: No, I'm in the parking lot. The front door's all busted in!

Dispatch: Okay, I need you to stay where you are, ma'am. Can I get your name, please?

Caller: Brenda, Brenda Lake.

Dispatch: Brenda, can you describe—

Caller: Oh shoot, there goes Dale. Whiter than a sheet! Dale! Dale! You all right? [*unintelligible*] Shit, ma'am, did you hear that? I think they got wild animals in there or something.

Dispatch: Do you see an animal?

Caller: No, but I can hear it!

Dispatch: What does it sound like, Brenda?

Caller: Hang on. [*pause*] Oh boy, oh dear, I got chills! It sounds like—it sounds like *wolves*.

CHAPTER 1

THE KIDS COME crashing out of the eastern Idaho woods like someone's chasing them. They're filthy. Barefoot. They dart across the highway, quick as deer. An old Toyota 4Runner honks and swerves, missing the boy by inches.

"What the hell?" the driver shouts after them. "You lookin' to be roadkill?"

The teen boy and girl tumble down the berm and sprint across the parking lot of the Grizzly Grocery and Bait Shop. The boy flings himself at the glass door, pushing it as hard as he can. It doesn't open. He snarls and spits in anger.

He pushes the door again. Snarls louder when it doesn't move.

Suddenly he bends down, picks up a rock, and smashes it into the glass. A spiderweb of cracks fans out. He hits the glass another time, shattering a small hole in it. He hits it again and the hole gets bigger. Glass daggers rain down onto the asphalt. He's about to land another blow when the girl pushes him aside.

She *pulls* on the door.

It opens.

For a second, the boy looks shocked. Then he cackles with wild glee. He throws the rock aside and runs barefoot over the glass into the store. The girl follows right behind him.

"Hey!" the store clerk yells. "Hey! What the hell're you doing? Get back here! I'm calling the cops!"

They ignore his spluttering fury. They burst into the candy and chips aisle, laughing maniacally. The girl swipes a bag of cheese puffs from the shelf and tosses it to the boy, who catches it in his mouth like a dog. He whips his head from side to side until the bag bursts open. Cheese puffs go flying. The girl grins and catches one midair with a *snap*. She grabs a handful off the ground and shoves them into her mouth. The chili-lime-spiked flavor makes her cough.

She pops open a can of Coke and guzzles it down. Then she bats cookie boxes off the shelves. Rips them open and shoves four Oreos in her mouth at once. The boy jumps up and down, jaws chomping on tortilla chips, eyes wide and wild-looking.

The store clerk appears at the end of the aisle. "Hey, you!" Dale Wilson yells. "Stop! Get out of here! You crazy shits!"

The boy twists the cap from a Gatorade. Red fruit punch flavor goes streaming down his face and onto his filthy shirt.

"Quit that!" Dale practically screams, his voice going girl-high with panic.

The boy turns and grins at him, and Dale's jaw falls open. The kid's got freaking *fangs*!

The girl starts laughing again as she shoves more food into her face. She's having the time of her life.

An old man makes the mistake of turning into the aisle with his cart full of prune juice and wet wipes. He goes white as a sheet when he sees two filthy kids in tattered clothing going nuts on the junk food. He leaves his cart where it is and runs gimpy legged out the door.

The kids can't stop laughing. The food's still flying every which way. The floor's a mess of crumbs and juice, dirt and glass and blood.

Dale's moved farther away, but he's still yelling at them. "Is this some kind of TikTok challenge bullshit? Because it's not freaking *funny!*"

The boy turns to him again. The kid's eyes have gone darker than midnight. They don't even look like human eyes anymore. His lips curl back from his mouth. And a low, bone-chilling growl rumbles up from his throat. It rises in volume and pitch as the kid comes toward him.

Moving on all fours.

Dale feels his bladder go slack, and the warm piss running down his leg. He turns around and runs.

CHAPTER 2

POLICE CHIEF CHESTER Greene streaks up to the Grizzly in his black-and-white. Officer Randall Pierce comes peeling into the parking lot ten seconds later.

"*Wolves*, Chief?" Randall scoffs, favoring a bum knee as he climbs out of his cruiser. "Brenda Lake must've had a few too many tequila sunrises."

"That's Brenda's Friday-night problem," Chester says. "Last I checked it's Tuesday afternoon." He notes the smashed front door, the glass sparkling on the ground. A wolf couldn't do that—*wouldn't* do that.

A bear might, though. He puts his hand on his pistol.

His boots crunch on glass as he goes inside. The store looks like a tornado hit aisle two. There's food and plastic food packaging everywhere, and a thin stream of red juice snakes along the floor. Chester looks toward the register. "Looks like Dale's long gone," he says.

Randall says, "I'd run, too, if I was him."

"Police!" Chester calls to the seemingly empty store. "Come on out now. Come slowly, and you won't get shot."

There's no answer.

Then Chester hears it: low growling coming from an aisle to the left. Randall peels off to come at the intruder—whatever it is—from the other side.

Chester grits his teeth. What's he going to find? It doesn't sound human, that's for sure.

He spins around the endcap and points his gun down the aisle. It takes him a second to process what he's seeing. Two skinny kids, dirty and disheveled—the girl's shoving chips into her mouth like she hasn't eaten in days, and the boy's crouched down and growling.

Randall appears at the other end of the aisle. Spotting the barefoot kids, he looks so surprised Chester almost laughs. "What the—" he says.

The kids freeze. Chester lowers his gun.

"My name's Chester Greene," he says calmly. "I'm the chief of police, and I'm going to need you to put down the Doritos."

The kids blink at him. They turn their heads to eyeball Randall, then back to look at Chester.

The girl reaches into the bag and shoves another handful into her mouth. And the boy—well, he *snarls* at Chester. His mouth's orange with Dorito dust.

"The chief said 'Put down the Doritos,'" Randall repeats.

Chester takes a step forward and the girl flinches. She looks about sixteen, with gray eyes set deep in a fine-featured face. The boy's younger, maybe thirteen or so, with uncombed hair that reaches past his shoulders. Chester knows all the kids in Kokanee Creek—especially the ones who do dumb shit like this—but he's never seen these two before.

He tucks the gun into its holster and takes another step in their direction. "What are your names? Where are your parents? Where're you supposed to be? You skipping school right now?"

The boy's growl gets louder. The girl presses herself against the shelves and bares her teeth at him like a dog would. Chester keeps walking, low and slow. "You must be really hungry," he says. He's moving toward them slowly, gently, the way he'd approach an animal caught in a trap. "But you can't just help yourselves to the chip aisle. You know that, don't you? You can't make messes like this. How about we go outside and talk about it?"

The boy's snarl turns into a warning bark, and it makes the hair on the back of Chester's neck stand up.

"Can you understand me?" Chester asks. "Do you speak English?"

They both growl at him.

Chester's still making his slow progress when Randall launches himself toward them. He's big and fast, in spite of his bum knee, a former Utah State wide receiver. The girl's faster, though. She dodges him as the boy trips him, and Randall lands hard and goes skidding on the floor toward Chester. The kids pounce on him like starving wolves on a goddamn elk.

Randall roars in rage as fists pummel him and nails rake his face. As Chester rushes forward to protect his fellow officer, Randall tases the girl. She falls off him, convulsing, her eyes wide in shock and pain. Randall gets to his feet. He's going for the boy next.

"Stop!" Chester shouts. "They're *kids*."

"That effing little animal bit me," Randall whines. He slips on the spilled Gatorade. The kids skitter away down the aisle and around the corner. "She could be rabid!" He reaches for his gun.

Chester says, "Keep it holstered," as he creeps forward.

If he can corner these two, he can calm them down. Talk sense into them. Maybe they were hiking and got lost. Maybe they were in a car accident. Or maybe they're high on something synthetic and weird and need a junk-food fix. All he knows is if they were actual criminals, they would've gone for the cash register.

He finds them cowering in the back corner of the store.

"Hey," he says in a half whisper. "We're not going to hurt you. Randall's sorry about the Taser."

They're huddled together, shaking. The boy makes a sound that's more like a whimper.

"Just put your hands where I can see them. Let's go outside together, okay?"

Chester's less than ten feet away from them when they run.

They're so freaking fast he barely sees them pass by as they dart for the exit. Chester lunges forward, sprinting faster than he has in years. He takes a flying leap and catches the girl's ankle. They go down. He rolls to the side and gets his hand around one skinny wrist, and then *snap*, he's got one cuff on. Before she can fight him off, he gets the other cuff on.

Randall's got the boy by the front door. He's cuffed too, and he's spitting and snarling. But he calms down when he sees Chester leading the girl toward him.

They have the same gray eyes. The same high forehead.

Siblings, Chester thinks.

But who the hell are they? Where the hell did they come from? And why haven't they said a single human word?

CHAPTER 3

THE KIDS ACT pretty calm—like they're in shock, maybe—
when they're put into the back of the police car. But the minute Chester shuts the door, they go apeshit.

The girl kicks the back of the seat with her dirty, bloody,
bare feet and the boy pounds on the window again and again.
His fists hit the glass with sickening thuds.

Chester puts his face right up to the window. "Don't do that!
Hey! You have to calm down! You're going to hurt yourself!"

The boy sends his forehead crashing into the grille part of
the partition. Chester winces. That must've really hurt.

"Where's a frickin' tranq gun when you need one?" Randall says. He's rubbing his wrist where the girl bit him. It's
bleeding. He spits a brown stream of tobacco juice into the
parking lot. He says, "I hope the little beast knocks himself
unconscious."

Chester smacks the window and yells, "Stop!"

The boy's still snarling and spitting. But then the girl stops kicking at the seat. She leans over and nuzzles her head against the boy's shoulder. Just like that, he goes quiet.

Chester waits a few beats. Then he walks around to the front of the car and slides in behind the wheel. Nothing happens. He can hear them breathing in the back seat.

Panting. Whimpering a little.

He turns around to face them, speaking through the grille. "I'd really appreciate it if you could stay calm for the duration of the ride. Do you think you could manage that?"

Silence.

"I've got a good feeling about it," he says. He's lying. "Also, while we're sitting here, I'm real curious about your names."

The girl's got a thunderstorm brewing in her eyes. But she doesn't speak.

Chester reaches way back to grade school memories, when he earned the alphabet in sign language. He spells out slowly, letter by letter, "Can you understand me?"

Both kids just glare at him. He drops his hand. All righty then. No ASL.

"I've got a few things to say before we start driving," Chester says, more for his sense of duty than for them at this point. "So I'm hoping there's some part of you that understands it. You two are in a little spot of trouble right now. Because here in Kokanee Creek, we don't smash doors. We don't eat things we haven't paid for. And we definitely don't bite officers of the law."

He still can't see a flicker of understanding cross their faces.

He turns on the car.

"We're going to take a little ride now," he says. "Try to keep calm. You're doing good right now. Real good."

When the engine revs, the boy starts to whimper again. And when Chester pulls out of the parking lot onto the highway leading into town, the whimpering gets louder.

"It's okay," he says over his shoulder. "We're just heading over to the station."

As the cruiser picks up speed, the kids look more and more freaked out. They start bouncing around a little. Chester can see the boy sweating in the rearview mirror, so he rolls down the window a crack. The boy lifts his face to the breeze, his nose twitching.

Chester thinks, *They* must *be on drugs. What kind, though?*

It's just a short drive into town. They pass the abandoned lumber yard, then the Wendy's billboard. LATE NIGHT GREAT NIGHT, it reads. TURN LEFT AT THE LIGHT.

The boy makes a noise that almost sounds like a word.

Chester turns and says, "Did you just speak?"

No answer.

"You two still hungry? You wish I could take you to Wendy's?"

There's silence for another second. And then the boy throws back his head and howls so loud that Chester's ears ring.

CHAPTER 4

THE KOKANEE CREEK police station occupies half a small brick building in the center of town; the other half houses the public library. Across the street there's a hair salon and a pub; down the block there's a cafe, an antiques store, a kayak rental place, two churches, and the Dollar General.

In other words, the town of Kokanee Creek isn't much more than a wide spot in the road.

Chester helps the girl out of the car and escorts her into the station, while Randall takes the boy. Pearl Riley's on dispatch, and her eyes go wide when she sees those rough-looking kids. "Are they from the Grizzly?" she gasps.

"Call Lacey," Chester tells her. "Have her bring food."

He turns to Randall. "I don't know if they *can't* tell us who they are, or if they *won't*, so we're going to have to figure it out for ourselves. See if anyone's reported missing kids. Runaways, maybe. Start with Washington, Oregon, Montana, Wyoming, Idaho—but go wide. They could be from anywhere. Call Dr. Meyer, too. We're going to need physicals.

Drug tests." He runs his hand through his graying hair. "We got any extra socks lying around?" he asks Pearl. "If not, see if Lacey can find some."

Chester takes the girl by the elbow and maneuvers her over to fingerprinting. As he raises her cuffed hands to the ink pad, he takes in how hard and calloused they are. She's got the palms of a weatherbeaten rancher. "Don't worry," he says gently, before pushing her thumb into the ink pad. "It's just for identification purposes."

She holds herself perfectly still and silent the whole time. So does the boy, for all ten fingers, but he pants audibly.

"You're doing good," he says to the kids. "I appreciate your cooperation."

The boy gives a little whimper. His ferocity's all gone. His thin shoulders slump.

"We're going to need to keep you here for a little bit," Chester goes on. "Till we figure out where you belong and find whoever's looking for you."

"If them two were mine, I'd say good riddance," Randall mumbles.

Chester glares at him before turning back to the kids. "I hope you can continue to stay calm, because it'll be a lot more pleasant for all of us that way." The girl glances nervously at the jail cells with their peeling paint, their old-fashioned bars and locks. "Yep," he confirms. "That's where we've got to put you for now."

As they approach the first cell, a figure calls out from one of the concrete beds.

"Who ya got there?" Dougie Jones rasps. Dougie lives ten

hard miles outside of town, so last night he'd put himself in jail to sleep one off. "Is that Ray? I *told* that fool not to drive." Dougie sits up and rubs his eyes. Does a double take. "Well, slap my ass and call me Susan, you're mighty young to be scofflaws!" He grins at Chester. "All you need is two more criminals and you'll have to hang a No Vacancy sign on the jail."

"Or you could *leave*," Chester points out.

Dougie considers this. "Maybe after snack time."

"There is no snack time," Chester says.

Dougie shrugs. "Hope springs eternal."

Once the kids are inside the cell together, Chester reaches through the bars and removes their handcuffs. "You're safe here now," he says. "When we find your folks, we'll do our best to get you out of here. Though that won't necessarily be the end of your troubles." He shakes his head. "What were you thinking, acting like that?"

The silent girl just stares at him. But the boy walks over to the far corner and turns to face the wall. It takes Chester a second to realize what he's doing.

"Hey!" The little shit's *pissing* in the corner, four feet away from the toilet. "What the fuck!" Then Chester shakes his head. "Okay, I get it. You had to mark your territory. Because you're a damn wolf or whatever."

The boy turns around and bares his teeth in what might be a grin.

"They ain't even housebroken?" Dougie cries.

"Pearl!" Chester yells. "Randall—one of you. Bring me some Lysol and towels." Pearl comes hustling over, and Chester takes the supplies and shoves them through the bars.

Chester watches the girl struggle to make the spray nozzle work. *Is she stupid?* he thinks. *Strung out?* Finally she manages to squirt the cleaner on the floor, and then she wordlessly directs her little brother to wipe it up.

Chester offers them soapy paper towels for their hands and faces next. It won't make them smell better, but he figures that at least it'll get the blood and dirt off.

By the time these various messes are taken care of, Lacey's walked down the street with takeout from her diner, and the smell of burgers overpowers the smell of Lysol. The boy comes up to the bars, sniffing madly.

"Miss Lacey brought you some food from her restaurant," Chester tells him.

"My cook called in sick," Miss Lacey adds, "so I made it myself."

The kid snuffles the bag all over, drooling, before his sister takes it away from him and opens it.

She looks up at Chester with her cold gray eyes. "Thanks, Officer," she says. "And thank you to Miss Lacey, too."

CHAPTER 5

"YOU CAN *TALK*?"

The poor police chief staggers backward like he's been slapped. I could probably knock him flat by blowing on him.

Yes, absolutely I can talk. But growling feels so *good*.

Now that we've established I'm capable of speech—and seeing as how this is my *life* we're dealing with—I'm going to take over the story. I think it'll work better that way.

For the record, my name's Kai, and I'm seventeen (I think). My brother, Holo, is fourteen, give or take. At this particular moment, we're all each other has in the world, and we are not happy to be here. Surely you can understand why.

The chief gets his balance back and immediately starts glaring at us. "What was all that howling about then? And all that pretending that you didn't know what I was saying to you?"

I hold up a finger. I'll consider talking again after I'm done getting whatever this delicious-smelling thing inside the bag is into my empty stomach. I pull out two paper-wrapped packages, and I smell fatty meat. Warm bread. Holo and I tear the packages open with our teeth.

"Hamburgers," the chief informs us. "With all the fixins."

I doubt anyone in the history of the world has eaten hamburgers faster than my brother and I did. Holo basically swallows the thing whole, and then he sniffs around the greasy paper bag, looking all sad and confused like he can't believe there isn't another hamburger in there waiting for him.

The chief pulls up a stool on the other side of the bars, and he patiently waits for more words to come out of my mouth. I chew the last few bites extra slow to show him that he's not as in charge as he thinks he is.

"Okay, you two," he says when I'm licking the last bit of grease from my fingers. "Why don't you start with your names? And then you can tell me where your parents are. After that, you can explain why they didn't teach you that you can't just break into a convenience store and start stuffing your faces with food you didn't pay for."

"Holo," my brother says.

"Ha," the chief says. "My mother used to tell me I had a hollow leg when I was hungry, too. Well, you're full up now, aren't you?"

"Not *hollow*. H-O-L-O. That's his name," I snap. "I'm Kai. And our parents didn't teach us that, because our parents have never been in a store."

"How do you figure that?" the chief says.

I look him straight in the eye. "We were raised by wolves," I say. "And wolves don't go shopping."

CHAPTER 6

THE CHIEF LOOKS surprised for about a millisecond. Then he starts laughing, hard, like I've just told the best damn joke in the world.

"I don't see what's so funny," I say.

"Sorry, you being raised by wolves strikes me as pretty unbelievable. And pretty humorous, too."

"It's the truth," I say. "There's nothing funny about it at all." I point to my clothes. They're old. Dirty. Claw-torn. "I found these in a dumpster. Because, remember, wolves don't shop."

The chief's about to say something, but then another officer appears, dragging some kid over to the cell opposite ours. The guy's about my age, and his hair's a messy sweep of brown with bleached ends. He's got big, sleepy eyes, like he's really tired or else he just woke up.

The chief goes, "*You* again?"

"Hey, Chief," the guy says, like it's no big deal.

"He was doing seventy-seven, and he got mouthy when I

pulled him over," the officer says. Then he looks over at us. "Are those the two juveniles that Randall's trying to ID?"

The chief nods. Holo bares his teeth. In wolf language, this means *I see you. Get lost.*

Meanwhile, the shaggy-haired guy makes himself comfortable in his cell. He takes off his worn leather jacket and kicks off his scuffed black boots. When he sits down on the bed, he leans back and looks right at me. Then he smiles, slow and teasing, like he thinks it's really cool that we're in here together. "I'm Waylon," he says.

Maybe it's his heartthrob smile or maybe it's because I ate six bags of chips and a hamburger, but my guts feel like something's twisting them.

I growl.

I didn't even mean to—it was instinct.

Waylon's grin gets wider. "Yeah, I get that a lot," he says.

Holo comes to stand next to me. He growls, too.

The police chief sighs. "Well, it looks like we're going to have a slumber party in the jail tonight. Unless I can somehow get the wolves on the phone and ask them to come pick you two up."

"Nah, they don't get good reception out in the woods," Dougie says, cracking himself up.

"*I* could call them," I say. "All I have to do is howl."

"Do it," Holo whispers. "I don't want to be in here anymore."

I put my arm protectively around him. "You know what would happen. They'd get shot the minute they set foot on Main Street."

"They could come at night when everyone is asleep," Holo insists.

"And how are they going to unlock the doors, Holo? I wish they could rescue us, too, but they can't. We're not going anywhere for a while."

Holo nods glumly and walks over to one of the concrete beds. There's a flimsy plastic mattress on top of it, and a yellowish blanket about as thick as the paper napkins that came with our burgers.

Watching my brother try to get comfortable on that skinny bed just about breaks my heart. I didn't know what would happen when we came out of the woods, but I sure didn't think it would be this. And as I lie down on my own hard bed, I worry that we've made an even bigger mistake than I thought.

CHAPTER 7

JAIL IS NOTHING like the forest. I can't sleep here. I almost can't breathe.

I lie awake on a sticky mattress that stinks of urine and rotting food. A TV is on down the hall. I hate TV and everything about it. The drunk, who *chose* to stay in this awful place, moans and talks in his sleep.

I toss. I turn. I twitch. I've never been locked up before. I'm an animal in a cage, and it sucks. I'm cut off from dirt and trees and sky. Who could live like this? We have to get out of here.

What would a wolf do?

I hear a sound from another bunk. My ears prick. Wolves hear everything.

It's Holo. He's crying, but he's doing it softly because he doesn't want me to know.

I hate hearing those frightened whimpers. But he wouldn't want me to comfort him, because crying is weakness. And in nature, weakness is death.

I close my eyes and breathe slow and steady. I imagine I can smell the forest. The river. The ancient rocks that hide our home from human eyes. I imagine I'm back there, miles away from this cold, stinking cell...

"I won't pretend it's the height of luxury, but maybe it's better than a wolf's den?"

I wake with a start.

The police chief stands on the other side of the bars, grinning. *What's he got to smile about?* I sit up and rub my eyes. I'm freezing cold. The napkin blanket had fallen off in the night.

I grab it and wrap it around my shoulders. It's itchy. It smells like pee, too.

"Lacey brought you something," he says.

I blink. Notice Lacey standing off to the side. She's short, with shiny black hair that falls past her shoulders. She lifts the lid of the basket she's carrying and says, "I don't know what you like, sweetheart, so there's a little bit of everything."

Sweetheart? Why's she calling me that? She doesn't know me from a tufted titmouse. But her voice is like honey, melting and sweet.

"She made lemon poppyseed muffins," the chief says, "and these little—what do you call 'em, Lacey?"

"Egg bites," Lacey says. "With cheddar and bacon." She peeks into the basket. "There's fruit, too, and a couple of bagels..."

By now Holo's jumped up from his mattress. He's pressed against the cell's bars, drooling at the food. Literally. Act more *human*, I almost say. But we've never worried about that before, so maybe we shouldn't start.

Dougie's still snoring, but Waylon across the way sits up and says, all smug and slow, "Ya'll going to share?"

Lacey turns to him. "Well, hello, Waylon, I didn't know you were in here, too," she says. "Let me guess. You didn't see the speed limit sign."

"Oh, I saw it. I just didn't agree with its message."

"The gray hairs you must give your mama!" Lacey exclaims.

"She's got the salon on speed dial," Waylon drawls.

The chief unlocks our cell door and opens it just enough for Lacey to slide the basket through. Holo snatches it from her fingers faster than you can blink.

We sit side by side on my rock-hard bed and dig in. I've never had a lemon poppyseed muffin before. It's amazing. It's also so sweet that it makes my teeth hurt. Holo shoves three egg bites into his mouth at once and chews with his mouth open.

"Looks like you appreciate my cooking," Lacey says. She sounds like this makes her happy, though I can't understand why she'd care.

Animals devour whatever they can as fast as they can. Wolves will gorge themselves on a kill until they can barely even move, because they don't know when they'll get to eat again.

Holo smiles at her, crumbs all over his face.

"If I smash up the Grizzly, can I get a muffin, too?" Waylon asks.

The chief says, "Treats are for first-timers only," and then he smiles at me again. All warm and kind, like he thinks we're *friends*.

That dumb smile just sends me over the edge. If I had fangs I'd bare them. Instead I lash out with words. "You're trying to fool us into thinking you're on our side, cop, but that's not going to happen. We're not stupid."

"I know that, Kai," the chief says.

"No, you *don't* know it," I growl. "But you will."

CHAPTER 8

THE CHIEF'S FACE darkens, and then he turns and walks away. Lacey shoots me a wounded look and trots after him.

Looks like I hurt some human feelings.

Can't say I care, though.

I sneak a glance over at Waylon. He's sprawled on the bed, using his beat-up leather jacket as a pillow and acting so relaxed you'd think he was enjoying himself.

"Why are you looking at me like that?" he asks. There's a hint of challenge to his voice.

I bristle. "I'm not."

This is a lie. I *was* staring at him. But it's not because he looks like some stupid teen heartthrob with perfectly messy hair and smoldering eyes. It's because I've never seen another person my age up close. Never talked to another boy besides Holo, who's so familiar to me that he might as well be my own shadow.

Now I'm staring down at my feet, but I can picture Waylon perfectly: his sharp cheekbones, his easy smile. His hint of a swagger when he moves.

Suddenly there's a bagel waving back and forth in front of my face.

"Are you going to eat this?" Holo asks. "It's the last one."

"What? No."

"Good," he says. He takes a giant bite of it. He looks happier than he did before Lacey brought food, but he's still afraid. I can smell it on him. If he had a tail it'd be tucked between his legs.

"—I'm telling you, those goddamn bastards are back!"

Holo flinches at the fierce voice. I go to the corner of the cell and press my face against the bars. Near the front door of the police station, there's a bearded man in overalls and a big dumb hat. He's pointing at the chief, yelling about how those "bloodthirsty bastards" need to be shot. Or trapped. Or poisoned. How they need to be "strung up from the trees as a warning to their bastard brothers."

Fear creeps up my spine.

"I've lost a dozen chickens in the last week," Dumb Hat yells. "Brady lost two lambs and a ewe, and Johnny Mills says they got his dog."

I'm praying that neither one of them says just one particular word—

"And you think it's wolves?" the chief says to Dumb Hat.

There it is—the word I didn't want to hear. Holo looks up at me, his eyes dark with fear.

"It's okay," I whisper. Meanwhile my blood's turning to ice.

It's not wolves, I want to scream. But why would they believe me? Especially since I'm not even sure I can believe myself.

You never know what a wild animal will do. That's why you call it *wild*.

"Raccoons kill chickens, too, Stan," the chief says.

"That's right!" I yell. "Those shits'll eat anything they can get their paws on." I loved raccoons until they devoured a hummingbird nest I'd been keeping my eye on. Not just the sweet baby birds, the whole perfect, tiny nest.

Dumb Hat ignores me, but the chief shoots me a look like *Please shut up, this is official police business.* "Foxes kill chickens, too, and coyotes can take down a calf," the chief adds.

"The howling the other night didn't sound like coyotes," Dumb Hat says stubbornly.

"I'm not saying it was," the chief says. "But you know as well as I do that coyotes are a lot more common than wolves around here, and they're first-class hunters. A couple of lambs and a mama is no match for a pack of 'em."

That's right, Chief—blame the killings on coyotes. Or foxes or bobcats. Anything but wolves.

"Eavesdrop much?" Waylon calls. He's grinning at me. His smile is electric.

I have to fight to keep my face stony. "There's nothing else to do in this hellhole."

I realize he's got his boots and motorcycle jacket on now. Does that mean he's getting out? Does it mean we're next?

Somehow I doubt it.

"You could get to know me," Waylon says easily.

I practically snarl at him. "And what would be the point of that?"

He shrugs. "We could become friends."

"And what would be the point of *that*?"

"I can't say for sure," he says. "But who knows? Maybe it'd change your life."

"Wow," I say. I'm thinking, *Are all hot teen guys this conceited?* "You've got a pretty high opinion of yourself."

Waylon laughs. "I didn't say it'd change your life for the *better*," he says. He leans against the bars and crosses one leg over the other. "I'm probably too dangerous for you, anyway. I've got a fast bike. I don't mind spending a night in jail."

Too *dangerous* for me? It's probably the most ridiculous thing I've ever heard. But I don't get time to tell him so, because a blond woman charges down the hall and starts banging her purse against the bars of his jail cell.

"My God in heaven, Waylon Eugene, when will you learn?" She gives the bars one last wallop and then turns to the chief. "I swear, Chester, sometimes I think my son is mentally challenged."

"More like behaviorally challenged, Mrs. Meloy," the chief says.

I'm thinking, *Waylon* Eugene *Meloy?* It almost makes me like him, knowing he's got such a bummer of a middle name. It's like he's keeping some kind of terrible secret.

"The sign said fifty-three," Waylon says calmly.

"When has fifty-three ever been an official speed limit? The sign said thirty-five and you know it," his mother snaps. "Anyway, you were going seventy-five."

"Seventy-seven," Waylon corrects, and then he winks at me. *Winks!* Is that a thing people do?

"Well, thank you for holding him," his mom says to the chief. "Scaring him a bit and whatnot."

The chief unlocks the cell and Waylon slowly walks out, not looking scared at all.

He thinks he's tough, I can tell. But he hasn't seen half of what I have. Hasn't done half of what I have. *He's* not the dangerous one here.

"Next time it's going to go on his record," the chief warns.

Waylon comes over to my cell and wraps his long fingers around the bars. Up close his eyes are a warm brown with golden flecks.

Almost like a wolf's.

"Maybe I'll see you around," he says.

I toss my hair over my shoulder. "I doubt it," I say.

He smiles, revealing a space between his two front teeth that makes another weird thing happen inside my stomach.

"If you say so. Well, it was nice being in jail with you," he says.

And then he's gone.

CHAPTER 9

"WHAT HAPPENS NOW, Kai?" Holo asks once it's just us and Dougie. He looks uncertain and small, like spending a night in jail shrunk him somehow.

A wolf in captivity is not a true wolf.

"Look," I say, "it's all part of the adventure, okay?"

Holo scowls at me.

I get it. Being in jail doesn't feel like an adventure. It feels like torture. When I reach out to ruffle his hair, he ducks away from me. He's too old for that now, I know. I just keep forgetting.

"They're going to let us out soon, I promise," I say. "What we did really wasn't so bad. No one's going to press charges."

I say it firmly, so we both have to believe it.

A little while later the chief comes down the jail hallway with a man so old and thin he looks like a spring breeze could blow him away. I'm wondering what this skeleton in a long white coat could've done to get himself arrested, when the chief leads him over to our cell and smiles like he's bringing us a treat.

"Kai, Holo," the chief says. "This is Dr. Meyer. He's going to take a look at you two. Make sure you're good and healthy." Then he says to the old man, "Dr. Meyer, this is Holo and Kai. I've never met anyone like them before. They're *very* interesting children."

You don't know the half of it, cop.

"You can't surprise me anymore, Chief Greene," the old man says airily. "I've seen everything under the sun."

"You seen kids raised by wolves?"

"You bet I have," the old liar says.

Holo and I press ourselves against the back of the cell when the doctor comes inside. I don't want that man anywhere near me. He's creepy and he smells like the stuff we used to clean up Holo's pee. Also we've never seen a doctor in real life before, and I have no idea what he wants to do to us.

"Don't worry, you two," the chief says. "Dr. Meyer is Kokanee Creek's most experienced physician."

"Because he was a doctor for the dinosaurs," I whisper to Holo.

"Doctor Dino," Holo snickers.

Dr. Meyer's too deaf to hear us making fun of him. He says, "Like Chief Greene says, I'm just here to give you two a little checkup—just to make sure you're healthy and happy."

"Healthy, yes," I say. "Happy, no."

We've got to get out of here.

He lifts his stethoscope and says to Holo, "How about you let me listen to your heart?"

Holo growls at him. If he had hackles, he'd raise them.

The doctor takes a step back and says, "It's not going to hurt, buddy."

"Holo doesn't care about *pain*," I say. I've seen my brother fall twenty feet from a tree, wipe off his bloody knees, and climb right back up again. "He cares about you keeping your veiny hands off of him."

Dr. Meyer blinks at me in surprise. "All right, I'll just take a seat. When you're ready, young man, you can come to me." He sits down on the edge of Holo's bed. He crosses one old, creaky leg over the other.

No one says anything for a long time. The chief clears his throat. Randall keeps looking our way. The doctor whistles jauntily. We ignore them all. Holo and I can sit quiet and still for hours. *Days.* The woods taught us how.

Finally Dr. Meyer looks at Holo and says, " 'You have brains in your head. You have feet in your shoes. You can steer yourself any direction you choose.' "

And Holo's eyes go wide, because he knows those lines by heart.

I butt in. "But my brother doesn't actually have *shoes*," I say. "The chief only gave us these dumb socks."

Dr. Meyer acts like he can't hear me. He smiles at my brother. "Do you know Dr. Seuss?"

Holo shakes his head. "No. I've never met him."

Dr. Meyer laughs, and the chief shushes him. "What Dr. Meyer means is, have you read Dr. Seuss *books*?" the chief explains.

Holo doesn't say anything.

"Holo, can you read?"

"Yeah, the wolves taught him," I say. "After a nice dinner of raw elk, we'd always have story time."

Holo giggles. Then he starts ripping up the napkins from our breakfast and throwing the pieces into the air like confetti. The chief looks annoyed. Good.

"I can recite every single one of Dr. Seuss's books," Dr. Meyer tells us. "The rhymes help distract kids when they're about to get their shots."

My whole body stiffens. "Keep your needles away from us, old man."

Dr. Meyer blinks watery blue eyes at me. "No shots today, dear. We must get to know each other better."

"I'd rather not," I say. "And don't call me dear."

The doctor sighs and turns to the chief. "Should I come back another time? Tomorrow's full, but I'm available the day after at four p.m."

Two *days*? I can't wait two more days to get out of here; I'll go insane. I step toward him. "Fine, I'm ready," I say. "You can examine me first."

"That's a good girl," he says.

I snarl at him for calling me "good girl." But I don't flinch as he takes my blood pressure and listens to my heart and lungs. Then he looks into my ears and eyes and down my throat.

"You seem to be in excellent health," he tells me. "The wolves must be taking very good care of you."

He says this like it's a joke. I growl.

He turns to Holo. "Young man, are you ready?"

My brother nods. He's nervous. The doc wraps the cuff around Holo's bicep and listens with his stethoscope. "Good, good," he says quietly. He peers into his ears. "Good, good, good."

But when he asks Holo to open his mouth, Dr. Meyer's face

goes white. He looks like he's about to have a heart attack. He calls the chief over to look.

"The boy's teeth appear to have been filed into the shape of *fangs*," the doctor says. He puts his hand on Holo's shoulder and asks gently, "Did you do this to yourself?"

Silence from Holo. Silence from me, too. Obviously my brother wasn't born with razor-sharp canines. But predators need every advantage they can get.

"It looks like the boy's got wolf teeth, doesn't it?" the chief says.

Dr. Meyer nods. "Indeed, his canines are distinctly...canine."

"You ever seen that before, Doc?" I ask.

He shakes his old white head.

"I guess you haven't seen 'everything under the sun' then."

CHAPTER 10

"YOU REMEMBER THE Griffin case a while back? Those missing kids?" The chief's sitting at his desk all the way near the door, but my hearing's sharp.

"That was before my time," says a female voice. I think it's the 911 operator. *What's her name? Pearl—that's it.*

"They were brother and sister, ages four and six, who disappeared from over in Wyoming. This was about ten years back."

My hands grip the bars so hard that my fingers turn white. A brother and a sister? Disappeared ten years ago?

"Don't tell me the details, Chester," Pearl says. "Not unless it's a happy ending."

I want him to tell all of it. Every last thing.

What if those two kids were us?

"Mom sends them out to play one day," the chief says. "After a while she realizes she hasn't heard them in a while. Usually they fight, and they can get pretty loud. So she goes outside to check on them, and they're gone." He snaps his fingers. "Just—*vanished.*"

Pearl gasps. "I'd have died of a heart attack right then and there. There *is* a happy ending, right?"

"Police looked everywhere. Search and rescue combed every inch of the forest near their house."

My hands are sweating now. *How old were they? What did they look like?*

Holo comes to stand beside me. "Are you okay?"

I shush him. I need to hear what the chief has to say.

"Did they ever find them?"

There's a long pause. "They found their bodies," the chief says finally. "They'd been murdered. Dumped in a river. The killer's still at large."

"God, Chester, I told you no details unless—"

"I'm sorry, Pearl. But suddenly I've got two reasons to wonder about missing kids, and they're both glaring at me from over in that jail cell. I know that a lot of missing kids are runaways, trying to escape bad parents or poverty or abuse. They don't always get happy endings, either. But it's the ones who get kidnapped that you really have to worry about. Most of them are dead within three hours of being taken."

Pearl's voice goes lower. "I'm guessing you think those two back there are runaways?"

"Either that," Chester says, "or else someone took them and they got real lucky and escaped." Then he shakes his head. "Or maybe they really *are* the children of wolves."

"I swear, sometimes my Andrew acts like he was raised by 'em," Pearl muses. "Teenagers! They aren't what I'd call civilized. Even the ones with two parents trying their best, like Lord knows Bill and I do."

My mind's a jumble of emotions as I walk back to my hard bed. For a minute, I'd thought the chief might be talking about Holo and me.

Do I really want to know the truth about who we are and where we came from? Honestly, I don't know if I do. I'm not sure I could handle it.

"When can we go home?" Holo asks.

I reach out to ruffle his hair but then stop myself. I tell him I don't know yet.

Because I have no idea what's supposed to be home right now.

CHAPTER 11

THE CHIEF BRINGS us another visitor in the afternoon, as if we wanted one. She's older than the chief but younger than the doctor, with bright-pink lipstick that clashes with her bright-red hair. She smells like fake flowers. It's better than the doc's chemical stink, but barely.

The chief tells us that her name is Ms. Pettibon. She's from some county social services organization. He brings out his set of keys and picks through the ring to find the right one.

This is our chance. We can escape. With an almost invisible nod of my head, I signal to Holo: *When the chief opens the door,* run.

The chief can't seem to decide which key he needs. Meanwhile Holo's gone into a half crouch, ready to spring. I've got a big fake innocent grin on my face, but every muscle is tensed. Once that door swings open, I'll be gone so fast that cop'll see nothing but a Kai-shaped blur.

He's finally sticking the right key into the lock when a low rumble comes out of Holo's throat. The woman puts a hand on the chief's arm and says, "Actually, if you don't mind, I think I'll feel safer on *this* side of the bars."

Shit. I glare at Holo. "Couldn't keep your hostility to yourself?" I mutter.

"Sorry," he whispers. "I don't like how she smells."

I get it. Wolves don't keep their feelings secret, either. As far as I know, humans are the only animals that try to.

The chief drags a folding chair over for Ms. Pettibon. She pulls out a clipboard and some kind of official-looking form, and then she asks us for our names.

I'm still pissed about losing our escape chance, so I cross my arms over my chest and keep my mouth shut. Pettibon and I play a staring game for a while. When she gives up and looks down, I decide to talk. Like a wolf, I've proven my dominance.

"Kai and Holo," I say.

"Last name?"

I shake my head. No such thing.

"And your address?" she asks.

"We live at 1101 Two Rocks Past a Stream," I say. "The Woods, Idaho."

Holo starts snickering. Ms. Pettibon knows it's a bullshit answer, so she grits her teeth and writes *Unknown* on the line.

She wouldn't last ten minutes where we come from. I look at her soft hands and her painted nails and try to imagine her gutting a fish. It's impossible. I can't see her grabbing that cold messy slime at the base of the head and yanking on it. Can't see her cutting out the liver and the swim bladder with a knife. She'd starve to death before she'd mess up her manicure. This makes me laugh.

"What's amusing you, Kai?" the woman asks.

Instead of answering, I start to whistle. I can do it way better than that crusty old doc.

"That's lovely—what's that song?" Pettibon asks. She's trying to make friends with me, even though we both know it's not going to happen.

"Robin."

"Robyn, the Swedish pop singer?"

"Who? No, robin the *bird*."

What kind of idiot can't recognize one of the most common bird songs there is?

The same kind of idiot who puts a bunch of paint on her lips and sprays herself with chemicals that pretend to be flowers, I guess.

"Well, you're very talented, Kai," Ms. Pettibon says tightly.

"Thanks. Not that your opinion matters to me."

Ms. Pettibon decides to see if Holo's going to be any friendlier. "Does your sister take care of you, Holo?" she asks.

Holo shrugs, like, *I don't know. Sort of.*

Maybe that's a fair answer. But what am I supposed to do, follow him everywhere? I don't have time for that. Creatures in the woods have to look out for themselves. I don't constantly dominate him, the way I would if we were wolves. And I definitely don't try to kill him, like I would if we were black eagles.

"How about your mom and dad?" Ms. Pettibon says.

Instead of answering, Holo pushes his nose through the bars and sniffs her. Then he makes a face of disgust. I don't get it—did he think she'd magically start smelling better?

"Did they hurt you? Is that why you ran away?" she asks him.

"They bit us when we were naughty," I say.

Her eyebrows disappear up under her straggly bangs. "*Bit* you?"

"Well, really it was more of a nip."

Snapsnapsnap go Holo's teeth. God, I love that kid.

Ms. Pettibon's pen scratches at lightning speed across her form. "In what other ways did they punish you?"

"Made us stay in the den," I say.

"The den of your house? Like the TV room?"

"The den *was* the house," I say.

Actually, only the littlest wolf pups sleep in dens, but what does she know?

Ms. Pettibon makes a sad face at me. "Oh dear, I am finding all this very hard to believe."

I lean back and cross my arms. "That seems like a you problem," I say.

Her face starts to go pink, then purplish. It's not a good look. Clashes with her hair and lipstick.

Holo gets down on all fours and starts growling. It's almost impossible to keep from cracking up. Ms. Pettibon's probably seen tough kids before, but how many of them acted like they wanted to gnaw on her ankles?

Ms. Pettibon stands up. "I think we should continue this interview later," she says.

"Great. You know where to find us."

When she stalks off down the hall, I turn to Holo. "Good job chasing her off," I say. "But you might want to start acting a little bit more like a human, or else they're going to take you out of jail and put you in the pound."

CHAPTER 12

"MAYBE THEY REALLY *do* live with wolves," Officer Randall says, rubbing his aching temples. He's spent hours trying to track down leads, but he keeps coming up empty-handed. Nobody around here's ever seen these kids before. There's no one matching their descriptions in the NCIC database. "I mean, they're dirty and smelly enough."

The chief sighs as he glances back toward the kids pacing their jail cell. The boy snarls and bares his teeth. He does that every time Chester looks in his direction.

Isn't anyone *missing these two?* the chief wonders.

Or did someone want them gone?

"My dog has better manners," Randall adds. "Shep knows not to snarl at people, or snap at 'em, or piss in corners."

It's true these kids seem pretty feral. But something isn't adding up for Chester Greene.

"I did some reading about kids raised by wolves," he says. "They don't act like human kids at all. They don't ever laugh or smile. They only want to eat raw food. Most of them can barely talk."

"Well, that boy hardly says a damn word," Randall points out.

"Doesn't mean he can't." The chief takes a sip of his coffee, forgetting that it's gone cold. He grimaces. "If these kids were really raised by wolves, we'd be lucky to get a yes or a no out of them."

"That girl's kinda mouthy."

"Exactly," the chief says. "And 'raised by wolves' isn't even what you'd call it, anyway. It's more like the kids I read about were *tolerated* by wolves. Not *raised* by them. All the wolves really did was decide not to eat them for dinner."

"So you're telling me wolves wouldn't win any parenting awards," Randall says.

"Yeah," Chester says grimly, "and you know who else wouldn't? Kai and Holo's parents. Who the hell are they, and where the hell are they, and why aren't they looking for their children?"

"Well, they're not exactly charming," Randall points out. "I mean, if they were *my* kids—"

"You'd spank 'em or ground 'em. You wouldn't abandon them in a forest."

The back of the chief's neck prickles, and he realizes he's being watched. He turns around. The kids have stopped pacing, and now they're just staring at him. Their eyes seem unnaturally wide in their thin faces. "You all right back there?" he calls.

The boy snarls. The girl hits the bars with her fist. "You act like we're zoo animals or something! But you don't have any right to keep us here."

Yep, she's mouthy all right. He admires her feistiness. Too

bad she doesn't know what she's talking about. "We do have the right, actually," he says. "Our little jail here is what we call a Type 1 detention facility, which means it's all set up to keep folks for a few days after they're arrested."

"No one's pressed charges, have they?" Kai demands.

"Not yet," Chester allows.

He doesn't tell her this, but he's asked the owners of the Grizzly to forgive and forget. They're not the nicest folks he knows, but he's hoping they'll come around. He's offered to pay for the damages.

"In that case, you'd better let us go," Kai says.

"For one thing, charges might be forthcoming. And for another, you're minors," he says. "I can't just open the doors and turn you loose."

"But you *can*," Kai insists. "We know how to take care of ourselves."

He looks pointedly at their filthy clothes and raises his eyebrows. "I'd say that's open to debate."

"We know how to hunt," Holo says.

Chester grins. "Yeah, you did a great job hunting down and killing all those bags of Doritos."

Holo flushes and turns away.

"You're not funny," Kai tells him.

Chester shrugs. "I thought that was a pretty good one. But we can agree to disagree." He takes another sip of coffee. *Damn it, still cold.* "Look, I don't like doing this to you," he tells her. "But I don't have any better options right now."

Kai steps up to the bars like she's ready to fight. "You'd better start figuring some out, then," she says.

CHAPTER 13

JANGLING KEYS STARTLE me from a dream of fangs. Fur.

Family.

I'm up and yelling at the cop before I'm even all the way awake. "This is cruel and unusual punishment! The TV's on all night! My bed smells like piss. I can't even see the damn sky!"

"Good morning to you, too," the chief says.

Holo groggily lifts his head. "Breakfast?"

I swear, all that kid thinks about is food. He'd stay in here forever if it meant daily hamburgers.

"Not quite yet."

Holo growls. But it's a quiet little rumble because he's still half-asleep.

The chief says, "Today we gotta hunt for it."

Does this cop think he's going to shoot some poor deer with his government handgun? Has he gone crazy?

Then the door to our jail cell swings wide open as the chief walks away down the hall.

Yes, he's definitely gone crazy.

And I'm so surprised that I'm frozen. All that time I spent thinking about how to escape, and the chief just opens the damn door! *Is he letting us go?*

And are we really going hunting?

"Do we get to go home?" Holo yells.

There's no answer.

"What now, Kai?" Holo asks softly.

I know we could run. We could sprint through town and vanish into the trees, and that small-town cop would never find us again. But we came here for a reason. And I'm not ready to give up on it yet.

Even though everything's been awful since we came out of the woods.

Except the grocery store. That was pretty fun.

"We follow him," I say.

"Are you sure?"

I can read a wild animal a lot easier than I can read a police chief. But I say, "Yes, I'm sure."

Outside the station, the sun's shining and the birds are going crazy. In the two days we were in jail, *spring* has taken over. I hate that I missed it.

Holo sniffs the air and sighs. "Finally I can breathe," he says.

The chief's waiting by his cruiser. He opens the back door. "Hop on in."

I narrow my eyes at him. They're watering from the brightness. "Where are you going?" I ask.

"We're going on a hunt for breakfast," he says.

"You can't hunt in a *car*," Holo points out.

The chief holds up his hands like he's surrendering. "All right, you got me there," he says. "I said a hunt, but I really meant a drive."

"Why would you say a hunt if you didn't mean it?" my brother asks.

Poor, innocent Holo. He doesn't understand that people hardly ever mean what they say. Me, I must've been born knowing it somehow.

Wolves can maim and kill and steal. But they can't ever deceive you, because they don't know how.

"The chief was making a joke," I say to Holo. "Not that it was funny," I add.

I give my brother a little shove. "Go on, get in." When he hesitates, I sigh and go in first, sliding across the hard plastic back seat. I pat the spot next to me, and Holo gives a whimper and climbs in.

It takes less than a minute for the chief to drive us through the town of Kokanee Creek, because it's only five blocks long. Then we're on the highway and the car picks up speed.

I grip the door. I hate seeing the world rush by so fast. Holo's turning green around the edges. Seems he doesn't like it much, either. Just when I think Holo's going to barf up whatever's left of last night's dinner, the chief pulls into the parking lot of a squat brick building.

"Wendy!" Holo says. "Wendy, Wendy, Wendy."

The chief grins at him in the rearview mirror. "Considering this might've been the first word you ever said in my presence, young man, I thought you might enjoy getting breakfast here at Wendy's."

"There's food inside?" Holo asks.

This seems like a dumb question, but in fairness my brother's never seen a restaurant before.

"You bet," says the chief.

"Is it any good?" I ask. I'm not as easily excited as Holo is.

"Not really. But it's hot, and you'll have it in your hands about thirty seconds after you order it."

"Wendy, Wendy, Wendy," says Holo in a singsong.

The chief's expression turns worried, like, *Is he okay in the head?*

I won't pretend I haven't wondered that myself once in a while.

I knock against the car door with my elbow. "Are you going to let us out?" There aren't any handles in the back. We're still caged animals.

"Patience," the chief says. He drives around to the back of the restaurant and comes to a stop in front of a big sign covered in pictures of food. HOT 'N JUICY CHEESEBURGERS," it reads, and MAKE IT A COMBO!

Whatever that means.

"Welcome to Wendy's," the sign says. "May I take your order?"

Holo jumps back. I start laughing at him; I can't help it, even though the voice scared me, too.

"What do you two want?" the chief asks us.

"Does the magic sign have any suggestions?" Holo asks.

The chief looks at him quizzically, then pokes his head out the window. "We'll have a couple of sausage, egg, and cheese biscuits, a hot honey chicken biscuit, and two breakfast Baconators. Two orange juices and one large coffee, black."

After the sign reads his order back to him, he drives forward again and stops in front of a small window. It slides open, and a pretty girl hands him a couple of white paper bags.

"Have a nice day," she says. When she spots us, her eyes widen, like she's surprised to see two kids stuffed in the back of a police car.

I bare my teeth at her. *Yeah, that's right—we're dangerous.*

The chief passes the bags through the partition. My mouth's already watering. I unwrap whatever little breakfast sandwich my hand touches first and take a giant bite.

"Whaddya think?" the chief asks, looking all pleased with himself.

"You were right," I tell him. "It's hot and it's fast. And it's not that good."

"Disagree," Holo says, his mouth full of biscuit. "*Absolutely* disagree."

CHAPTER 14

INSTEAD OF GOING back into town, the chief turns east. We start driving toward the foothills of the mountains, and the road gets narrower and bumpier. The houses and ranches get fewer and farther between. The trees start closing in as we climb.

Holo seems almost happy now. His stomach's full, and we're heading into the wilderness—what's not to like about that? But I feel queasy, and I don't think it's the greasy biscuit.

Where's the cop taking us?

I'd asked him, but he already told me I'd find out soon enough.

I gaze nervously into the woods. I don't know where we are, but I'm looking for a flash of gray—

A big bump in the road jolts us hard. I practically hit the ceiling, and the last of Holo's Baconator goes flying from his hands. But he just grabs all the pieces from the floor and pops them into his mouth.

Wolves eat *everything* from the ground.

After another few minutes, the chief takes a left onto a gravel road. We bounce along that for a while until we come to a small clearing in the woods. "Welcome to my place," he says.

That's when I see the little log cabin, tucked right up against the edge of the forest. Smoke curls up from the chimney. Spring violets bloom around the porch.

"Pretty, isn't it?" the chief says, letting us out of the back.

It's even better than pretty. It's actually beautiful. Peaceful. But I'm not going to say so. I'm still pissed about jail, and about him not telling us anything unless he feels like it. "Your fire's not hot enough," I say.

The chief goes, "Huh?"

"Your smoke," I say. "Look at how brown it is. Either your wood's too wet or you made a really sad, dumb fire this morning."

His jaw works a little, like he's stopping himself from snapping at me, but one glance toward the chimney tells him I'm right.

I climb up on a tree stump and look all around. I need to get my bearings. Need to figure out where we are versus where Holo and I come from. But the trees block most of my view. I spin around, looking for any land feature I recognize. In the distance I see the craggy top of a mountain, and nearby, the spine of a ridge dotted with lodgepoles. "I'll bet you had a forest fire here about twenty years ago," I say.

"What makes you say that?"

"A lodgepole pine will grow just about anywhere, but it really loves growing in burned dirt. And those trees look like they're a little bit older than I am."

Now the chief looks more impressed than annoyed. "You're

right. A forest fire's heat releases lodgepole seeds from their cones," he says. "Supposedly it was a lightning strike. But I always thought it was a Hardy."

"What's a Hardy?" Holo asks.

"Not what, *who*. The Hardys are a local family," the chief says. His expression darkens. "But between you and me, if I could run them out of town—make 'em *not* local—I would. They're nothing but trouble."

"Is the kid who was in jail with us a Hardy?" I ask. He had kind of an outlaw vibe.

"No, Waylon's a lead foot, but he's a good kid. Wouldn't hurt a fly unless he ran into it with his motorcycle."

"Why can't you chase the Hardys out of your territory?" Holo asks. "It's what a wolf would do."

"It doesn't work that way, kid," the chief says. "I watch over Kokanee Creek, but it's not *my* territory. And people pretty much get to live where they choose."

Holo uproots a green plant with white flowers. "You could try poisoning them," he says. He holds the plant out to the chief, who looks alarmed.

"He's kidding," I say quickly. "But that's meadow death camas, and you have a lot of it growing around here."

"Shoot," the chief says. "I thought those were wild onions."

"Wild onions don't cause vomiting, diarrhea, and death," I say.

"Good thing I never got around to eatin' 'em," the chief says.

Holo throws the plant into the woods. "You really should know what's growing in your yard," he scolds.

The chief folds his arms across his chest. "Maybe you can teach me."

And Holo, who's always been the smallest and weakest of our pack, suddenly sees a chance to be something bigger. He smiles so brightly that his whole face lights up. "Maybe," he says. "Just maybe I could."

Out of the corner of my eye I see a flicker of movement. I spin around, focusing all my attention on a single spot in the underbrush. A branch sways back and forth, like something's just pushed it.

I squint. Then I see the flash of an ear. A pair of yellow eyes. My heart starts thudding in my chest.

"Holy shit," the chief whispers. "Who's he?"

I swallow down my dread. "Not he, *she*. That wolf is a female," I say. I wave my arms and shout. "Go! Go!"

She melts into the shadows. She's safe—as long as she doesn't get any closer.

Holo and I may have come into the world of humans, but we don't want our family following us.

CHAPTER 15

A STELLAR'S JAY squawks from a tree as Holo and I follow the chief to his house.

Before we go inside, he turns to us and says, "Now that you're my guests, you should call me Chester."

And my little brother says, all polite, "Okay, Mr. Chester."

If Holo were a wolf, he'd be the omega—the one who tries to please all the other wolves. Meanwhile I think, *I'm* never *going to call you Chester. And we'll see how long we're your "guests."*

"Not mister," the chief says. "Just Chester." He opens the door onto a small, neat living room, with a big soft couch and a couple of faded armchairs. "Come on in."

The room smells like woodsmoke and cedar. Comforting. The chief walks over to the cast-iron stove and puts another log inside. He looks up at me, kind of sheepish. "We have electric heat. I just thought a fire would be nice."

He probably thinks I'll be touched by his thoughtfulness. But I'm not. I'm just confused. And a little freaked out. Why did he bring us here? What's his plan?

A cabin's a lot nicer than jail, obviously. But it doesn't mean we're *safe*.

Holo flicks a light switch, and a lamp in the corner of the room goes on. My brother grins in delight. He flicks the switch off. Flicks it back on again. "Did you see that, Kai? Look!" On-off, on-off goes the light.

"I sure did." I'm not as impressed as Holo is. I like the sun better.

The chief smiles at my brother like he's still wondering if the kid's an idiot or not. "I've always taken electricity for granted," he says. "But it's kind of like magic, isn't it? I mean, you flip a switch and suddenly a dark room's bright." He motions us into the kitchen. "If you want to see something that'll *really* blow your mind, though, you should check out the kitchen faucet."

Maybe the chief thinks he's just going along with a game we're playing. But it's not a game.

Indoor plumbing, it turns out, is pretty amazing. Holo makes the water stop and go about five hundred times and it still delights him. And later, with a turn of a handle, I fill a big tub with water and take the first truly hot bath of my life. I sink into a cloud of soap bubbles and close my eyes. I decide that I will never get out again.

But then the water gets cold.

And I can see Holo's feet going back and forth on the other side of the door. Pacing.

"Kai?" he calls. "What are you doing in there?"

I rise dripping from the tub and wrap myself in a soft towel. "Bathing. You should try it sometime."

"I jumped into the creek!" he says.

I yank open the door. Sure enough, my brother's hair is dripping wet and his face looks actually clean. He's wearing new clothes that are much too big for him. I sniff. "Are those the chief's pants? You look ridiculous, but at least you smell better than you did before."

"You smell *weird*."

"It's called soap," I say. "And I like it."

I'm dreading putting my gross jail clothes back on. But it turns out that I don't have to. While I was in the bathtub, Lacey came home and laid out a clean outfit for me. The pink sweatsuit's ugly, but at least it's not covered in dirt and grass and canine slobber.

I walk into the kitchen in my new wool socks. Lacey's got her back to me. She's washing dishes in the sink. When I clear my throat, she jumps. But then she turns around, smiling.

"You look mighty comfortable, Kai," she says in her honey voice. "Are you hungry?"

"Always," I say. "But not as always as Holo."

She grins and offers me a plate of apple slices. "*Mi casa es su casa*," she says. "That means my home is your home."

She's so welcoming. I wonder how she really feels about having two feral kids in her house, though.

Dinner is roasted chicken and vegetables. Holo chews with his mouth open and totally forgets to use his fork, but no one mentions it. Instead the chief and Lacey talk to each other about their days. Occasionally they ask us a question, which usually we don't answer. We're too busy eating.

Plus our secrets are none of their business.

After Holo's had three helpings of food, he pushes himself

back from the table and lets out a giant burp. He's sucked every molecule of marrow out of the chicken bones and licked his plate so clean it shines. If he were a wolf, he'd have to sleep the feast off.

"Good stuff, huh?" the chief says.

"Great," Holo says. "But Kai's the best cook there is."

"Most teens I know can barely boil a box of Annie's Mac," says Lacey.

"I'm not that good," I say. "Holo's just really loyal. Kind of like a dog."

Or a wolf.

My brother kicks me under the table.

The chief says, "Lacey and I talked it over last night, and we figure you two can stay here until we work things out."

Holo looks over at me, waiting to see what I'll say. I've always made the decisions for us. What do I say? Should we stay? It seems crazy to me. But Holo wants to, I can tell. And I—well, I don't really have a better plan.

"Before you answer," the chief says, "I should point out that your only other option is going back to jail."

Or running away, I think.

But I know that I don't want to run. Not yet.

My mouth's full of bread, so I just nod. *Okay, fine.* I'm not thrilled about moving in with the guy who arrested me. But maybe that's what you get when you break a bunch of laws and you don't have any parents to rescue you.

"We want your lives to be as normal as possible until everything's figured out with the Grizzly," Lacey says. "And with . . . where you belong."

I choke on a bite of bread. Normal? Lacey doesn't understand that *none* of this is normal to us.

Later, lying in a big, soft bed for the first time ever, I can't fall asleep. I keep thinking I hear the wolves pacing around outside.

Looking for us. Missing us.

I get up and go to the window. The sky's gone black, and I can see a thousand stars and the blurry wash of the Milky Way. We're not so far away from where we were raised, but somehow it feels like I can't get there from here.

CHAPTER 16

IN THE MORNING, Lacey and the chief feed us a hot breakfast and then take us somewhere even worse than jail.

High school.

The principal's name is Mrs. Simon. She's hugely tall, and she shakes my hand with a grip so strong I wince.

"So you want to be a Kokanee Creek Cougar," she booms at me.

No, I can't say I do.

But Mrs. Simon looks like she could wrestle a cougar and win, so instead of answering I shrug. There's no need to get on her bad side on purpose; I'm pretty sure I'll do it soon enough by mistake.

"The chief tells me you two have never been to school before."

I shake my head no. My brother just stares at her. I can tell he's trying hard not to snarl.

"And you are"—she glances down at a piece of paper covered in notes—"seventeen and fourteen?"

I nod. Sounds about right.

Mrs. Simon turns to the chief and Lacey. "They do *speak,*

don't they? When we talked on the phone, you said nothing about them being mutes."

"Yes, ma'am, they speak," says the chief. "They're quiet on the whole, but if you piss 'em off, you'll hear about it."

"I'll ask you to watch your language in my office, Chief Greene," Mrs. Simon says briskly. "We must always be role models for our youth." Then she walks over to the door and opens it. "And now I'd like to speak with Kai and Holo alone."

Holo shoots me a fearful glance as the chief and Lacey obediently leave. I'm not worried, though. What's the worst Mrs. Simon can do to us? Enroll us in school?

"I hear you've had an unusual upbringing," Mrs. Simon says to us.

You don't know the half of it, lady.

"Frankly, I don't care about that. All I care about is how you act now, inside my halls. We are a high school, grades nine to twelve, and we are a community of— *What* are you doing, young man?"

Holo has grabbed a multicolored cube from her desk, and he's turning it over in his hands, staring at it in fascination. "What's this?" he says.

"So you *can* talk. That's good," Mrs. Simon says. Then, quick as a snake, she snatches the cube away from him. "It's called a Rubik's Cube, and you should never take it—or anything—off my desk without asking."

If he weren't so fascinated by the cube, Holo would've growled at her for sure. "What does it do?" he asks, unable to take his eyes off it.

"It's a puzzle," Mrs. Simon says. "You twist the blocks around in order to get only one color per side."

Holo's fingers reach for it. "Can I—"

"*May* I."

"May I hold it?"

Mrs. Simon gives the cube back, and Holo immediately starts twisting and spinning it. Then she hands me the newspaper off her desk. "Read this out loud, please."

I open the paper and stare down at the tiny letters. I can hear Mrs. Simon's heavy breathing. I stall. I sigh.

Unless I lie, she's going to find out the truth. I feel like I'm spilling a secret when I open my mouth.

"'The North Pines baseball team played a doubleheader last week,'" I read. "'On March 28, they swept the Kokanee Cougars, 6–2 and 9–1.'" I look up from the paper. "I'm not really familiar with the sport, but it sounds like your baseball team sucks."

If she's surprised, Mrs. Simon doesn't act like it. She takes the paper from me and throws it into a blue recycling bin. "Okay. The wolves taught Kai to read. Excellent. Holo, how's your math?"

Holo shrugs and places the Rubik's Cube back on her desk. He's never seen one before, yet he's solved it in about forty-five seconds.

"What's the square root of 121?" she asks him.

"Eleven," he says instantly. "Eleven is the fifth prime number, after two, three, five, and seven. A prime number is a number that has no divisor besides one and itself." Then he looks at me nervously, like he's afraid he's said something wrong.

At first I'm annoyed. We're freaks already, and now he's going to start tossing out math facts?

But then I soften. If we want to stay in the human world, we're going to have to go to school. The chief made that clear to us on the way over. Which means we need to prove to Mrs. Simon that we belong here.

"Very impressive," Mrs. Simon says.

Holo smiles shyly. "Thank you very much," he says. Every once in a while, the kid can really turn on the politeness.

She hands us each a pencil and a piece of paper covered in questions.

Evaluate 8x + 7 given that x - 3 = 10
What are the three branches of the US government?
What is a preposition?

I don't know if Holo gets the same questions as I do, but I race through mine.

When Mrs. Simon checks my answers, her eyes get narrow. Wary. "Do you know what I think?" she asks coolly.

"No, I haven't learned how to read minds yet. Do you teach that here? Because that would be cool."

Mrs. Simon scowls. She doesn't appreciate my sarcasm. "I believe that you're very clever, Kai. But I don't believe you were raised by wolves, and I don't think that anyone in their right mind would."

Holo's done with his test now, but instead of handing it to her, he starts ripping it into pieces. Mrs. Simon doesn't seem to notice.

"I think you two are running away from something," she says. "And I don't know what it is, but I'll find out."

CHAPTER 17

A BEDROOM IS much better than a jail cell, but it's nothing like the woods. My bed is too freaking soft and I'm alone. The cheerful yellow walls feel like they're closing in on me. The air is hot and still.

Last night was the first time I'd ever gone to sleep without Holo right next to me. I tossed and turned for hours, but I fell asleep eventually. Tonight, sleep isn't coming. I lie awake listening to the chief and Lacey talking in the kitchen. Every once in a while I hear our names. There's confusion and worry in their voices. Who are we? Where did we come from?

Look, I can barely answer those questions myself. But I'm used to that. What I want to know is this: am I crazy not to take Holo and run? Right *now*. It was me who wanted to come into this world. But Holo's the one who's really starting to like it. Earlier tonight he tucked himself between Lacey and the chief on the couch, and they all watched some dumb cop show together on the TV. It's like he already belongs here.

I'm not sure that I'll ever belong anywhere.

"Lacey?" my brother calls in a half whisper. "Lacey?"

I hear Lacey coming down the hallway and opening the door to Holo's room.

"What do you need, sweetheart?" she says.

No one's ever called Holo sweetheart before.

"I don't know," he admits.

Her laugh's low and sweet like her voice. "Let me tuck you in," she says.

"Okay," he says.

It hurts that Holo calls for Lacey instead of me.

Does your sister take care of you, Holo? Ms. Pettibon had asked. And Holo hadn't said yes.

But I taught him how to read the sky. I showed him how to look to the clouds for weather and the stars for directions. I taught him how to trap rainwater. I taught him which mushrooms are delicious and which are deadly. I taught him how to hunt and kill.

Isn't *that* taking care of someone?

"Are you glad to be here, Holo?" Lacey asks my brother.

"Yes," he says.

I've spent my life protecting Holo. From hunger. From wild animals. From loneliness. But how am I supposed to protect him from getting used to this comfortable, *human* life?

We're here now, but we can't stay forever.

I'm afraid he's going to forget that.

"I love you, Miss Lacey," he says.

He *loves* her? *Already?*

I turn my face to the wall. I don't believe in crying. So I just close my eyes and will myself to sleep.

Later I wake suddenly, all senses alert. Moonlight streams through my window. I wait—breath held, ears pricked. Then one lonely, haunted cry pierces the night. A moment later, it's joined by another. Then another.

Soon a howling chorus fills the air. The sound is so familiar to me, and it sends a chill up my spine.

It sounds like heartache. It sounds like home.

CHAPTER 18

POUNDING ON THE front door wakes Chester at 7 a.m. He groans and pulls the covers up over his face. It's the weekend, damn it, and he's supposed to be able to sleep in until eight. But the knocking won't stop.

Grumbling, he puts on his robe. Lacey sits up. "Who is it?" she asks sleepily.

"No one I want to see, I know that much," Chester says.

Sure enough, he's absolutely right. There are two men in dark suits standing stiff legged on his porch. One big, grizzled guy and one younger, shorter one. Nobody in Kokanee Creek wears a suit, not even to church. Chester takes an instant dislike to them.

"Chester Greene?" the grizzled one asks.

"Yes."

"I'm Special Agent Dunham," he says, flashing his credentials. "This is Field Agent Rollins."

Rollins lifts his chin in greeting and holds up his badge. "Good morning, Chief Greene."

Not anymore it isn't, Chester thinks. "What's the FBI doing in Kokanee Creek?"

"We hear the fishing's good," Agent Rollins says.

"It's still catch-and-release on the lake," Chester says, playing along. "And don't get your hopes up for any Kokanee salmon. It's going to be another bad year."

Agent Dunham doesn't care for the small talk. "We need to speak to the juveniles you have staying with you."

Chester's scowl turns to a look of surprise. How the hell do they know about Kai and Holo?

"Can I ask why?" There's no way a little B&E at the Grizzly Grocery would bring down the feds. The damage didn't even top five hundred bucks.

"You could," Agent Dunham says flatly.

"But there'd be no point, because you're not going to tell me."

"You're a quick study, Chief."

Chester reluctantly lets the men inside and wakes the kids while Lacey makes coffee for everyone.

By the time Chester comes out with a sleepy, rumpled Holo and a wary Kai, the men are sipping coffee on the couch. Lacey asks if she can make them breakfast, but Chester tells her that the FBI doesn't want any scrambled eggs.

"I do," Holo says, overhearing.

"Later," Chester says. His voice comes out sharper than he means it to.

Agent Dunham asks to speak to the kids alone. But he's not really *asking*. Chester leaves the room, but he stands as close as he can on the other side of the wall.

JAMES PATTERSON

He can hear Agent Rollins trying to put Kai and Holo at ease. "You're not in any trouble," he says.

He must be the Good Cop, Chester thinks.

Agent Rollins asks them to talk about where they come from. About how they've survived. And Kai tells the agents the same story she'd told Chester—how she and her brother lived deep in the woods. They hunted and fished. They fended for themselves. They'd done it for as long as they could remember.

"I'm sorry," Agent Dunham keeps saying, "can you go over that again?"

Okay, so the older one's playing Dumb Cop, Chester thinks. He knows the strategy: you make someone repeat their story, again and again, and pretty soon you'll find inconsistencies. You watch their body language carefully. Are they getting nervous? Do they ever seem confused? Did they just catch themselves in a lie?

The kids' version of their lives never changes. Kai answers in as few words as possible, and every fact is consistent. No, they're not runaways. No, they haven't stolen to survive— barring the Grizzly break-in, of course. Yes, they're all alone in the world. Yes, they like living with Chief Greene.

That's the answer that really surprises Chester. *Huh*, he thinks. *Who knew?*

Of course, they could be lying. They could be lying about everything. But if they are, they're very good at it.

After half an hour or so, the agents come into the kitchen, where Lacey and Chester are sitting at the table picking at their cold toast.

"Thanks for your time," Agent Rollins says. He tips an imaginary hat.

"Sorry to come by on your day off," Agent Dunham says insincerely.

"What'd you need to talk to those poor kids about?" Lacey demands. Her dark eyes flash.

Chester expects them to brush her off. But Dunham says, "The FBI never forgets a missing child, Mrs. Greene, no matter how long they've been missing."

"Hernandez," Lacey says icily. "My last name is Hernandez."

Chester says, "These kids just *got* here. What are you trying to say?"

But Dunham and Rollins are walking away before he even finishes asking the question.

CHAPTER 19

"TODAY'S A SPECIAL day," Lacey chirps as she hands us our new backpacks.

I sling the bright-blue pack over my shoulder. "Not so special for us."

"I think Miss Lacey meant to say 'scary,'" my brother whispers.

We'd rather face a pack of rabid coyotes than go to Kokanee Creek High School. We're not ready. We're not properly *trained*.

But the chief keeps telling us that we'll figure it out just fine. And Lacey insists we're going to love it.

"Say cheese," she says, waggling her camera at us.

"Why?" Holo asks. "Do you have some?"

Lacey laughs because she thinks he's joking. He's not.

"No cheese," I tell him.

"Really?" he asks. "But that's confusing."

I put my arm around my brother. "It's okay," I say. "We'll get you cheese soon."

"On a *burger*," he says.

"Sure thing."

We pose on the porch steps, wearing hand-me-down clothes and fake smiles. Holo keeps messing with his hair. Last night Lacey took a pair of kitchen shears to it. It's shorter than it's been in ten years.

After Lacey takes about a million pictures, we climb into the chief's truck. He's quiet as he drives into town. He looks tired. I wonder if the wolf chorus kept him up last night.

I wonder if he knows they were calling for us.

Or maybe the chief's quiet because he's more worried about sending us to school than he wants to admit. When he drops us off, he shakes our hands, which is weird, and he says, "Good luck, you two."

He must know how badly we need it.

There's a crowd of Kokanee kids hanging out in front near the flagpole, but Holo and I keep our distance. We don't want to be seen yet. We're nervous.

"We don't have to do this," Holo reminds me. "We can always run."

I tighten my backpack straps. "No, we can't," I say. "Not yet."

A school bus pulls up, brakes screeching, and even more high school kids get off. The crowd in front of the school gets bigger. Louder. They call out to one another. Jostle one another. It's a giant surging herd of humans.

A wolf looks for signs of vulnerability when picking its prey. The newborn elk calf. The lame bull. The yearling deer who stumbles on a rock in a dry riverbed.

I watch the crowd with hunter's eyes—but for what? Holo and I both know that the only vulnerable animals around here are us.

Wolves who trespass on other wolves' territory will be attacked. The goal is to be accepted by the pack.

A bell rings, and the front doors swing open. My heart gives a sickening leap. My brother grabs my hand, and I give his fingers a quick squeeze.

Then I let go and we start walking.

Inside Kokanee Creek High School, kids are shouting, laughing, slamming their lockers. Someone's playing loud and terrible music. Noise swirls around me. Voices ricochet off my skin.

"He says Michael kissed me, which is bullshit!"

"Yo, Gunner—where's my twenty?"

"Gedney seriously needs to give us a break."

"I didn't study, did you?"

I smell soap and perfume and sweat. Bodies brush against me. Someone steps on my foot. I start breathing too quickly. My hands start to shake. It's too loud. Too close. Too much for my senses to handle.

"Kai," Holo says, "are you all right?" He knows I'm not.

"I'm fine," I insist. "I just have to get to room 112."

He presses his shoulder tight against mine. Wordless, wolfish reassurance. And then we start walking again, weaving through all the people. We're doing okay until a grizzly-sized guy in a camo T-shirt steps in front of us, blocking our way.

He says, "Who the hell are you?"

He's so tall I've got to crane my head back to see his face. He's got tiny blue eyes and a short, fat nose. Blond hair cut close to a pink scalp. Small, mean teeth.

My jaw clenches. Holo starts to growl.

He laughs harshly. "Oh shit, never mind," he says. "I know who you are. You're the new *freaks*." He takes a menacing step forward. His smell washes over me. Musk. Sour milk. Crotch.

I freeze. I don't know whether to run or fight. We're in enemy territory. Holo crouches down and bares his teeth. He looks ready to spring.

Okay, I think. *Fight it is.*

I'm scanning the giant kid's body for where to hit first when suddenly there's a teacher in between us and him. "Mr. Hardy," she says, all sugary sweet, "your classroom is down that way. I wouldn't want you to be late again. Would you?"

His pink face gets pinker with rage. Then he turns and lumbers away down the hall, muttering under his breath.

Hardy, I think. *That means he's one of* them.

In a normal voice, the teacher says to me, "Are you Kai? I'm Ms. Tillman, your ELA teacher." She's kind of old, but her hair's dyed turquoise. There's a tattoo of a mountain bluebird on her freckled forearm.

"Yes, I'm Kai," I say. *What's ELA?*

"Come on in," she says, gesturing to her classroom.

I don't move. What about my brother? Every cell in my body screams *Don't separate the pack*. As if he can hear this silent cry, Holo steps closer to me. His bony elbow pokes my ribs.

"Do you know where your classroom is?" Ms. Tillman asks him.

Holo looks blankly down at his schedule. "No," he says.

"I think you must be upstairs with Mr. Williams. He teaches the ninth graders."

"He's staying with me," I say.

Ms. Tillman blinks at me in surprise. "Well, I don't know if that—"

"You should definitely just agree, Ms. Tillman," says a voice right behind me. "These two get pretty mad when they don't get what they want. They'll definitely growl, and I think they might actually *bite*."

The voice is low and amused. It's also familiar.

I turn around, and Waylon Eugene Meloy's brown-gold eyes lock on mine. He gives me a lazy smile. "Hello, Kai," he says. "Remember me?"

My cheeks flare hot. My stomach wobbles. I want to turn and run away into the woods. I want to reach out and press my palm against his chest.

Instead I shake my head. "No," I say. "Can't say I do."

Then I grab Holo's sleeve and pull him toward two empty desks in the back of Ms. Tillman's classroom.

"Liar!" Waylon calls after me.

Laughing.

CHAPTER 20

I DON'T GET school at *all*.

It's not about being stupid. I've got an answer for any question the teachers throw at me. What I can't understand is why you'd shove a bunch of teenagers into a room and expect them to sit quietly while some boring old guy drones on about a subject they don't care about.

I'm not saying that kids *shouldn't* care about chemistry or civics. I'm just saying that they *don't*. The kids at Kokanee Creek spend half the class playing games on their laptops and the other half looking at their phones. Except, every once in a while, they take a break to stare at me and Holo.

The new freaks.

Usually I stare right back.

Usually my brother growls.

Mrs. Simon, the principal, doesn't appreciate the animal noises. She pulls us aside right after lunch and wags her finger in my brother's face. "If you are to be a member of the Cougar community," she says, "and I do mean *if*, then there will be no more growling."

"It's a natural response to a threat," I say.

"It is an *animal's* response, and you are not an animal."

"Actually, last time I checked, we all are."

Mrs. Simon smiles thinly at me. "You know what I mean." Then she takes my brother by the elbow—"Let's have you attend *your* classes this afternoon, dear," she says—and steers him away down the hall. As Holo looks back at me, alarmed, Mrs. Simon calls over her shoulder, "Anyway, they are no *threats* to you here at Kokanee Creek High School!"

Really? Are you sure about that?

That's my first thought when I get to PE class and see that Hardy monster leaning against the gym wall, glaring at me.

Apparently his name is Mac. Short for MacDougal, which is an even worse name than Eugene.

I turn my back to him. I want him to know that I'm not afraid.

The PE teacher, Mr. Chive, blows his whistle at us. "Timed eight-hundreds today," he says. "Everybody out to the track!"

I don't know what this means. But everyone in the class groans, so it must suck. A girl in a bright-purple sweatshirt sinks to the floor. She looks like she's about to cry.

"Outside, everyone!" Mr. Chive roars. "Get up, please, Lucy."

Lucy rolls her eyes.

"What's a timed eight-hundred?" I ask when she's gotten to her feet.

She rolls her eyes again.

"Okay, cool, thanks," I say. Maybe *she's* the mute one.

I follow Lucy and the rest of the class out to the red oval track behind the school. Mr. Chive starts leading warm-up stretches "to get the blood flowing." I'm doing arm circles when Mac starts scratching himself all over.

"I think I've got fleas," he calls to his friends. "The wolf girl must've given them to me."

I ignore him. A basic rule of the forest: whenever possible, don't piss off an animal that's bigger and stronger than you are.

Mr. Chive says, "All right, everybody stretch your hamstrings!"

I copy what everyone else is doing. I grab my ankle and lift my foot until the back of my heel touches my butt. I've never really stretched anything before. It feels kind of good.

Mac hops closer to me on one leg. He's panting now, and his tongue's lolling out. "*Yip, yip, yip,*" he whispers. His eyes linger on my chest. I hunch my shoulders and turn away.

"Bend down slowly and touch your toes," Mr. Chive calls. "Then roll up to standing, one vertebra at a time."

I follow his directions. By the time I stand up, Mac's moved even closer. He's right behind me. I can feel his hot, humid breath on my neck.

"You'd better watch your *back*, freak," he mutters.

I stay rigid. Silent.

Don't engage the larger animal.

Then we're done with stretching, and Mr. Chive counts us off into running groups. Mac's in the first one. He struts to the starting line, bragging about how fast he is. How he's going to make everyone eat his dust. He looks too big to be quick, but then again, an eight-hundred-pound grizzly can run at twice the speed of a man.

When Mr. Chive blows the whistle, group one takes off running. They start at a sprint, the guys jostling one another, each of them wanting to get out in front and stay there. When they round the first curve, Mac's already got a ten-foot lead.

Chive calls, "Group two!" and the next crew of kids goes. After that bunch turns the corner, Chive yells for group three to go.

That's my group, and I don't hesitate. I shoot forward, arms and legs pumping. Ahead of me, the red track's smooth and flat.

Running in the woods, I have to dodge branches. Swerve around rocks. Jump over streams. A misstep could mean broken bones. Death. But this—this is like flying. I don't have to do anything but find my speed and settle into it.

In a hunt, it's the lighter, faster female wolves who drive the prey. The bigger, stronger males who bring it down.

The wind whistles in my ears, and the trees rush by me in a blur of green. I'm not even breathing heavily. I catch up with group two. Pass them.

Group one's a couple hundred feet in front of me when I finish my first circuit of the track. Mac's still way out ahead of them, running gracefully for how big he is. His feet fly over the ground.

Overtaking him isn't going to be easy. His legs are twice as long as mine.

I lean forward. Lift my knees a little higher to drive power from my hips. Push my foot strikes faster. Breathe hard but steady. Wish for four legs instead of two. A wolf can run at thirty-five miles an hour around this track without breaking a sweat. And that's not because wolves *can't* sweat.

I'm catching up to Mac Hardy. My legs burn, but I don't care. I could run like this forever. There's nothing to think about but the speed and the breath. The body knows what to do.

I'm right behind him.

I stay there as we sprint down the back straightaway. *Thanks for blocking the wind for me, Mac!*

He doesn't realize I'm there. We lap the stragglers from group three.

A wolf knows that if it follows a herd of elk long enough, eventually one of them's going to panic. If it leaves the trail, it's dead meat.

"*Hi*," I call to Mac's back.

He flinches like he's been hit. He puts on another burst of speed. He thinks it's going to be enough. But I know it's not.

As we round the last curve, I swing wide. I pass him on the right. Then I'm down the final stretch alone, lungs screaming. Arms pumping. Feet pounding. Hair streaming out behind me.

People are shouting, but I can't tell what they're saying. When I cross the finish line first, everyone goes quiet.

"Holy shit," someone whispers. "Did you *see* that?"

Mac crosses the line five full seconds behind me. He stumbles to the edge of the track and bends over, hands on his thighs. He's gasping. Wheezing. Cursing whenever he can get enough air in his lungs to talk.

My heart pounds and my throat's raw, but I feel amazing. I

walk toward him, smiling. And I lean in close so only he can hear me. "I guess you had to watch my back for me, didn't you?"

And then I leave him there, still hunched over—and now throwing up into the grass.

CHAPTER 21

HOLO'S WATCHING A raven preen itself when Lacey pulls up in her hatchback. The old Volkswagen belches a cloud of exhaust. Holo chokes on it. He's not used to machine and engine smells. He hates them. They sear his nose and burn his throat.

"Hey, you, how was school?" Lacey asks, beaming.

Holo blinks. How's he supposed to answer that? He'd felt trapped. Scared. Confused. The food was weird and soft—though he ate it, whatever it was (some kind of meat, sitting in a salty, brown puddle)—and he'd had to take something called a quiz. He'd gotten yelled at for growling. And then he'd met another Hardy, younger than the big one but just as mean. Logan Hardy had said that all wolves should be shot on sight, and that anyone who thought otherwise deserved to get their freaky asses kicked.

"Ummm . . . It was okay," Holo tells Lacey.

"Good! Where's Kai?"

Holo glances back toward the school. He hasn't seen his

sister since Mrs. Simon led him away from her after lunch. But the bell rang twenty minutes ago, and he watched all the other kids go home. He can't help the thought he has next: *What if she ran?*

But she wouldn't, not without him.

Would she?

The raven rasps from the tree branch. Holo looks up to watch it flap away and disappear into the blue sky.

"Should I go in and look around?" Lacey asks.

Holo shakes his head. She wouldn't be able to find Kai unless Kai wanted to be found. And he doubts that she does. "We have to wait," he says.

Lacey says, "All right, we've got time. Hop in, why don't you?"

"No thanks." He doesn't want to breathe car air. He doesn't want to hear the car radio. He stands there, fists clenched. *Kai, where are you?*

Lacey sings along to the radio. Something about a guy named Bruno and how no one's supposed to talk about him.

Kai, you didn't leave me, did you?

Did you?

Ten terrible minutes later, his sister finally appears. Relief floods Holo's body. *She didn't run.* But when she gets close, Holo sees that she has thunder in her eyes. Kai's scary when she looks like that, so he doesn't tell her how worried he was. He just presses his shoulder tight against hers.

She doesn't speak the whole car ride back to Chester and Lacey's house. She stares out the window. But that's okay, Holo tells himself. They've gone days without talking before. Nature doesn't care about words.

When they turn onto the gravel road, Kai starts whis-
tling. Yellow-rumped warbler. Then song sparrow. House
finch. Holo takes this as a good sign. He thinks her mood's
improving.

Which is why he doesn't react quickly enough when Lacey
stops in front of the cabin and Kai flings open the car door
and starts running. He just stands there, his mouth hanging
open. Shocked.

"Kai?" he calls, stupefied. "Kai?"

She's heading for the woods. In the underbrush he sees a
flash of gray. A pair of golden eyes.

"Kai!"

By the time he gets his feet moving, his sister and the wolf
have vanished into the trees.

CHAPTER 22

RUN.

It's my first instinct. I leave my brother behind and race toward the two silvery shadows already fading into the woods. Try to touch the tails as they disappear into the underbrush.

I run even faster than I did on the track. They're only fifty yards ahead of me. They flow through the trees, graceful as wind. They could let me catch up to them if they wanted to.

But they don't want to. They speed away from me like I'm just another human. A stranger—or an enemy.

"Come back!" I cry. "It's me! Wait!"

But wolves aren't dogs. They don't come when you call them.

They get smaller and smaller and soon I can't see them at all. I stop and bend over, gasping for breath. My lungs scream. My heart aches.

They left me, I think, *they left me*.

When I stand upright again, the forest is quiet.

I'm utterly alone.

But I can feel how the woods welcome me. How the ground knows my footsteps. I feel a weight lift from my shoulders.

There's no school here in the woods. No Hardys. No Chief "You Might Still Face Criminal Charges" Greene. I'm just another animal in the wilderness. A creature without paws or fangs or fur, but an animal all the same.

What if I keep on walking? What if I don't go back? Will Holo know to come find me? Can we—should we—pretend that all this never happened?

The piercing cry of a red-tailed hawk interrupts my thoughts. Of course I have to go back. If I'm going to give up now, then we shouldn't have come out of the woods in the first place. We should've stayed lost forever.

Maybe that would have been easier.

Just walk, Kai. Put one foot in front of the other. You know where you have to go.

By the time I get back to the cabin, Lacey's making dinner. Holo, sitting at the kitchen table, looks at me accusingly. "Where'd you go?"

Lacey says, "And why'd you go there so damn *fast*?"

I dump an armload of roots and leaves on the table. "I went foraging," I tell them. "I just suddenly had a craving for wild greens."

"Oh," Lacey says, as if this is perfectly reasonable.

Holo can tell that I'm lying. But he doesn't say anything. We know how to keep each other's secrets. We always have.

"What is all this?" Lacey says, picking up a long, thin root and looking at it curiously.

"Biscuit-root," I say. "It grows by the lodgepole pines and in the meadow. And that's lamb's-quarter from near the stream. And dandelions from your garden."

"Neat," she says brightly. "But what do you do with them?"

"You eat them, obviously," I say. My hands are dirty. I start to rub them on my pants, but then I remember the kitchen sink. I may not love the human world, but I love its running water.

"For dinner?" Lacey asks, sounding uncertain. "I was making burgers."

"I love burgers," Holo says dreamily. "Especially when they have cheese on them."

"They'll keep," I say. "I'll just put them in the—the thing."

"You mean the refrigerator?"

"I forgot what it was called," I admit. Can you blame me? I've never used one before.

The chief comes into the kitchen after I've stashed the wild food next to the plastic packaged food.

"I think I saw your friends just now," he says.

"We don't have any friends," I remind him.

"I'm talking about the wolves," he says.

They've come back? Then why did they run away from me?

"They were checking me out," the chief says.

"They don't care about you, don't worry," I tell him. "They just want to make sure we're okay."

"Well, why don't you tell them that you are, so they don't keep coming around?"

The chief's right: they shouldn't be getting this close to houses. They ought to stay deep in the wilderness where they belong. But I can't help bristling at his tone. "Is my *family* bothering you?"

"They're dangerous animals, Kai." The chief reaches into the thing—the refrigerator, whatever—and gets a beer. "Wouldn't want to have to shoot one."

Before I even realize I'm doing it, I've grabbed the knife that Lacey was using to chop carrots and I'm pointing it at his chest. "No offense, Chief," I say, "but if you do that, it's going to be the last thing that you do."

The chief frowns, but he stands his ground. "You're a fierce one, huh, Kai?"

The knife's shaking in my hand. Maybe I've gone too far. Maybe he's going to throw me in jail again.

Let him try.

"She's fierce as fuck!" Holo says.

Lacey and the chief whip around and stare at him in shock. "Holo!" Lacey exclaims. "We don't use that word in this house."

"Why not?" Holo asks innocently. "I learned it at school."

Then the chief bursts out laughing, and all the tension in the room suddenly breaks. "Well," he says, "I guess that doesn't surprise me. But it's a bad word, Holo. A curse word, and we don't use it around here."

"Oh. Sorry," Holo says.

"Did you learn any other words today?" I ask my brother.

Holo nods. "Yeah. Shitass, dickface—"

"I think that's enough," the chief says. "Thanks, Holo." He's still smiling.

And I slowly put down the knife.

CHAPTER 23

SATURDAY APPARENTLY MEANS something special to people around here. In the woods, every day was the same: we'd wake up, we'd survive, and when darkness fell we'd sleep. But the weekend is different in Kokanee Creek. Kids don't go to school, Lacey serves a buffet brunch at the KC Diner, and the chief drinks an extra cup of coffee before he goes out on his rounds.

He's halfway out the door when he asks if I want to come along.

"Me?" I say, confused.

"You see anyone else around here?"

"No." Lacey's gone, and Holo's still snoring upstairs.

"Come on, then," he says. "I could use your help."

I can't imagine what he thinks I can help him with, but I've got nothing better to do. I put on my shoes.

The chief turns on the radio as we drive. I recognize the song and start singing along. "*Maybe you're the problem...*"

"Did the wolves teach you that one?" the chief asks.

He thinks he's funny. I shoot him a sideways glare and don't answer. Last year I stole a radio from an illegal campsite and listened to it every night until the batteries died. But that isn't any of his business, is it?

The chief turns off at a sign that says RABBITS and heads us up a dirt driveway alongside a stubbly pasture. A few cows are standing off in the distance looking bored and fly-bothered. As we drive up to the house, a flock of chickens scatters in every direction. White feathers swirl up into the air.

"You tend to see the gun first with these folks," the chief says. "But if you greet it—and them—respectfully, it'll be all right."

"And you're bringing me along *why*?" I ask as I follow him out of the car.

The chief takes his turn not answering. He goes up to the door and knocks loudly, *one-two-three*. I hang back at a safe distance. Sure enough, I see the barrel of a gun come out first.

It lowers when whoever's inside sees that it's the Kokanee Creek police chief on the porch. The door opens wider and a woman steps out, barefoot and scowling.

"If this is about Charlie, he's eighteen now and he don't answer to me no more," she says. "Not that he ever did. Just like his daddy—more stubborn than a mule in concrete, and only about half as smart."

"It's not about Charlie, Mrs. Hill. I'm here about your daughter, Julissa. Is she here?"

Mrs. Hill looks halfway over her shoulder like she's checking the hall behind her. "Nope."

"When was the last time you saw her?"

Her eyebrows knit together. "Earlier this week, I guess."

"Can you tell me the day?"

"No, sir, I can't. But she's sixteen. Old enough to take care of herself."

"Not legally," the chief says. "And she hasn't been in school since last Friday."

"Huh," Mrs. Hill says. She doesn't sound concerned.

The chief turns and looks at me. Beckons me forward. "I brought along one of her friends. This is Kai. She misses Julissa a lot."

I nod enthusiastically. *Julissa! Love that girl! We go waaaaay back.*

Mrs. Hill just looks at me like I smell bad. Admittedly, I might.

"It didn't occur to you to mention Julissa's absence to anyone?" the chief asks her.

"Hell, no, I was enjoying the peace and quiet." She lumbers down the porch steps and starts walking around to the back of the house. "That girl's attitude! She don't get what she wants, she gets meaner than a rattlesnake."

The chief and I follow Mrs. Hill into a big dirt yard lined with dozens of homemade chicken-wire cages. Inside the cages: hundreds—thousands?—of rabbits. As we get closer, they hop nervously back and forth. Their little ears and noses twitch adorably. Mrs. Hill picks up a bucket of feed and starts pouring it into the nearest cage.

"Julissa's gone off before and always come back," Mrs. Hill says. "I don't think no harm's going to come to her."

"What if it does?" the chief asks.

"No one looked after me, and no harm came. I turned out just fine."

It's obvious the chief doesn't entirely agree with her on this count. "This is an unofficial visit, Mrs. Hill. What one neighbor would do for another. But if you file a missing persons report, there's a lot *more* that I can do."

I walk over to the nearest cage. A fluffy brown rabbit sniffs my fingers. I touch its soft cheek through the wire.

"If she don't turn up, I'll give you a call," Mrs. Hill says.

The chief sighs. "I hope I hear from you soon. Actually, I take that back—I hope you hear from your daughter."

"Uh-huh." Mrs. Hill moves on to the next cage, dumps more pellets in.

Another rabbit, a gray one, hops over to check me out. "You've got a lot of pet bunnies," I say.

Mrs. Hill turns around with the bucket in her hand and shoots me a look like I'm crazy. Then she barks out a laugh. "*Pets?*" she says. "Ha, that's a good one."

The gray rabbit nibbles my thumb. Its whiskers tickle. *If you're not a pet*, I think, *then you're—*

"Come along, Kai," the chief says. "Let's go."

As we walk back to the car, the chief looks worried. Angry, too.

I don't know this Julissa person, but I can sympathize. "If that was my mom, I probably wouldn't hang around much, either," I say.

But isn't a bad mom better than no mom? It's the tiny thought that I quickly push away.

The chief gives a heavy sigh. "Being a police officer teaches you a lot about human nature, Kai," he says as we drive away.

"I know why people steal and cheat—even why they fight and kill. I'm not saying that it's right. I'm saying that I can *understand* it. But I'll never get why folks don't do better by their kids. 'You *made* them,' I want to say to these people. 'Why can't you take care of them?'"

Then he looks over at me like he's just realized that he's said something wrong.

And sure—maybe for a second there's another little tiny thought that goes: *Why didn't my parents take care of* me?

But that's an old question. An old wound. I don't pick at it anymore.

"Kai," the chief says. "Are you okay?"

I stare out the window at the trees going by, the green world that Holo and I left behind. The world of dirt and stone and sky. "I'm just thinking about all those rabbits," I tell him.

"Did that upset you?"

"You mean because they spend their whole entire lives in pens, and then they end up in a stew?" I say.

The chief grimaces. "Yes."

I can still feel the rabbit's soft gray fur on my fingertips. Still picture its bright black eyes. But nature's nature, right? We all need to eat.

I shake my head. "Chief, mountain cottontails taste great, but they run *fast*. It's a lot easier to catch a rabbit for dinner if it's already in a damn cage."

The chief looks a bit queasy now. But he just says, all quiet and pleading, "We don't say that word, either, Kai, okay?"

CHAPTER 24

DRIVING BACK INTO Kokanee Creek, the chief asks if I want to keep riding along on his rounds. "I've got to check on a report about a sick raccoon in someone's garage. Then I'll go make sure Dougie isn't causing trouble. It's ten a.m., so he's sure to be drunk already."

The chief sounds like he actually wants me to come along. I can't quite figure it out. Is he trying to prove he's a nice guy? I guess by now I can *tell* that he is, but that doesn't mean I have to be nice back. I'm planning on holding that jail experience against him forever.

So that's the first reason I'm not sticking around while he protects Kokanee Creek from drunks and vermin. The second reason is that I hate riding in a car. Being strapped inside a tiny, moving room that smells like gasoline makes me feel like I'm going to be sick.

"I better go back and check on Holo," I say.

Does your sister take care of you, Holo? Yes! Yes, damn it, I do.

"Okay," the chief says, nodding. "Sure." He seems disappointed.

Sorry, Chief.

Sort of.

By the time we get back to the meadow, Holo's sitting on the porch looking pissed. "You can't keep running off like that, Kai," he fumes.

"Blame Chief Greene," I say. "He totally forced me to go."

Since the chief's already pulling away, he can't deny it.

"You could've left a note," Holo points out.

"I thought you'd still be asleep." I sit down next to my brother. The air smells like pine, the wooden steps are warm from the sun, and a trio of cedar waxwings make high-pitched whistles from a nearby tree. My mood lifts immediately. Being outside's *so* much better than being inside.

Unless, of course, it's the middle of the Idaho winter. In that case, you'd better have really good shelter or else you're going to be saying goodbye to half of your toes.

Holo's ripping stalks of prairie June grass into tiny pieces. "I'm bored," he whines.

"Seriously? You just discovered the human world a week ago. How can you be bored already? Go turn some lights off and on."

"I did that when I woke up. I experimented with the garbage disposal thing, too." His eyes widen. "It grinds up everything."

Uh-oh. *Don't ask*, I think. *Don't ask*.

His face turns serious. "What are you supposed to do when you don't have to collect water to drink or make a fire to keep warm? What do you do when the food just gets *handed* to you?"

When someone's really, truly *taking care of you.* That's what he means. Fine, I get it. It's new to both of us.

I pat his bony knee and then get up and start walking toward the trees. "Come on," I say, "let's go not be bored."

We push our way through the underbrush. The light gets dimmer and greener the farther we go into the woods. Our footsteps are silent. We leave no tracks behind us.

After half an hour, Holo stops and looks around in dismay. "No one's here," he says.

By no one, he means no wolves.

"They know where to find us if they want to," I say sharply. I'm still mad at them for running. "Let's keep walking."

Holo and I go another half mile and then we come to a wide, deep creek. We pick our way along the edge until we find a bend where the water has eaten away at the bank to form an overhanging ledge of dirt and roots.

"Yes," Holo whispers, because this is exactly what we need right now.

I lie down on the ledge, belly to ground. My fingers trail in the cold water.

Holo knows what he's supposed to do next. He walks downstream a ways, and then he steps into the creek and starts wading in my direction.

He's herding any fish toward the shelter of the ledge . . . and my waiting hands.

Shadowy trout slip away from him through the water. They slide under the stream's bank, thinking that they've escaped danger.

They haven't.

I'm right above them.

I wait, my hands unmoving in the water, until I feel a brush against my wrist—and then my fingers snap closed around a fish's belly. I pin it to the bottom of the undercut while it struggles. I work my fingers into the gills so I've got a good grip, and then I fling it over my shoulder onto the shore.

Kai 1, rainbow trout 0.

Holo lowers himself into the water so he can reach under the bank and grab them from below. He moves slowly, slowly, sloooowly—until suddenly he doesn't.

"Pinned one," he says, grinning. Water streams down his happy face.

We repeat the herd-and-grab process until we've got a little pile of speckled rainbow trout. While Holo guts and cleans them, I look around for more things to eat. I don't have to look too hard to find morel mushrooms and a bunch of miner's lettuce.

We rest creekside for a while, and then we walk back to the cottage with our arms full. In the early evening we make a fire in the yard. And by the time Lacey and the chief get home, there's a feast waiting for them.

Lacey looks like you could knock her over with a sneeze. "Did you two—"

"Yes," Holo interrupts, so excited to surprise her. "We cooked dinner!"

"I don't think anyone's cooked me dinner in a decade," Lacey says, and then she gives the chief the side-eye.

He says, "Oh, come on now, Lacey, I grill us steaks."

"Okay," she acknowledges. "But you sure don't know how to make a salad or a side dish, do you?"

"A what?" the chief says, and then they're laughing, and he

kisses her cheek before she goes into the kitchen and brings out a bottle of wine. The chief spreads out a blanket on the grass. Then he goes inside and comes back out with plates and forks.

"Why are you bringing all that stuff out here?" Holo wants to know.

"When it's a nice day, sometimes you eat outside on the ground, and it's called a picnic," Lacey says.

"I guess wolves have picnics all the time, then," Holo says.

Lacey laughs, but of course Holo isn't trying to be funny; he's just figuring stuff out. And considering we've never lived in an actual house before, or been to actual school, we're not nearly as ignorant as we could be.

The food we made is a thousand times better than Wendy's or the slop they serve in the cafeteria. Lacey's licking her fingers when she says, "You know what, Holo, you might just be right."

"About what?" he asks eagerly. He's so excited to be right about something—*anything*.

"About Kai being the best cook there is," she says.

Then she grins at him and ruffles his hair, and my brother doesn't duck away. Instead he smiles back at her, and then he rests his head on her shoulder.

The compliment ought to make me feel good. But suddenly I'm afraid. I'm convinced that the human world is going to tear my brother and me apart.

CHAPTER 25

BACK AT SCHOOL on Monday, I can't stop thinking about that missing girl. Julissa. When did she disappear? And why?

Her mother seems to think that sixteen years is old enough to leave. If you ask me, she's probably right. Hell, a wolf might leave its pack when it's two.

But the chief seems pretty worried. Like maybe something bad happened to her. I wonder if Julissa's okay, and if she knows people are wanting her back home. Maybe she thinks that no one's even noticed she's gone.

Did anyone notice when Holo and I disappeared? I don't know. All I know is that it's a lonely thing to wonder.

I must've had a weird look on my face, because suddenly Waylon plops down next to me in the cafeteria and says, "Look, I know you prefer growling to talking, but you've obviously got something on your mind." He leans closer and says confidentially, "I have to warn you, I don't speak Wolf. But I get straight As in English and solid Bs in Spanish."

I'm so surprised that he snuck up on me that I just stare at him. How could I let my guard down like that? But his body language says *friend*, not *foe*. Okay, fine, good—but what am I supposed to say back? The woods taught me a lot of things, but the art of conversation wasn't one of them.

"Hi," Waylon says, holding out his hand for me to shake. "*Again.* Do you remember me this time?"

Just play along, I think. *Try to act like a normal teenager. Whatever that is.*

I cock my head to the side and look thoughtful. It'd be too much to take his hand. "I'm not sure," I say, squinting at him. "You seem vaguely familiar."

His grin's brighter than electric light. "Well, I'm part of your criminal past. So I can understand why you'd want to forget," he says. "I'm Waylon Eugene Meloy. Nice to meet you. *Again.*"

"I'm Kai," I say. "Just Kai."

"Trust me, I remember your name," Waylon Eugene Meloy says. He scooches closer to me. "So, what's on your mind? Are you still trying to figure out what it was you just ate? Cafeteria food is never fantastic, but today's lunch was especially... *mysterious.*"

"'Mysterious' is a nice way to put it. I've had slugs that tasted better than that."

"You've had *what*?" Waylon says.

"Never mind," I say quickly. It's time to change the subject. And maybe it's time to be honest, too. "I was thinking about a girl named Julissa," I admit. "Do you know her?"

"Yeah, she's in my math class."

"Have you seen her at school lately?"

Waylon ponders this for a second. "No."

"Her mother doesn't know where she is. And she doesn't seem to care, either."

"I'm jealous," Waylon says. "If only *my* mom didn't care."

"I don't know a lot about parents," I admit, "but isn't caring a main part of their job?"

Waylon looks intently at me. He seems like he's going to say something. *Ask* something. But then he gives his head a little shake and says, "Julissa. Right. You should talk to her friends. See if she's been in touch with them. Look, they're right over there."

I turn to where he's pointing. There's a corner table of girls looking at something on a phone and giggling. They have shiny ponytails and painted lips and they're clustered tightly together. A *pack*.

"Do I just go over there and ask them?"

"Yeah," Waylon says. "Girls love being approached by people they don't know."

Girls are different than wolves then, I guess.

And so I walk over and I take a deep breath, and I ask them if they've seen Julissa lately. They don't seem to hear me, so I ask it again.

One by one, they lift their heads. And they just stare. They don't say a single word. They look at me like I'm a foreign species. An invader.

"Julissa?" I repeat. "Do you know where she is?"

My answer is just dead-eyed silence.

I walk back to Waylon. "That didn't work," I tell him.

He laughs. "Of course it didn't!"

"Then why did you tell me to do it?" I cry.

He brushes his bangs away from his face. "Maybe I was getting back at you for not remembering me. Or maybe I thought you should learn something important about high school, which is that a lot of people in it are assholes."

"The Hardys already taught me that, thanks," I say.

"Gotta love those guys," Waylon says. "They're *champion* assholes. They take their duties very seriously." He stands up; the bell's about to ring. "I do have a real idea, though," he adds. "About Julissa."

"I don't believe you."

"I'm telling the truth this time. I think we can find her."

"Where?"

"Meet me in the parking lot after school," he says.

CHAPTER 26

"I DON'T GET why you're so worried about her, though," Waylon says as we walk east along the road toward town. "You've never even met Julissa Hill."

"Well, the chief's worried." I point to the rangeland, the mountains, the forest—all the wilderness that surrounds Kokanee Creek. "It's dangerous out there."

And I know all about it.

"She didn't get eaten by a bear, Kai."

"How do you know?"

"Because we're juniors at Kokanee Creek High School. We aren't elk and wolves in a nature show about how only the strongest survive."

"For your information, *no one* survives," I say. "Nature's a battle that all of us lose."

"How cheerful," Waylon says sarcastically.

"Sorry for being honest."

"Uh, you're obviously not."

"Okay, I'm sorry that I'm *not* sorry. Maybe living in a city cuts you off from the realities of life and death, but it's a fact."

"Last time I looked, Kokanee Creek wasn't actually a city."

He has a point—what's the population, three thousand? But still. "It might as well be Paris as far as I'm concerned."

Waylon laughs and knocks his shoulder into mine in a friendly, maybe even flirty way. When his skin slides against mine, I feel its smooth, delicious warmth. And I just *freeze*. Every muscle in my body goes tense. I actually stop breathing.

"Kai?" he says. "Are you okay?"

No, no I'm not.

My heart's pounding.

Get it together, Kai. Breathe.

"What happened?" he asks.

I inhale and blink at him. Try to smile and brush it off. Start to move again. "Tonic immobility," I say.

Waylon looks at me blankly.

"After a predator has made contact with its prey, the prey freezes to prevent further attack," I explain. "It's called tonic immobility."

He shakes his head. "Kai," he says, "I'm not a predator."

"I know," I say. *Of course you're not.* "I just—oh, never mind. I'm sorry." I start to walk faster. I can hardly admit that one touch of Waylon's skin sent me reeling. Made me feel something I'd never felt before.

Get it together, Kai.

Waylon hurries to catch up to me. "Don't growl at me for asking, but don't you think it's ironic that you've gone from being a convict to an aspiring crime solver?"

This ridiculous question breaks the spell that Waylon doesn't even know he put on me. "I'm not a convict, because I was never even charged with anything, let alone convicted," I say. "And I *really* hope there's no crime we're going to uncover."

As we walk past the diner, I catch a glimpse of Holo through the window. Lacey had promised him ice cream after school. I wave, but he doesn't see me.

You don't need fangs for three scoops of ice cream, Holo. Hell, you don't even need teeth.

But why am I annoyed? Isn't this what I wanted for us—to live like everyone else? I shake off my weird feeling of unease and keep walking.

"Do we have far to go?" I ask Waylon when we've reached the far edge of town.

"Define 'far,'" he says.

I think about this. "Ten miles."

His mouth drops open. "You're joking."

A wolf pack's territory is a hundred square miles or more. "No."

"We'll be there in ten minutes," he says.

"There" is a faded yellow house overlooking a weed-choked pond. A couple of dogs on the front porch get to their feet as we approach. I check for stiff legs and raised hackles. But I don't see those signs of aggression.

The dogs sniff our legs as we climb the steps. One of them wags its stumpy tail. Waylon gives it a pat and then knocks on the door.

After a while a twentysomething guy with pale, scruffy cheeks and a confused expression opens it and says, "What are you doing here?"

"Hey, Carl," says Waylon. "How's your score on *Red Dead Redemption*?"

"Better than yours, bro, that's for sure," Carl says. His blood-shot eyes shift over to me. "You two selling Girl Scout Cookies or something? I only like Samoas, so fuck off with your Thin Mints and your peanut-butter whatevers."

Waylon gives a tiny shake of his head and mouths *He's not my bro* at me. I try not to laugh. Then he says, "I had to quit the Girl Scouts, Carl. I just couldn't earn my sewing badge." Then he gets serious and his voice goes lower. "I'm wondering if you've seen Julissa around."

"Julissa?" Carl repeats. "Who's asking?"

"Us, obviously," I say sharply. I don't like this guy. He smells sour. Weak. He wouldn't survive a day in a state park, let alone a lifetime in the wilderness.

Carl frowns and starts to close the door on us. But Way-lon puts his foot in the way and turns to me. "Carl is Julissa's secret boyfriend, Kai, so we should be polite to him."

I look more closely at skinny, greasy Carl in his sweat-stained T-shirt. *That guy? Ewww.*

Carl starts to protest, but Waylon calmly keeps explain-ing things to me. "Carl's twenty-five, so Julissa hasn't told her mom about him. She hasn't told her friends, either. They *definitely* wouldn't approve. No offense, Carl."

"Then how do *you* know about him?" I demand.

"Because I'm an observant person. Generally I'd rather watch people than talk to them."

How come you keep talking to me, then? I think. But I say, "You didn't notice that Julissa was gone."

Waylon ducks his head, acknowledging this. "True. But she skips school a lot."

Carl says to Waylon, "So you're Nancy damn Drew now, huh?" He looks mad.

"I guess," Waylon says good-naturedly.

Carl stares at Waylon for another minute, like he's trying to decide whether to punch him or invite him in to play video games. Eventually—probably because he knows he'd lose the fight—Carl opens the door wider and says, "All right."

Inside, the living room's dark and it smells like old cigarette smoke and stale beer. There's a dark-haired girl lying on a lumpy brown couch with a Coke balanced on her stomach. She turns to Waylon and says dully, "What are you doing here?"

"Funny, that's just what your boyfriend asked us," Waylon says. "I told him we were looking for you."

Relief floods my body. *Julissa's safe.*

Well, mostly.

Julissa yawns. "Here I am," she says.

"Your mom misses you," Waylon says.

"Bullshit."

Waylon goes, "Fine, your mom sucks. But you really need to call her."

Julissa rolls her eyes.

"Seriously," Waylon says.

"*You* call her," Julissa says. "Tell her I said hi."

"You want me to send Carl's best wishes, too?" Waylon asks.

Julissa puts the Coke on the floor and sits up. "You little shit," she says.

"I'm not little," Waylon points out. "The shit part I'll give you."

"You should go back home, and tomorrow you should go back to school," I say.

My voice wakes Julissa up a little. "Who're you?" she practically snarls.

I shrug. "Just the new freak in town."

Julissa waits a beat and then—total surprise—she actually smiles a little. "Okay, freak," she says. "Whatever."

"I'll see you in math class tomorrow, right?" Waylon asks.

"Whatever," she says again. But she's still smiling.

It's a nice smile.

"The way I see it," Waylon says as we walk back toward town, "is that people want to disappear sometimes. But that doesn't mean they don't want someone coming after them. It doesn't mean they don't want to be found."

I reach down and grab a fistful of pigweed from the roadside. I start stripping the leaves from the stems. What I don't point out to Waylon is that it's possible to be found *and* lost at the same time. And Holo and I know all about what it feels like.

CHAPTER 27

"WHEN ARE YOU going to go to the class you're *supposed* to be in?" I ask my brother as he follows me into Ms. Tillman's room.

"Never," he says. He waves to Ms. Tillman, snatches a book from her desk, and wanders over to the corner beanbag.

"Remember to cite textual evidence, people," Ms. Tillman calls to the rest of us. "Don't tell me that Hamlet can't make up his mind without quoting his famous 'To be or not to be' speech. Although I hope your essay topics will be slightly less obvious than that."

I sink down into my desk. I've never written an essay before, and I don't really want to start now.

Outside I can hear two ravens calling to each other. The thing about a raven's call is that it can sound like a kid screaming.

I feel like screaming. What am I doing here? I should be in the woods, watching spring explode all around me.

"You have forty-five minutes," Ms. Tillman says. "Drafts *will* be graded."

I look around at the other students. How many of them

could cache rainwater, start a fire with a handmade bow drill, or skin a big buck?

None, that's how many. They're helpless and lazy, and they can't peel their eyeballs away from their phones long enough to *spot* prey, let alone hunt it.

Maybe Julissa had the right idea. Not by going out with Carl, obviously, but by refusing to regularly attend Kokanee Creek High School.

"*Arghhhhhhhh!*" the raven screams. "*Oarghhhhhhhh!*" calls his friend.

I want to be outside. I want the sky as my roof.

"Focus, Kai," Mrs. Tillman says.

I sigh and pick up my pen. Instead of writing, I draw a pair of eyes at the top corner of my paper. Then a long dark snout. Fangs.

"That doesn't look like textual evidence," Waylon whispers.

He's taken the desk next to mine, and I've been trying to ignore him. I was doing pretty well for a while.

I cover my paper with my forearm. "No looking."

He raises one dark eyebrow. Smirks a little. "Are you afraid I'm going to copy your answers?"

"Very funny."

"I thought so, too."

When he gives me a full-on smile, my stomach jumps like a fish. I angle away from him. Still blocking my paper from his view, I draw a furry body. A wagging tail. Pricked, eager ears.

"What do you think about ol' Hamlet?" Waylon asks.

"I don't think about him at all."

"Personally, I think if you put him in a forest," Waylon says, "he'd debate about whether or not to kill a rabbit until he starved to death."

"Then he's an idiot."

"Waylon," Ms. Tillman calls, "are you distracting your neighbor?"

"Define 'distract,'" he says sweetly.

Ms. Tillman rolls her eyes. "Cease and desist, Mr. Meloy," she says.

"Sure, no problem," he says. He's quiet for no more than fifteen seconds before he turns to me and whispers, "'Why, what an ass am I!'" He taps the cover of his Shakespeare book. "That's a Hamlet line, you know."

"Waylon," Ms. Tillman warns.

"Sorry."

We work quietly for the rest of the class. Well, Waylon does; I keep listening to the ravens and drawing. I'm going to fail this class. But I'm not going to pretend that I care. I know how to *survive*—what class can teach me anything more important than that?

"You're a good artist," Waylon whispers.

He's leaning close, and I can smell him. Soap and toothpaste and warm, human skin. His attention makes me jittery. I feel vulnerable—and that's not something an animal ever wants to feel.

I bare my teeth at him and growl.

CHAPTER 28

HOLO ISN'T STUPID; he knows the other kids think he's weird. He takes his shoes off and walks barefoot down the halls sometimes. He doesn't talk enough.

And he definitely stares too much.

But that's what animals do: they watch things. They stay alert to threats.

He's been trying to act more normal, though. He wants to be accepted by the herd. So when he sits down at an empty lunch table—Kai's nowhere to be seen—he doesn't lift his head and look around constantly, the way a grazing deer does. The way he used to. He pays a lot of attention to his sandwich instead. The menu said it was turkey, but he's never seen a turkey in a round gray slice like this. And the white, greasy smear on the bread—what the heck is *that*?

He's so busy inspecting this soft, almost colorless food that when the lunch tray goes flying up and away from the table, he doesn't react right away. He's too surprised.

Then Logan says, "Whoops, you dropped your lunch. *Freak*."

Holo's furious at himself. He let his guard down and allowed Logan to sneak up on him. But he stays calm. "Why did you do that?" he asks. He's still trying to understand human ways.

Logan's cheeks and ears are red. His big fists are clenched. "Because I don't like you." He steps closer.

Holo stands up. The top of his head barely comes to Logan's shoulder. He sees what looks like a fading bruise on Logan's cheek.

Someone hurt him, Holo thinks. *And he doesn't want to be the lowest-ranking animal, so now he's going to hurt me.*

"I said I don't like you," Logan repeats. "And I don't like your sister. You don't belong here. What are you going to do about it?"

Holo's pulse quickens. He says, "What do you think I should do about it?"

"I think you should crawl back into whatever forest hole you crawled out of," Logan says. "You fucking freaks."

Holo scratches his head. He doesn't really like his short hair. He thought it'd help him fit in, but he was wrong.

"You gonna growl at me now?" Logan taunts. When Holo doesn't say anything, Logan shoves him hard in the chest. "You gonna *bite*?"

Holo takes a deep breath. He feels the blood rising in his veins. *Never be the weakest in the herd.* "No," he says quietly. "I'm going to do this."

He tucks his chin, lowers his head, and charges. He rams Logan in the guts with his skull. Shocked, Logan goes reeling backward, arms swinging wildly as he tries to catch his balance. He can't do it. He falls onto his back with a thud. Lands on Holo's turkey sandwich.

Holo stands over him, quiet but furious. "You wouldn't last a day where I come from," he says through gritted teeth. "You're weak. You're *nothing*."

CHAPTER 29

EVERYONE'S FUSSING AND shouting, and they're saying it's my brother's fault. That he started it. Logan Hardy's getting up from the ground, cursing. And—*crying*?

I wrap my arm around my brother's shoulders and push through the crowd. I'm trying to get us out of here, but there are too many people. I can't even tell which direction to go. My adrenaline levels are through the roof. **Where is the damn door?** Someone's screaming in my face. Someone tries to pull my brother away from me.

Then Mr. Chive blows his ear-piercing whistle. "Quiet!" he shouts, shoving his way toward us. "Enough!"

Everyone backs away, and now we're surrounded by a ring of kids who stare at us like we're wild animals. I can hear their low, mean murmurs. "*Freak.*" "*Fucking animals.*"

Chive yells, "I said *quiet!*" Then he turns to me and Holo and shoves his finger toward our faces. "This behavior is unacceptable! We're calling your parents!"

I say, "Where have you been, Chive? We don't *have* any."

Suddenly Principal Simon's right next to me, her face twisted in anger. Spittle flecks her lips. "This is *way* beyond growling," she shouts.

No shit, lady.

"Kai—Holo—you're suspended for the rest of the week!"

Her hand closes like a vise around my bicep. She grabs Holo with her other mitt and leads us outside. "Chief Greene is going to be even more disturbed by your behavior than I am!"

I clench my jaw so I don't say something I'll regret. Holo looks like he's about to cry.

Mrs. Simon makes us stand on the sidewalk right outside the cafeteria. All the kids stare out the windows at us until the chief pulls up in his cop car. It looks like we're being arrested.

"Lock them up!" someone calls.

"Why'd they call the police?" says someone else. "They should've called animal control."

I can see Logan's brother, Mac, standing off to the side. He's not saying anything. His eyes do the talking instead. *You're dead*, they say.

"Get in," the chief says.

Holo and I climb into the back and the chief slams the car into gear. He's holding the steering wheel so tight it looks like he's trying to strangle it. Beside me, Holo's shaking. He may be good at fighting, but he isn't used to it.

"What happened back there?" the chief finally asks.

Before my brother can answer, I say, "Nothing."

"Kai, the principal doesn't call me for *nothing*."

I glare at him defiantly in the rearview mirror. "Logan told the truth about us," I say. *We're freaks.* "And so Holo beat the hell out of him."

CHAPTER 30

DINNER'S TENSE THAT night. The chief chomps his grilled cheese like he's mad at it. He answers Lacey's questions about his day in grunts.

Lacey finally puts down her silverware and says, "Will you stop *stewing*, Chester? Logan Hardy's an ass, if you'll excuse my saying so! He got what was coming to him." She turns to Holo. "I don't approve of fighting, young man. But I know you didn't mean to hurt him."

You don't know us, I think. *You don't know anything.*

"Maybe you should lock us up again," I challenge the chief. "Keep us from getting into more trouble."

The chief's eyes flash with anger. "If you end up in jail, it won't be because of me," he says. "It'll be because the Hardys decided to charge Holo with assault."

Holo goes pale as snow.

Lacey swats the chief on the arm. "Don't scare them like that, Chester. Reginald Hardy'll admit his son got his butt beat on the day he'll tap-dance in a tutu. Now, Holo, you and

Kai clear the table and then head on up to your rooms. Chester and I have things to discuss."

For once I don't mind doing what I'm told. Better to be alone than sit around with a pissed-off police chief.

If he were a wolf, he'd have just bitten me and been done with it. Anger's a human thing.

So is regret—and revenge.

Upstairs I flop down onto the bed and stare at the ceiling. I can hear Lacey and the chief doing the dishes together in the kitchen. Later they go into the living room, and the big recliner squeaks as the chief sinks down into it.

Lacey's honeyed voice floats softly up the stairs. "They don't have anyone but us, Chester."

I roll off my bed and tiptoe to the landing so I can hear better.

"They've got each other," says the chief gruffly.

"But no one else is looking out for them."

"They've done pretty well so far. I've seen kids with two parents doing plenty worse."

Yeah, like Julissa Hill. Her mom's nicer to those rabbits than she is to her own daughter. Well, up until the point that she kills and eats them, anyway.

The chief starts making a weird noise. It takes me a minute to realize that he's *laughing*. "God, I would've loved to have seen that fight. Logan Hardy must have six inches and seventy-five pounds on Holo—but that scrawny little kid kicked the living daylights out of him."

They're quiet for a while, and I'm getting ready to go back to my bedroom. Then I hear Lacey say, all gentle and wondering, "Chester? Honey?"

"Huh?" the chief grunts.

"I don't want to give them up."

The chief goes, "What do you mean?" which is exactly what I'm thinking.

"I mean I want them to stay, Chester. I want them to be ours."

Ours?

"Ours?" the chief asks, echoing my thought.

"Yes," Lacey says. "Do you think we could adopt them?"

"Lacey," the chief says calmly, "I'm still looking for their parents. Even if I don't ever find them, there are a lot of steps between letting someone sleep in your house and making them an official part of your family."

"I know that," says Lacey. "I'm ready for all of them."

A gasp escapes my lips.

"Did you hear something?" the chief says. He gets up from his chair. Calls, "Kai? Holo?"

I zip back to my bed and dive under the covers. My heart hammers. But no one comes upstairs.

She wants to keep us.

Lying there, it's like I really see my room for the first time. There are alphabet watercolors on the pale-yellow walls: *A is for aadvark, B is for bat.* There's a pile of stuffed animals in one corner and a rocking chair in another. The realization hits me like a headbutt to the stomach: This wasn't supposed to be a guest room. This was supposed to be a nursery.

Poor Lacey.

She wanted a baby. But what she got was us.

And we can't be trusted.

We can't be kept.

CHAPTER 31

"HOLO, HOLO, WAKE up."

"Huh?" My brother rolls over but keeps his eyes closed.

"We have to go."

"Go where?" he mumbles sleepily.

I grab his jacket from the closet and throw it at him. Since he still hasn't opened his eyes, it lands on his face.

Holo groans and pulls the jacket down. "I'm asleep."

"No, you're not. Get up."

We have to get out of here before we wake anyone. I'm already layered up—long underwear, sweats, a jacket. Spring nights can be cold, and hypothermia is real. I've got a backpack stuffed full of food and water, too.

"Ugghhhhh," my brother moans. "Ughhh."

"Use your words."

"I was having a good dream. Bim and Ben were there, and Beast, and Harriet..." His voice trails off.

"Well, you're awake now, so get up," I say. I have to be a little mean about it, or else he'll just ignore me.

Grumbling, with eyes still half-closed, he starts getting himself ready. I peer out the window. The sky's clear and the moon's nearly full. The forest's calling.

When Holo's finally dressed, we creep downstairs. We tiptoe past Lacey and the chief's bedroom. I can hear the chief snoring.

The floor creaks and the snores stop.

I freeze. *Don't wake up, don't wake up.*

Holo and I stand still as trees. We barely breathe. The minutes tick by. Finally there's another snore.

"*Go*," I whisper.

The front door's noisy, so Holo opens the living room window instead. I clamber out first and drop to the ground. A moment later, Holo lands in the dirt next to me. We don't hesitate; we head for the forest. Holo doesn't ask what we're doing or where we're going. That's because he's tired.

But also because he knows.

We walk parallel to the stream, stepping carefully but surely. We're used to traveling in darkness.

Wolves like to hunt at night.

An owl hoots from somewhere to the north. Holo cups his hand around his mouth and calls back. Nothing.

"Nice try," I say.

"Dumb owl," Holo growls.

"More like *smart* owl."

We head east along a deer path, moving at something between a walk and a jog, for an hour or two. The forest is quiet, but I can sense how alive it is all around us. Eyes I can't see watching us. Little creatures slinking and burrowing and hunting.

I inhale the scent of leaves and bark and water and dirt. *This is where I belong.*

We cross where the stream narrows, hopping from rock to rock. I hear a splash behind me.

"Shit," Holo says.

His right foot slipped and now he's wet halfway up his leg.

"Good thing it's not winter."

"It's still freezing, though," he grumbles.

"We don't have much farther."

Ahead of us the ground slopes down and—if I'm right—it'll open into a meadow that we know. We push through underbrush. Blackberry brambles snag my clothes. I'm hurrying now, and I stumble over a fallen branch. My ankle twists as I land. *Ow.*

I'm limping a little as we come out of the trees into a small clearing. The grass is silver in the moonlight. It's beautiful.

And it's empty.

"They're not here," Holo whispers.

"No, but they will be."

And I throw back my head and howl.

CHAPTER 32

WE WAIT.

And wait.

And *wait*.

I start to get cold, even with all my layers. I shiver. Move closer to my brother. Wish for the hundredth time that I had a thick pelt of fur.

"Call them again," Holo urges. "Your howl's louder than mine."

I snort. "Remember when you sat in a tree for a whole day waiting for a woodpecker chick to hatch? City life did *not* ruin your attention span already."

"But I'm so tired," he says.

"Quit whining. Even if they're six miles away, they heard us. But I think they're closer. And if they want to come, they will."

Annoyed, Holo sticks his tongue out at me. What a stupid human expression. I answer it with a growl. Because I'm tired, too, and I'm also scared. *What if they don't come?*

"They'll recognize us, right?" Holo whispers.

"Of course they will."

"They won't attack?"

"No, Holo. We're still family."

Aren't we?

But I realize that's not up to me to say. If you leave the forest, you become something else.

Maybe, to a wolf, you might even become an enemy.

Are we making a huge mistake?

There's no way to tell. Not yet, anyway.

Wind rustles the leaves above us. Something skitters through the underbrush. A branch cracks.

Was that a pawstep?

I freeze. Hold my breath. Listen.

Everything's dead quiet.

Suddenly I'm thrown sideways by impact. I land hard on the ground, and all the breath goes out of my lungs. I'm on my back, half-blind with fear. Something huge is on top of me. I can't move. I can't even breathe.

Sharp white teeth come snapping toward my face—I try to block them, and I feel my sleeve shred. I scream. Then a long warm tongue slobbers its way up my cheek.

Oh my God, I'd know that kiss anywhere.

"Harriet, you practically killed me! And now you're getting me all wet!" I'm laughing and crying as the big female wolf licks my nose and mouth. Greeting me. Welcoming me back to the pack. I reach up and wrap my arms around her neck and bury my face into her thick, musky ruff. I didn't even realize how much I missed her until now.

"Oh, my sweet girl, I'm glad to see you, too," I cry.

Harriet yips and wags and wiggles. She licks the tears from

my face. She keeps stepping on my arms and chest. I try to push her away but she's much too strong. I laugh and try to duck out from under her paws. She headbutts me and knocks me over again.

"Ooof! Get off before you squish me to death, you giant, beautiful mutt!"

Finally she backs away from me, tongue lolling and tail wagging madly.

Ten feet away, a giant black wolf has her front legs wrapped around my brother's neck in a bear hug. Or maybe I should say *wolf* hug. I recognize Bim, with her brother Ben off to the side, whining and turning in excited circles.

"I think Bim rolled in dead fish," Holo gasps, holding his nose.

"Of course she did," I laugh. Wolves will roll in anything that stinks. Dead things, rotting stuff, poop—the smellier, the better.

Ben trots over and greets me with a tail wag and a hard nip on my knee. Wolves play rough, and Ben never seems to understand that I don't have a thick layer of fur. That I bleed much easier than his sister does. I wipe the blood from my leg as he starts sniffing eagerly at the backpack.

"Yes, I brought treats," I tell him. Then I glance around. "Where's your mom? Where's Beast?"

Holo stops wrestling with Bim and looks up. Beast is the alpha female, the mother of Bim and her brother. She's brave and bossy. Normally she's the first to greet us. My pulse, which had finally gone back down after Harriet's ambush, quickens again. In the wild, a wolf lives an average of eight or nine years.

Beast is seven.

"Beast?" I shout.

Bim's ears go up, then down. Ben does a little dash toward the trees, then comes sprinting back, whimpering.

"Where is she?" I demand. I can hear the panic in my voice. I squint into the dark. Is that something moving by the line of trees?

Harriet starts whining and presses her shoulder against my leg. Bim and Ben yip and prance. The wolves are anxious.

And I'm filled with dread.

Then I see Beast coming out of the trees. Moving too slowly. Stopping and starting again. Turning to look back behind her.

"Is she hurt?" Holo whispers.

I squint.

And then I gasp.

There are two clumsy balls of dark-gray fluff following her. Nipping at her heels.

I sink to my knees—I can't believe it. Beast has pups!

"Keep still," I whisper to my brother. Beast loves us, but if we threaten her babies she'll rip out our throats.

We stay where we are, barely breathing. The pups hop and stumble and fall over each other, tiny tails wagging. As Beast approaches, watching us carefully, the bigger one inches toward my brother's foot. Then Holo coughs, and the pup yips in fear and trips over its own paws as it darts backward. Bim raises her hackles, and a growl builds in Ben's throat.

Holo looks at me in alarm. *Don't move*, I mouth.

The pup presses itself against Beast's front legs. She bends her great head and licks it, reassuring it. The pup gives a tiny hiccup and prances forward again. Curiosity overcomes fear. It sniffs my brother's feet, and then my fingers. Its sibling does the same. The cuteness might just kill me.

The pups are only a few weeks old, and this is probably the farthest they've ever been from the den. They were born deaf and blind. But soon they'll follow their parents on the hunt, learning by watching. Sharpening their little teeth on the adults' kills.

I hear the sound of fabric ripping. I turn and find Bim getting into the backpack. "Shoo," I say, laughing. She darts away and I reach into the bag, pulling out cold hunks of raw meat and tossing them to the wolves. "There's enough for all of you."

Harriet tries to steal Ben's steak anyway.

"I hope Chester doesn't mind you took all this stuff," Holo says, as a baby wolf gnaws happily on the toe of his sneaker.

"I don't care if he does," I say.

I'm full of love and full of relief.

The chief and Lacey could never adopt us.

This is our family.

CHAPTER 33

THE SUN WAKES me early. I'm wet with dew and shivering under the blanket that I took from the cabin. I roll over in the grass. Holo's already awake and staring at the clouds.

"I think we should call the pups Thing One and Thing Two," he says dreamily.

I grin, remembering those sweet babies and their proud mama. There's nothing more adorable than wolf pups—they're all fluff and fang and feet. "Sticking with the Dr. Seuss names?"

"It's tradition," Holo insists.

Sam I Am was the first wolf we named. He was ornery and lovable. He died a long time ago, though.

Holo turns to me, and his eyes are suddenly dark with worry. "Do you think they'll make it?"

A lot of wolf pups die before their first birthday. But I nod. "Beast is a good mom. She'll protect them, the way she protected Bim and Ben."

I'm more worried about the adult wolves, because they're

the ones that people in Kokanee Creek talk about shooting. They don't have mothers looking out for them.

Of course, neither do Holo and I.

"I didn't see Ernie," he says softly.

Ernie is Beast's mate—the pack's big, silver alpha male. "You know how he likes to be alone a lot," I say. "And maybe he was just tired from minding the pups."

"You think?"

I don't know. "I hope."

"Excuse me, but what the *hell* are you two doing sleeping in my yard?"

Startled, I sit up. The chief's standing over us, looking confused and more than a little annoyed.

"Um," Holo says, blinking.

It's a reasonable question. Too bad I can't really answer it. I wanted to sleep under the stars again, but why did I lead us back here? Why didn't we just stay in the woods?

Because we don't belong there now.

I rub my eyes. Take in the carefully mown grass, the pretty tended flower garden, the neat little space that the chief and Lacey have carved out of the woods.

But I don't belong here, either.

The chief gives us a headshake and a resigned-sounding sigh. "Next time you want to camp out, I'll put up the tent, okay?"

Holo lifts his face and sniffs. "Is Lacey cooking bacon?" he asks eagerly.

"Yes. Now come inside and get ready for school."

I slowly get to my feet. I'm cold and stiff. "We're suspended, remember?"

"No, you're not. Mrs. Simon and I had a long conversation, and she agreed to let you come back. You just have to remember what you promised: No growling, no biting, and no fighting."

"We didn't actually promise that," I tell him.

"You will now. Go on, get up and get dressed." He reaches down and swipes the blanket away from Holo's legs.

I scan the trees as my brother and I trudge into the house. The wolves are long gone. I don't know when we'll see them again.

"Eat," the chief says, gesturing to the giant breakfast Lacey made us before she left for the diner.

Holo devours his food at wolf speed, but I just push my eggs from one side of the plate to the other. Now that Beast has pups, it's more important than ever that she keeps the pack far away from civilization.

From us.

The realization makes me feel like crying.

"Eat," the chief says again.

I glare at him and shove my plate away.

Holo takes a huge bite of toast. "Kai's growling at you in her mind," he tells the chief.

"I don't care, as long as I can't hear it," the chief says. Then he frowns. Because now a sound a lot like a growl is coming from outside the house.

I follow the chief as he goes to open the front door. My brother stays put and helps himself to my breakfast.

"Shoot," the chief says, sounding surprised. "What are you doing here?"

Waylon Meloy is on the porch, leaning easily against the railing, one leg crossed over the other. Behind him I can see two helmets dangling from the handlebars of his motorcycle. "Good morning," he says, with a sly half smile.

The chief braces himself in the doorway like he's trying to keep me inside. "Let's try that again. Why are you on my porch when it's not even seven a.m.?"

Waylon peers over the chief's outstretched arms to catch my eye. He winks. *Why does he always do that?* Then he gives the chief a little bow that seems polite and mocking at the same time. "Well, sir, I heard Kai's suspension got revoked, and I thought she should return to school in style. So I'm here to give her a ride." He gestures to the extra helmet. It's purple with gold stars. "I'll go very, very slowly. Ten miles under the speed limit at least."

The chief scoffs. "You can go whatever speed you want. You're not taking Kai."

"Doesn't Kai have a say in it?" Waylon asks reasonably.

The chief starts to close the door. "No, she does not."

Waylon sticks his foot out to block it and cranes his neck to see me again. "Hey, Kai," he calls. "I thought you might like to try riding on a motorcycle, but this cop here says you can't."

I manage to smile at him—maybe because he's at a safe distance. "So I heard."

"It's definitely not against the law, so I'm not sure what his problem is."

The chief tries to move so he can block my view of Waylon. But Waylon ducks down low so he can peer at me through the chief's legs. "Do *you* know what his problem is?"

I can't help laughing, even though I can tell by the chief's body language that Waylon's kind of pissing him off. "I'm not really sure," I say. "Maybe keeping a couple of wolf kids is a hassle or something."

"Waylon Meloy," the chief says, ignoring my comment. "Please get the hell off my property before I find some reason to object more officially to your presence."

"I've never been arrested for trespassing before," Waylon says. "Could be exciting."

"It won't be," the chief says.

"Okay, fine, Chief Greene," Waylon says, sighing dramatically. He calls over his shoulder to me as he walks away. "See you in class, Kai!"

"Bye," I say, but so quietly that he doesn't hear me.

The chief shuts the door. "I should've let you stay suspended," he grumbles.

"Great," I say. "Call the principal back."

Even if it means seeing Waylon again, I don't want to go back to Kokanee Creek High. I don't like those people and they don't like me.

But the chief shakes his head. "You're going to school. And you're going to smile and be nice. And you're going to make friends."

"That's impossible," I say. "They think we're freaks. And they're totally right."

"I don't know why you'd say that, Kai."

"Because it's true. I don't know how to talk to them without growling, and Holo stares too much, and we're nothing like them. They'd die without their *phones*, let alone without gross plastic food being handed to them three times a day. Holo and I might as well be from a different planet."

"Isn't there anyone you like there?" The chief's eyes look suspiciously twinkly all of a sudden.

I bristle with annoyance. I can't even admit to *myself* that I might like Waylon, so I'm hardly about to say it to the police chief of Kokanee Creek.

"No."

The chief rests a big hand on my shoulder. "Well, that's too bad for Waylon Meloy, isn't it? Because I think he's making it pretty obvious that he likes you."

"He's just being nice to the new freak."

"You're not a freak, Kai," the chief says.

I shrug his hand off. "I can't be a real wolf, and I don't know how to be a real girl," I say bitterly. "So yeah, actually I am."

CHAPTER 34

SOMEHOW I MAKE it through the school day. I do what they tell me to do. I don't growl. And Holo doesn't fight.

But we still don't fit in.

When the bell rings, I'm the first one out the door. I breathe deep, clearing the school's chemical stench from my nose. I roll my shoulders and shake out my cramped legs. I'm not used to sitting for hours at a time.

And what did I learn today? How to say *Odio la escuela*.

It means *I hate school*.

A raven lands on a nearby trash can and starts pecking at a Cheetos bag, searching for crumbs.

"Shoo," I say, waving my arms at it. "Get out of here!"

The bird seems to glare at me before it flaps its big black wings and takes off.

"Poor guy, why'd you chase him away?"

Startled, I turn. Waylon's followed me outside. His motorcycle jacket's slung over his shoulder, and his expression's amused. The sun turns the bleached ends of his hair golden. They match the gold flecks in his eyes.

I try to act like he didn't surprise me. Like my heart isn't beating faster and being near him is just like being near anyone else. Still, I cross my arms over my chest like I need to protect myself. "That bird should be eating carrion, not Cheetos."

"Okay, but that's kind of gross."

"Not to a raven. The way eating your mom's regurgitated dinner isn't gross if you're a wolf pup."

Waylon winces a little. "Baby wolves eat barf?"

"Yeah, when they're too young to eat from a kill. They lick an adult wolf's mouth, and the adult immediately coughs up part of its last meal."

"'Here, son, have some raw deer meat mixed with stomach acid!'" Waylon gags a little.

"It doesn't even have to be the wolf's actual son. Any adult wolf will do it for the pack's pups."

I don't admit that the wolves used to bring my brother and me bits of their kill. That I've eaten raw deer meat, too. Waylon already thinks I'm strange enough.

The raven comes back, heading for the Cheetos bag again.

Another thing I don't tell Waylon is that ravens sometimes imitate wolves, calling them to carcasses the birds can't break open themselves. When the wolves finish eating, the raven gets the leftovers.

"Hey, bird, I saw some sweet roadkill on Route 20 this morning," Waylon calls. "You should go check it out." Then he turns to me, and his sudden, gorgeous smile is almost impossible for me to look at. He grabs one of my hands and holds it lightly between his. "All this talk about carrion and vomit is making me hungry," he says. "How about we go get something to eat?"

Warmth floods my body, and all of my attention rushes to where his skin touches mine. *He's holding my hand*, I think stupidly. *Waylon Meloy is holding my hand. No one's ever done that before.*

"Well, what do you say?" Waylon nods over to his motorcycle, the one I'm technically not allowed to ride. "That right there is a 1975 Norton Commando, electric start," he says. "You can't find a more classic bike. It was the only thing I got from my dad when he died. I had to rewire it, though, because a lot of old British motorcycles have shit electrical systems. Next I'm probably going to swap out the Amal carbs for a Mikuni carburetor—" Then he stops. "Sorry, this doesn't mean anything to you at all, does it?"

I shake my head. I understand raven language better than motorcycle terminology. But I can tell Waylon really loves his bike. And I also wonder what happened to his dad.

"Look, all you really need to know is that it's a killer bike," Waylon says, "and when the chief says you shouldn't ride it, you should *not* listen to him." He lets go of my hand, and my skin misses his warmth.

Touch me again, I think.

"So," he says, "are you going to get on or what?"

I shouldn't do it. The chief would kill me.

I can't bring myself to say yes.

But I can manage a nod.

"Great," he says happily. "Let's go."

Excitement and fear take turns flooding through me as I put on my helmet. Waylon slings his right leg over the seat. Awkwardly I slide on behind him. The seat's hot from the sun. The bike smells like gas and leather.

"You're going to have to hold on," Waylon tells me.

I feel around the side of the seat for grips or handles. There aren't any. "To what?" I ask, confused.

I can hear the smile in his voice when he answers. "To *me*," he says.

CHAPTER 35

FOR HOLO AND me, survival meant following three life-or-death rules.

Be prepared.

Stay in control.

Don't do anything stupid.

As the trees rush by and the motorcycle rattles between my legs, I realize that I'm violating all three of them all at once.

This is a terrible mistake.

And there's nothing I can do about it now.

Leaning forward, I press my chest closer against Waylon's muscular back. I wrap my arms tighter around his waist. The bike picks up speed. The world turns into a green-and-blue blur.

I can actually feel Waylon's voice against my rib cage. But I can't hear what he's saying, because the roar of the engine drowns it out. My eyes tear up from the wind, and I don't know where we're going. If he hits a bump wrong, we're dead.

Yep, I'm pretty convinced I'm going to die.

Hey, raven, there's some really *fresh roadkill on the Kokanee Highway!*

But I also feel more alive than I've ever felt before.

Then Waylon slows down, the bike makes a leaning turn, and we come to a gentle stop. He cuts the engine and I half fall off the motorcycle, my legs weak with relief.

"Well?" Waylon asks. "Did you love it?"

What am I supposed to tell him? My brain can't process what I just went through. A wolf risks its life because it has to eat. A human risks its life for—*moving to a different location?*

"It was... intense," I say. I'll leave it at that.

Waylon reaches out and lifts the helmet from my head. He frowns. "You look like you were crying."

"The wind," I say.

And, okay, maybe just a little bit of panic. Before a few weeks ago, I'd never gone faster than I could run.

When he gently wipes the tears from my cheek, I freeze. I can't help it.

"You're doing that thing again," Waylon says. "Tonic whatever it is."

"Immobility," I manage. "Sorry."

He steps closer to me. It's overwhelming to be so near him. I don't understand why, and I don't know how to control the feelings flooding my body.

He must sense that something has changed between us. He brushes a tangled strand of hair from my face. "It's okay, Kai," he says softly. "I like you, too."

When I was little, I used to spin in circles until my stomach churned and my eyes watered, and when I stopped I could barely stand up. For years, that dizziness was the biggest feeling I knew.

This feeling is bigger.

I can't bear it, and I turn away. And when I do, I realize that we're standing in the parking lot of the Grizzly Grocery.

Suddenly I'm not overwhelmed by desire anymore. I'm just angry.

"Why'd you bring me here?" I demand. "Is this some kind of joke?"

"No!" Waylon says. "Never. I told you, all that carrion talk got me hungry." He grins. "Seriously, though, the Grizzly has the best doughnuts in town. They make them fresh on Mondays, Wednesdays, and Fridays, and I'm going to buy us a dozen. Maybe even *two* dozen. I'm feeling dangerous today."

And now I'm feeling slightly stupid.

I glance over at the door my brother smashed. The glass hasn't been replaced yet. Instead there's plywood nailed to the doorframe, and I'm pretty sure I can see the rock that Holo used lying a few feet away on the sidewalk. Guilt flushes my cheeks. "Um, maybe I should wait outside."

Waylon's eyes follow mine. He nods in agreement. "Yeah, that's probably not a bad idea."

When he comes back, he's holding a brown paper bag spotted with oil. He reaches in and hands me a warm, sugar-coated circle of dough. "Next time you rob the place," he says, "just remember that the doughnuts are the only thing worth stealing, and they're at the end of aisle five."

CHAPTER 36

THE CHIEF LOOKS so grim as he starts to leave the house on Saturday morning that I stand in front of him and block his way. "What's wrong?" I demand. "Is the Grizzly pressing charges after all? Are we going to jail again?"

I never should've let Waylon take me there, even if those doughnuts were the greatest things I've ever eaten.

The chief shakes his head. "I've been talking to Fish and Wildlife," he says. "Ranchers in the area are reporting new wolf attacks."

My stomach's suddenly full of lead. "What do you mean?"

"I mean that calves are disappearing. Sheep are being killed."

"*Here?* In Kokanee Creek?" I gasp.

My wolves would never do that.

Would they?

"Apparently so," the chief says, slipping past me and stomping outside.

I shove my feet into a pair of Lacey's shoes and follow him.

"How do they know it's wolves?" I demand. "Has anyone seen them?"

"They don't have to, Kai," he says, exasperated. "When they find a bloody, half-eaten ewe, they know it didn't die of natural causes." He yanks open the cruiser door and gets in.

"But you said it yourself—foxes kill lambs, and coyotes can take down a calf! There's bears in the woods, too, and cougars, and all kinds of predators—"

The chief starts the engine. Revs it a little to warm it up. Leans out the window to lecture me. "But people don't *hate* those predators, Kai, not the way they hate wolves. They want to blame wolves for everything they can. Wolves are bloodthirsty and vicious and evil—that's what people around here think."

"That's ridiculous!" My hands are balled into fists and I'm actually yelling at the police chief. "Wolves live in families! They play together and love each other and trust each other! And they *take care* of each other, unlike most of the people I've met. How's that vicious?"

The chief shoves the car into gear. "When a pack of them kills the sheep you're trying to raise up, I guess it seems pretty damn vicious."

I run around to the passenger side and fling myself into the car. I'm not letting him leave without me. Wolf business is *my* business. "Then maybe someone should tell those people to quit raising their stupid livestock on land that's supposed to belong to wolves and other wild things!"

The chief sighs. "Coming along for the ride, are you? Okay. Look, Kai, I'm on your side. I don't want people poisoning wolves, or shooting them with machine guns, or chasing them down with helicopters. But the fact is, you can kill a wolf the minute it steps onto your property in Idaho. It's more than legal—it's encouraged."

People are *encouraged* to use machine guns? Invited to murder animals who are only trying to live? As the chief drives away from the cabin, I feel so sick I can barely stand it. It's humans, not wolves, who are the vicious ones.

The chief says quietly, "Just so we're clear, this isn't my jurisdiction. I'm not supposed to police wildlife, and no one's broken any laws. I'm just going around to check in with folks."

My mind races as we drive. I think of Sam I Am, shot by a man who'd tracked him for months, convinced the wolf was preying on his calves. What if there isn't enough wild prey to feed Beast's pups? What if the pack came down the mountainside and onto a rancher's land? A deer has evolved to be wily and quick. A cow's been bred to be heavy and slow. It's obvious which one makes the easier meal.

But Beast is smarter than that. Isn't she?

Eventually the chief turns down a dirt track that ends in front of a ranch house painted faded yellow. A man comes out, shading his eyes from the sun. He's got a red face and a bow-legged, tough-guy swagger. As the chief climbs out of the car, he says, "You come about the vermin?"

I shoot a glance at the chief. Is he calling wolves "vermin"?

The chief shakes his head at me. *Keep your mouth shut, Kai*—that's what he's saying.

Sorry, chief, I can't make any promises.

"Come on out back and have a look," the red-faced man says.

I've never seen him before, but somehow his mean eyes look familiar.

We hop a barbed-wire fence and follow him a few hundred yards through the dirt. Then he stops and puts his hands on his hips. "There," he says furiously. He kicks an unmoving reddened lump on the ground with his boot.

I look down at the gruesome mess of wool and flesh and guts. A cloud of flies feast on the dead sheep's eyes. Hungry vultures circle overhead.

"If it was up to me, I'd kill every single one of them bastards," the man spits.

The smell of rotting sheep fills the air. Good thing I didn't eat breakfast, or it would've come back up again.

The chief doesn't answer him. He eyeballs the dirt around the carcass, probably looking for wolf prints. "You'll be compensated, Mr. Hardy."

He's a Hardy! I *knew* I didn't like this guy.

"Uncle Sam'll send me a check, sure. He should send me an army instead."

I kneel down to take a closer look at the dead sheep. Immediately, relief—and more nausea—flood through me. "This animal wasn't killed by a wolf."

Both men look at me in surprise.

"Who the hell are you?" the man asks. Apparently he's only just noticed me.

"This is Kai," the chief says. "She's...shadowing me on the job today."

I stand up and brush off my dusty knees. "I know what a

wolf kill looks like," I tell the chief. "And this isn't it." I turn to red-faced Hardy. "Do your neighbors have dogs?"

"Reckon they do."

"Then ask them where their dogs were the other night, because a dog killed this sheep."

"How do you know?" the chief asks, surprised.

I point to all the meat left on the animal, and to the puncture wounds dotting its side. "Because wolves would've *eaten* it. Whoever killed your sheep wasn't hungry. And those triangular wounds? Those are from golden eagles. Scavengers. Your killer went home and ate . . . what's it called? *Purina.*"

"Bullshit," Hardy says.

The chief's staring at me, like *I thought I told you to keep your mouth shut.*

I shrug. I never made any promises, did I? And I'm not going to let my friends take the blame for some runaway mutt. Especially not when the dead sheep belongs to the father of the two biggest assholes in high school.

But then Hardy laughs. "You think it wasn't no wolf? I got something else to show you, then," he says.

"Not another sheep, I hope," the chief says.

"No sirree. I got the wolf who killed her."

CHAPTER 37

I SWEAR MY heart stops.

The chief makes a strangled sound in his throat. "I don't think we want to see that," he says. "We can take your word for it."

"But I did a real nice job skinnin' him," Hardy says. "Might make myself a fur coat." He grins horribly. His teeth are yellow and crooked. I want to kick every last one of them down into his throat.

"I want to see," I growl. I *have* to see.

I need to know who it is.

Hardy looks so smug and ugly, I feel my fists clenching again. He stalks back toward the barn. "Come on, then," he says over his shoulder.

My stomach's knotted up and my feet feel like they're made of lead. I know all the wolves around here, so my only hope is that this one's a disperser—a wolf who left its pack to form a new one and ended up getting killed for it.

But you didn't see Ernie the other night, Kai, did you?

I push the thought away.

The chief comes up alongside me. "I think you should go back to the car. Wait for me there."

"No way."

Now that my heart's beating again, every thud of it hurts like a punch. But I tell myself that Ernie's a wise wolf. He's the alpha. Aloof, intelligent, strong. He wouldn't let himself get killed by an idiot.

The chief reaches for my hand, grabs it, gives it a quick squeeze. "It's going to be okay," he whispers. "No matter what."

Of course I want him to be right. But why wasn't Ernie with the pack? He wouldn't have missed the chance to show off his beautiful babies, would he? When Bim and Ben were born, he strutted back and forth across the meadow, his tail waving like a flag.

Hardy yanks open the barn door. The smell of hay and manure rolls out. And there's another smell I recognize.

Death.

"Right this way," Hardy says. And he gives a mocking bow.

It's dark in the barn. A few dusty shafts of light fall down through the cracks in the plank walls. The smell's overpowering now. A lump rises in my throat.

"There he is," Hardy says proudly. "Or what's left of him, anyway."

Nailed to the barn wall is the pelt of a giant, silvery-gray wolf. The tail's stubby and tinged with black at the tip. Just like Ernie's. I grab onto the chief to keep from falling.

No, no, no.

"Kai?" the chief whispers.

Hardy stands there, bowlegged and proud. "A wolf's no match for a Winchester," he says. "Though it did take him a long time to die."

With a growl that turns into a scream, I charge toward Hardy. When our bodies collide he goes stumbling backward. I hook a leg behind his and give him another hard shove. Falling, he reaches out—grabs my shirt—tries to pull me down with him. I land a hard chop to his forearm. He lets go. Falls. Lands hard on the barn floor.

You think it's hard to wrestle a man? It isn't—not if you practice with wolves.

I go crashing down on top of his chest. Dust and hay fly up. Hardy curses and struggles. He slaps me hard but he can't get himself free. I'm punching and scratching at his face like a wild animal. "You killed my friend!" Tears are streaming down my face. "He was a *dad*!"

Hardy bucks beneath me. My nails scratch bloody lines on his cheek. I grab his hair and hold him still with my left hand while I punch him with the right. It feels so good, I could do this forever.

Humans are the only animals that understand revenge.

Suddenly I'm yanked backward by big, strong hands. I kick and scream. I want to kill Hardy and I'm about to do it, too.

But the chief pulls me away. He yanks me up and shoves me against the wall and holds me there. He says, low and fierce, "If you don't stop, Kai, I will take you to jail and I will *not* let you out."

I go limp. All the anger drains out of me, and grief fills up the space it left behind. My shoulders shake with sobs. Snot pours out of my nose. I can barely breathe from crying.

Hardy lies in the straw, cursing. "I'll sue!" he spits. "You and the county and all of you bastards!"

Still holding me by the shoulders, the chief says calmly, "Mr. Hardy, with all due respect, you got a little kitten scratch just now. You want to press charges for that? I don't think you do. Because investigations look very carefully at the accused— *and* the accuser."

"It ain't over," Hardy hisses. He rolls over and retches into the straw.

"It is for now," the chief says. And then he guides me toward the door.

I can barely see through my tears.

"Why'd you pull me off him?" I cry.

The chief smiles grimly. "In case you didn't notice," he says, "I took my time in doing it. You're welcome, Kai."

CHAPTER 38

THURSDAY AFTERNOON, WHEN he's supposed to be working the speed trap out on Highway 20, Chester is instead stomping up the steps to Kokanee Creek High School. The secretary wouldn't tell him what the matter was when she called. Just said: *If you can just come to the office, Chief Greene. Mrs. Simon wants to speak to you.*

What is it this *time?* he's thinking as his boots ring down the hallway. He's expecting the worst, of course. Holo biting and drawing blood. Kai ambushing someone in the hall. The two of them jumping a kid who made the mistake of insulting wolves.

Chester's seen how strong Kai is, and Holo's probably not much weaker. But if they hurt someone, whose fault is it really? Theirs—or his, for sending them to a place where everyone knows they don't belong?

He strides down the long hallway to the office, cursing himself for his stupidity. Why did he ever think this would work?

The secretary, Suzy Garcia, waves him toward the principal's door.

Kai and Holo are already in the office. Holo looks confused. Kai looks defiant. Chester's jaw clenches.

We had an agreement, he thinks, feeling the fury growing inside him. *No acting like animals!*

He turns to Mrs. Simon. He's angry at her, too. Hasn't she dealt with unruly kids before? Can't she handle these two for a measly six hours without calling him in to deal with whatever mess they've made?

"What'd they do?" he demands. He just wants to get this over with.

Instead of answering, Mrs. Simon hands him a piece of paper. Chester takes it, but he doesn't know what he's looking at. There are rows of numbers and percentages and graphs. He sees a lot of 99s.

"What the hell is this?" he asks.

"I'll ask you not to curse," Mrs. Simon says prissily. "It sets a bad example."

Chester *supremely* resents being told what to do. But he reminds himself that he needs to be civil to this woman; he's the one who handed her these two feral kids. With exaggerated politeness, he sets the paper back on her desk. "Sorry, what the *heck* is this?"

Mrs. Simon slides it into a folder on her desk. "We had state-mandated testing last week," she says. "Kai and Holo's scores were...surprising."

"Look," he says, "you know they haven't been in school before now. They're smart kids—they'll catch up. You just have to give them a chance."

Mrs. Simon gives him a thin-lipped smile. "That's not the

kind of surprising I'm talking about, Chief Greene. What I mean is, their scores blew everyone else's away."

Chester's first feeling is disbelief. It's quickly followed by chest-swelling pride. *Their scores blew everyone else's away!*

Maybe he shouldn't feel this way—they aren't *his* kids—but right now he's as proud of them as he would be if he had raised them up himself. "Well," he says gruffly, "that *is* surprising."

"Thanks a lot," Kai grumbles. "I guess you thought we were stupid or something."

"Because we're not," Holo says. "We know all kinds of things. You think Spanish is hard? We had to learn to speak *Wolf.*"

Mrs. Simon tucks the test scores into her desk. "Though they still struggle with appropriate behaviors, Kai and Holo are excellent students. They remember everything. And they've clearly been educated by . . ."—here she glances over at the sullen-looking teenagers—"*someone.*"

"Or some*thing*," Kai mutters.

"How do you do it?" Chester asks them.

Kai looks up at him, her expression resentful. Her mood's been dark ever since the visit to Hardy's farm. "Are you asking how we live up to this school's low expectations?" she says. "It's simple. We don't have our faces in our phones all the time. We pay attention. We listen. It's what we've always done."

"I think they were homeschooled," Mrs. Simon says over Kai's head.

Kai rolls her eyes.

"We were woods-schooled," Holo retorts. He grabs a Rubik's Cube from Mrs. Simon's desk and starts twisting it around. "Wolf-schooled. World-schooled."

Mrs. Simon looks for a second like she's going to scold him, but then she turns to Chester. "I'm sure it's challenging, taking care of these two," she says. "But they're doing much better than I ever would have expected."

"Again," Kai says bitterly, "thanks a lot."

"I'm very proud of them," Mrs. Simon goes on, ignoring her. "It's seeing improvement like this that keeps me coming back to this job."

Chester smiles at Kai and Holo. "Good job, you two," he says gruffly.

Holo grins back. Kai doesn't. But Chester could swear he sees the tiniest hint of a gleam in her eye. *Maybe she's not quite as hard as she pretends to be*, he thinks. *That wouldn't be a bad thing.*

CHAPTER 39

AFTER SCHOOL, HOLO and I walk into town and find a booth at the diner. Lacey hustles out of the kitchen to greet us. She cooks, waits tables, and seems to basically run the place by herself.

"Fries and Cokes?" she asks, wiping her hands on a stained white apron. "In celebration of your incredible test scores? Chester called me right away. I'm so proud of you!"

I really can't understand what the big deal is. "Fries, yes please. Cokes, no," I say. After a lifetime of drinking only water, I can't get used to Coke's fizzy sweetness.

"But I want a Coke," Holo whines as Lacey hurries off to get our fries.

I try to ruffle my brother's hair, but he dodges my hand. "You don't want to turn into a regular, normal human, do you?" I ask. My tone's light, but my question's dead serious: *How much do you really want to be just like everyone else?*

"I don't know," he mumbles grumpily.

The booth behind me creaks. "And what, exactly, does it mean to be a so-called regular, normal human?"

When I twist around in my seat, I'm completely *not* surprised to see Waylon Eugene Meloy there, grinning and looking pleased with himself. He seems to enjoy sneaking up on me. And he's better at it than I'd like to admit.

My cheeks get hot. What do *I* know about what being normal means?

"Well, if I think about the kids at school," I say, "it means eating junk food all the time and being obsessed with video games and cell phones. And taking self-portraits constantly, and watching nonstop Knock Knock videos—"

Waylon bursts out laughing. "Let me stop you before you say anything else ridiculous. For one thing, they're called selfies and TikTok. Also, plenty of regular people do other things with their time. Me, I specialize in restoring motorcycles, ignoring speed limits, and being both charming and dangerous."

His teasing grin is infectious. I can't help smiling back.

"I don't really think you're regular, though," I tell him. "I think you're weird, too."

He slides into the booth next to me as Lacey sets our fries down. He helps himself to the first handful. "I never said I wasn't," he says, shoving about twenty fries into his mouth at once. Then he holds up a hand for my brother to hit. "Freak high five," he says.

Holo slaps his palm, giggling.

"Here," Waylon says, digging into his pocket and handing my brother a five-dollar bill. "Go play some good songs on the jukebox."

"On the what?" Holo says. He has no idea what Waylon's talking about. Honestly, I don't really, either.

"That machine with the blinky lights over there. You'll figure it out."

Holo stares at him for a second. Then he snatches the money and disappears.

Waylon turns to me and says, "So what are you doing tomorrow night?"

I think about this for a second. "I'm probably going to sit in the chief's living room, staring out the window and wondering what I'm doing living in the house of the man who put me in jail."

"Sounds like fun," Waylon says.

I shrug. "I've had worse nights." Like the time Holo and I got trapped in a snowstorm halfway down the mountain and had to spend the night in a snow cave—

"Well, I've got a great idea," Waylon says. "I think you should come to the school dance with me." He shrugs. "It's stupid and lame, but everyone goes to it anyway."

"If it's stupid and lame, why do people go?" I ask. Meanwhile my mind is going: *A gorgeous juvenile delinquent just asked me to a dance!*

Waylon contemplatively gnaws on a fry. "Sometimes you just feel like you're *supposed* to do something, even if you don't really know why. Like maybe you do it because you know you're supposed to have certain *regular, normal* human experiences."

It's annoying that he's throwing my words back at me, but I ignore it. "What happens at a dance?"

Waylon brushes his hair off his forehead; it flops back down immediately. "Well, they play music, and people hang around and talk to their friends, and every once in a while they dance with each other."

"I don't know how to dance." Also I don't really have any friends.

"That makes two of us," Waylon says. "Actually that makes the whole high school gym full of us. Those kids have no rhythm; you should see them."

And then he gets up from the booth and starts jumping around, kicking out his legs and swinging his arms. It looks like he's being stung by a swarm of bees.

"Is that what it's supposed to look like, or are you just really bad?" I ask when he stops.

He looks offended. "Let's see you try it."

"No thank you."

"OK," he says. "Let's try it together."

I look around the diner. "Here?"

"It's as good a place as any. Hang on." He walks over to the jukebox, exchanges a few words with Holo, and then presses a few buttons. The diner fills with the sound of a piano, then a smooth, smoky voice.

Waylon returns and holds out his arms. "Alicia Keys, 'If I Ain't Got You,'" he says. "Classic slow-dance song."

I don't know what to do. Why are his arms out like that? Is he trying to hug me?

"Step closer," he says. "Okay, good, now put your hands on my shoulders."

When I do, I feel his warm skin through his T-shirt, and the strong, shifting muscles beneath. He puts his hands on my waist. I give a tiny, involuntary shiver.

"Now we do this," he says, his voice husky. He starts sort of rocking back and forth, side to side, and I mirror him.

It feels awkward.

And also—amazing.

As we hold each other and sway, I feel pulled magnetically toward him. Our bodies move closer together, until there's barely an inch between his chest and mine. By now my pulse is racing.

Do I dare?

I take that last step toward him. I press myself against his long, lean torso, and I tighten my arms around his neck. I feel his muscles tense and then relax. His steady breath ruffles my hair.

All the years I was so lonely—why did I wait so long to find someone to hold me?

I close my eyes. I press my face into his chest and nuzzle him, hard. And suddenly he steps back.

"What are you doing?" he blurts.

I'm horrified. I was acting like a *wolf*.

I drop my arms to my sides. "Um, my nose itched and I, um, scratched it on your shirt. I'm sorry."

He looks at me quizzically for a moment, and then he laughs. "Sure, that's a totally regular, normal thing to do," he says lightly.

My cheeks are hot with shame. "Isn't it obvious that I don't know *anything* about what's regular and normal?" I practically yell.

"Hey," he says, "it's no big deal. Come on, the song's not

over." He looks at me pleadingly, his arms held wide. "Let's keep dancing."

I shake my head and sink back down into the booth. If I could make myself disappear, I would. "Thanks," I say. "But I'm done. So you'd better find someone else to take to the dance."

CHAPTER 40

HOLO'S JUST SETTLING into his beanbag on Friday morning when the classroom phone rings. Ms. Tillman looks between him and his sister while she listens to whoever's on the other end. When she hangs up, she says, "Holo, Kai, you're to report to the counselor's office."

Holo closes his book and gets up. He's seen the school counselor in the hallways. His bald head is very shiny, and he picks his nose when he thinks no one's looking. But Holo's always looking.

He glances over at his sister, who scowls as she gathers up her books and papers. Are they in some new kind of trouble? He hopes that whatever this meeting is about is her fault, not his.

Out in the hall he says, "Did you do something?"

"Not that I'm aware of."

"Why would the counselor call us in?"

"Don't ask me."

"I already did."

"Well, I don't know," she says huffily. "But I'm sick of getting pulled out of classes."

"You don't even like your classes," he reminds her.

She says, "So?" Then she leans over and sniffs him. "You stink."

"I tried the chief's cologne." It was a mistake. He smells like fake pine trees. He should roll in something rotten to cover it up.

Mr. Johnston is waiting for them in the doorway of his office. His head looks especially shiny today. "Please, come in," he says.

"What's this about?" Kai demands.

"Just a few questions," he says.

But Mr. Johnston's not the one who's going to be asking them. Sitting in the counselor's office, on school chairs much too small for them, are the FBI agents who came to Chester's house so early in the morning.

"Hello again, Holo," says the gray-haired, grizzled one. "Kai."

Kai spins around and tries to leave, but the little one's too fast for her. He shoots up and grabs her arm. Leads her to another chair. "Sit," he says. "Remember us? Rollins and Dunham?"

Of course Holo does. He remembers Rollins's small, mean eyes and threatening posture. And Dunham's lean, hungry face and gray, close-cropped hair. If it wasn't a compliment, Holo would say there's something wolfish about Dunham.

"Make yourself comfortable," the older man says.

"Impossible," Kai says.

"I just keep thinking about your stories," Agent Dunham

says. "About being raised up by a ferocious pack of predators. I want you to tell me more about it."

Kai's mouth is a thin hard line. She looks at Holo. *You take this one,* her eyes say.

Holo clears his throat. He still finds it hard to talk to anyone but Kai, Chester, and Lacey. And he doesn't really want to tell these men about wolves. They won't understand.

"I'm waiting," Dunham says.

"That makes two of us," says Rollins.

Holo stares down at his hands. "When you call them a pack, you make it sound like they're a mob or something. But they're just a family." He remembers Ernie, and he clenches his fists. It's easier to feel anger than sorrow. "They're just parents and their kids, working together to survive."

The death of an alpha can destroy a pack. It's up to Beast to hold them together now.

"And how would you describe your relationship to this pack?" Dunham asks.

"They watched over us. They protected us. They brought food for us, the way you bring home food from the store for your family."

"You'd think they'd've killed and eaten you," Rollins says dryly. "I mean, you'd be so easy to catch."

"Would you kill and eat your kids?" Holo shoots back.

Kai snickers, and Holo feels a surge of pride.

"How did you survive the winter?" Dunham asks.

"Wolves are like four-legged fur blankets," Holo says. He smiles a little, remembering the nights he lay cuddled up between warm, luxuriously furry wolves, breathing in their musky, comforting scent, feeling their paws twitch in dreams. He'd dream of running. Hunting. Feasting.

"But prey must be scarce," Dunham says.

"It's harder to find, but it's easier to catch," Holo says. "A pronghorn can't run very well in snow, but wolves' paws are so big and fluffy they're like—what do you call them? Snow-shoes. And a wolf's jaws can break bones."

"This is all pretty fascinating," Dunham says. "Okay, so the wolves fed you and kept you warm. But they sure as hell didn't read Dr. Seuss books to you. So how are you going to explain that?"

Holo's hands begin to sweat. "I'm not," he says. He looks over at his sister. She nods almost invisibly at him.

You're doing great, she seems to say. *Don't cave.*

Agent Dunham leans close. Holo can smell the coffee on his breath and the mint of his toothpaste. "We think you're leaving out some crucial information," he says.

"We might even say that you're lying to us," Rollins adds.

Holo wipes his hands on his hand-me-down jeans. Keeps his mouth shut. So what if he is? They can't make him betray his pack.

"Lying to federal agents could result in false statements charges," Dunham says. "Did you know that? So I want you to think very carefully before you answer this question: Do you know a woman named Wendy?"

Holo gasps. Kai jumps up from her chair and grabs his hand.

"What I *think*," she says through clenched teeth, "is that we don't have to answer that question."

She gives her wild, dark hair a toss and yanks Holo out the door. She kicks it shut behind them, and then they start to run.

By the time the agents burst into the hallway, brother and sister are gone.

CHAPTER 41

WE THINK YOU'RE leaving out some crucial information.

We might even say that you're lying to us.

I slam my shovel into the dirt. Dunham and Rollins don't scare me. I just don't ever want to see them again.

I fling the dirt to the side, grab a green seedling, drop it into the hole, and cover up its roots. Planting tomatoes in Lacey's garden is chore number one on a long list the chief left for us before he went back to work a second shift. Guess I was wrong about what I told Waylon I'd be doing on a Friday night.

"We have to be ready to run," I tell my brother.

Holo pinches off a leaf of a chard plant and pops it into his mouth. He chews and makes a face. "This isn't as good as miner's lettuce."

"It's because you're supposed to eat it cooked, dummy. And I don't think you're taking this threat seriously."

He gives me a wounded look. "I did a good job today, though, didn't I? I didn't give anything away."

I soften. I never want to hurt my brother. He's all I've got right now. "You did great."

Lacey leans out the kitchen window. "Do you kids want chocolate or vanilla frosting on your cake?"

"Cake?" Holo yelps, brightening immediately.

"You bet," Lacey says. "We're *still* celebrating your test scores. You could go to Harvard with scores like that."

"What's Harvard?" Holo asks.

"A place only very smart people go. Now, chocolate or vanilla?"

"We've never had frosting before," I tell her.

"Obviously chocolate then," Lacey says, withdrawing her head.

Holo digs and plants happily for a little while, thinking about cake. But then his face gets serious again. "Do you think those men know anything?"

"I'm not sure. But I don't trust them."

But what if they knew who we were? Then *would I want to see them again?*

I look down at my hands. My fingernails are filthy, but my cuts and callouses are pretty much gone by now. I've almost got the hands of a regular, normal girl.

"I don't really want to leave," Holo says quietly.

Waylon Eugene Meloy's smile flashes in my mind. For a second, it's like I can still feel his arms around me.

"I don't think I want to, either," I say. Not yet.

CHAPTER 42

ONCE HOLO AND I get all the tomatoes in the ground, Lacey goes out to check our work. I think it's funny that she's so obsessed with her garden when the whole meadow is edible. I wonder what she'd say if I told her that the cattails by the pond are delicious. Or that the plantain herb she calls a weed is good for poison ivy, or that the yarrow helps fevers and heals wounds.

"When's that cake going to be ready?" Holo wonders.

I eyeball the timer. "Ten minutes."

"I'm starving."

"When *aren't* you starving?"

He shrugs. "When I'm asleep."

I swear he's grown two inches since we came out of the woods.

And the wolf pups are gaining about three pounds a week.

Assuming they're still alive.

"Can we take the cake out early?" Holo asks, gazing longingly at the oven.

I'm about to scold him—*no, that's a stupid question*—when a short, high yelp rips through the air. Then comes a longer, low wail.

I hear, "Kai? *Kai!*"

I run outside to find Lacey lying in the dirt at the edge of the garden. Her face is shiny with sweat and very white.

I drop to the ground beside her. A rock slices into my knee. I ignore it.

"Something—bit me," she gasps. She's clutching her left arm to her chest. Then she rolls over on her side, curls her knees up, and vomits.

Panic lights up my nerves. *A rattlesnake*, I think. But I manage to keep my voice calm. "Is it your arm? Your hand? Can I see it?"

Lacey doesn't seem to hear me. She's shaking, and now she's crying in fear and pain. I gently tug on her arm, pulling it toward me. She squeezes her eyes shut and moans, "*Oh God oh God oh God*—" A trickle of bile runs out of the side of her mouth.

There. I see it. Two deep puncture wounds on the fleshy part of her palm near the thumb. There's no blood, but her hand is already starting to swell.

"Holo," I shout over my shoulder. "Call the hospital!"

Lacey's face is going from white to green.

Does the kid even know how to work a phone?

"It's okay, Lacey, you're okay," I say urgently. "Hang on, I'll be right back."

I rush over to a clump of plantain herb, grab a few leaves, and shove them into my mouth. They're disgustingly bitter and tough. I chew them for as long as I can stand it and then spit them into my hand. I run back to Lacey and press the green fibrous pulp against the bite.

"This is plantain," I tell her. "It's good for stings and snakebites."

But she's hyperventilating. Her legs start spasming. There's no meadow herb that's going to help her now.

"Holo!" I scream. "Are you calling?"

Once the chief showed us a movie where someone cut an X through a rattlesnake bite on someone's leg and sucked the venom out. But that was a *movie*, and this is *life*, and what we need is an ambulance.

"It's not working!" Holo shouts through the window.

"You idiot, you just press three buttons! 9-1-1!"

He's crying and then he disappears from the window, and the next thing I know he's shoving the phone in my face. The screen is dark.

And I realize that it's dead.

"Isn't there a cord?" I shriek.

"No, I looked everywhere!"

Lacey's hand is getting bigger by the minute. Now there's blood running down from the wounds, and it looks pale and watery because it's been thinned by the venom. *That must have been one big goddamn snake.*

She's sweating and groaning. She rolls over and vomits again.

"Then get me a towel and the car keys!"

But my brother just stares at me.

"Do you need me to *bark* it at you? Get the car keys! And a damp towel!"

"You don't know how to drive!"

"I'm about to learn, aren't I?"

With one final terrified glance at Lacey, Holo runs into the house. When he comes back, he's got what I asked for. "Wrap that tight around her hand," I tell him. "Keep the plantain on it." I push Lacey's hair off her damp forehead. "It's going to be okay," I whisper.

But I don't know if it is.

I pull her to a seated position and then, with Holo's help, I half carry, half drag her over to her car. We push her into the back seat, fold her legs up, and put a blanket over her. I feel her wrist. The pulse is so faint I almost can't tell it's there.

Holo gets in beside her. She's almost unconscious now. "I turned off the oven," he tells her. "The cake's perfect." Big fat tears start rolling down his cheeks. "Is she going to die?" he asks me.

God, I hope not. I grit my teeth and turn the key.

CHAPTER 43

NOTHING HAPPENS. *DAMN it, damn it!*

I yank it out and stab it back in again. Turn. Nothing.

I've watched Chester start a car before—I can do this. Can't I?

"We're going to get help, don't worry," Holo tells Lacey. "It's going to be okay."

It's not going to be okay if I can't get us out of here.

I can see my brother's terrified eyes in the rearview mirror. "Make sure her arm's hanging down off the seat! Keep the bite below heart level—the venom moves slower that way!"

"I've got it! Just start the car!" Holo yells.

"I'm trying!" I start pressing pedals with my feet while turning the key at the same time. The car still doesn't start.

I have to twist around to check on Lacey. Her arm's going purple—a sign of internal hemorrhaging. "Lift up her head!"

"Drive the fucking car!" Holo screams.

I have to focus. I have to figure this out. Panic makes my fingers shake. I'm overdosing on adrenaline.

Just calm down for one second, Kai. Which is the gas? Stomp on it!

Nothing happens.

Brake. Try that. *Press. Turn.*

The engine roars to life.

"D stands for drive, right?" I yell. "Wait, why am I asking you—you don't even know how to work a phone."

"It was *dead*," Holo yells back.

I hear the awful terror in his voice.

I'm sorry, Holo.

I have to calm down.

I push the stick to D and press what I think is the gas. We go shooting forward. Reflex makes me stomp on the other pedal. Holo yelps as he crashes into the back of my seat. But Lacey's dead silent.

"Sorry, it's just going to take me a minute—"

I press the gas again, more gently this time, and we start to move forward. When I press it harder, we go faster.

Okay, this is totally fine, I can do this.

"You're about to hit a tree," Holo cries.

I have to learn how to steer, too.

By the time I get to the end of the chief's long driveway, I'm getting the hang of it. I pull out onto the road. My hands are white and shaking, but I'm driving.

"Which way is the hospital?" Holo says.

I don't know.

"Holo, is she breathing?"

"Yes," Holo says. "Barely."

I press the gas harder. The trees go whipping by. Nausea fills my stomach, my chest. I'm freaking carsick! And I'm going seventy miles an hour. Lacey's old VW shudders as I give it more gas. I pass a truck. Another truck. I keep my hand on the horn. *Get the hell out of my way!* I swallow down vomit. Tears stream from my eyes.

"Faster!" Holo cries. "Her skin's cold!"

I unclench my jaw. Bile rises up. I snap it shut again. We're almost there.

When we pull up to the police station I'm out of the car almost before it stops, screaming, "Chester! Chester!" And then I throw up on the sidewalk.

The chief bursts out, saying "What the hell?" His face is dark with anger.

"Lacey," I gasp, pointing to the back seat. "Snakebite."

The chief looks at me wiping barf from my face and then sees his partner lying in the back seat, looking dead already. He dives into the driver's seat and I take the passenger side, and he peels out. He keeps his hand on the horn the whole time, too, and I'm halfway out the window, screaming "Get out of the way!"

Twenty minutes later, we're screeching to a halt in front of the emergency room doors. The chief's still honking the horn and shouting like crazy, and people come pouring out of the hospital. They swarm around Lacey, and they get her onto a stretcher. When they rush her inside, the chief goes running after them.

And then, just like that, everything is quiet. Holo and I stand on the sidewalk, alone.

Just the two of us.

Like always.

All the adrenaline drains away. It *aches*. My vision goes dim, and my legs give out.

CHAPTER 44

LACEY'S LYING IN a white bed in a white room. She's pale and motionless. It seems like about a hundred plastic tubes are going in and out of her body.

The chief gets up from his chair when we walk in. He looks terrible. He opens his mouth to say something, but then he turns away. His shoulders shake.

Is he crying?

Holo looks to me in panic. "Is she—?" he whispers.

"She's going to be all right." A young nurse comes into the room and walks over to Lacey's bedside. She pulls the blankets up and gives Lacey's shoulder a gentle pat. "We've given her medicine to help her sleep."

She checks the IVs and monitors and then nods, satisfied. "She's much more stable now." Then she spins around to the three of us. "Who put all that stuff on the bite?"

I hesitate. *Stuff?* That was *medicine*. But maybe it didn't look good, bringing Lacey in with a bunch of chewed-up leaves on her hand.

"What are you talking about?" the chief demands. He wipes furiously at his cheeks.

Yeah, he was crying.

The nurse looks at me and Holo.

I slowly raise my hand. "It was a poultice," I say. "I thought—I just—"

"What was it?" she interrupts.

"Plantain herb."

Instead of scolding me, the nurse actually smiles. Nods. "Well, you did a good thing. Using what you had and then getting her to us. Who knows, maybe you'll be a doctor someday."

"That's what Kai's always wanted to be," Holo practically shouts. "Ever since she was little."

"Shut up," I tell my brother, my cheeks flushing.

"But it's true," he says huffily.

Then the actual doctor walks into the room, white coat and everything. She confers for a moment with the nurse while I stand there, watching Lacey lightly breathe.

"Plaintain herb?" the chief says to me, looking confused. "Where'd you get that?"

"Your yard," I say. "There's all kinds of medicine in it."

When the nurse leaves, the doctor turns her attention to us. "It's extremely rare to have a reaction like this. But the venom went into a vein." She glances back at Lacey. "It was good luck that Ms. Hernandez got here when she did. Any longer with that venom in her and the outcome would have been very different."

The chief comes over to me and puts his arm around my shoulder. I stiffen at first, but I do my best to relax.

"Good *luck?*" he says fiercely. "You've got it all wrong. It wasn't luck. It was *Kai*."

CHAPTER 45

THE NICE "I saved someone's life" feeling doesn't last very long.

It starts on Monday with Mrs. Simon telling Holo that he has to go to his own language arts class. The kid growls a little—I don't blame him; it's a hard habit to break—and then it's detention for him, plus for me, too, because I tried to stand up for him.

On the bright side, the chief doesn't get mad at us for getting in trouble again. He's too distracted, because Lacey's still in the hospital, recovering. Her blood pressure hasn't quite stabilized, and her entire arm's black and blue and green, and so whenever he's not at work he's sitting at her bedside.

On the not-bright side, it means that I'm in charge of taking care of the house and keeping Holo fed and bathed. This last part isn't easy. He's a bottomless food pit—he ate Lacey's entire cake in one sitting—and he has a weird fear of the shower. He says it's "not natural" that hot water rains down from the ceiling. Since he grew up bathing in rivers, he has a point. But just because something isn't natural doesn't mean it's not *nice*.

And even worse, every day at school, I hear stories of more dead sheep. More missing calves. Suddenly it seems like every kid lives on a ranch or a farm, and every single one of them is losing livestock.

Wolves are to blame, they say. And something's got to be done.

When I hear that kind of thing, my blood turns to ice. I think about Beast and her family. Would she leave the safety of the forest? Would she kill a cow?

She's the fastest wolf in the pack. But Ernie was the strongest. And now he's gone. He didn't kill Hardy's ewe but he died for it anyway.

And it's not like Beast understands *ownership*. She can't comprehend that a sheep isn't hers to hunt and kill.

So if she had to hunt livestock, she would. Anything to keep those babies alive.

I have to warn her, I think.

It's the last period of the day, and I'm still worrying about the wolves as I jog around the track in PE. I'm coming down the backstretch, trying to figure out how to warn her, when I feel Mac Hardy's sour breath on my neck.

"My dad says we should kill all wolves," he says.

My shoulders stiffen. *Your dad is a murderer*, I think.

He pulls up beside me. He's red and sweating. "'Yeah,' I go, 'just don't forget the wolf girls.'" Then he passes me, laughing. His stupid friends turn and leer.

I give them all the finger. So far, this gesture's the best thing I've learned in school.

But I keep my distance from Mac for the rest of the class. I don't want another confrontation, and I don't need any more detentions. I jog so slowly around the track that even Lucy can keep up.

"He sure doesn't like you," she says, huffing alongside me.

"Maybe because I beat him in a race and then I kicked his dad's ass."

She lets out a braying laugh. "I wish I could've seen that."

"I wish I could do it again."

She pants awhile, then says, "Are wolves nicer than high school kids?"

"That's a weird question."

"I'm a weird person. Like you are."

"Thanks," I say sarcastically. "I was hoping not everyone noticed."

"Sorry," she says. "But we all noticed." She elbows me lightly. "So—are wolves nicer or what?"

I think about Beast, and how she keeps the pack in line, with aggression if she needs to. How she kills by necessity and without any remorse. And how Ben bites, and Bim steals...

"I wouldn't call a wolf nice," I say, "but they don't understand cruelty, either."

"You mean they aren't assholes just because they can be? I'll take that as a yes, then."

I grin. I'm starting to like Lucy.

When PE is over, we walk together back toward the school. Lucy is telling me about her pet chinchilla, an animal I've never even heard of before.

"His name is Squeaky, because he squeaks when he—" She stops in her tracks. Her eyes go wide.

Mac Hardy is looming by the entrance to the school. And we both know he's waiting for me.

"I'll see you later," she gasps, and then she runs off faster than I've ever seen her go.

I could follow Lucy to the other door, a hundred yards away. But I refuse to let any Hardy scare me. So I stare straight ahead and keep walking. As I try to pass him by, Mac throws out an arm and stops me.

"Animals belong *outside*," he says.

"I hope you're not planning on going in then," I say.

He spits a thick wad of phlegm onto the asphalt. "You think you're smart," he says.

"Actually, I know I'm smart."

"You don't belong here," he says.

I sigh. "Are you bringing up *that* argument again? Look, we fundamentally agree with each other about it. But for better and worse, I'm here now, so you might as well get used to it."

"I don't have to get used to anything," he says.

He moves quickly toward me, and suddenly there's something sharp and cold jabbing into my stomach. I look down.

It's a *gun*.

CHAPTER 46

I SHOULD BE terrified, but instead I'm just *pissed*.

"Did you bring your daddy's toy to school for show and tell?" I ask mockingly.

He jabs it harder into my ribs. I wince involuntarily.

"I brought it as a warning," he growls.

I look him in the eye like I'm daring him to shoot. "Never pull out a weapon you aren't ready to use."

"I was born ready."

I really, truly can't stand this kid. "You were born a helpless, stupid baby"—I grab his wrist and twist it so the gun's pointing at him now—"and you haven't changed a bit." Then I drive my heel down onto the small bones on the top of his foot at the same time as I crash my elbow into his solar plexus with all my strength. He gasps and bends over, nearly dropping his weapon. I take my chance and run, bursting into the gym just as the final bell rings.

Okay, maybe that wasn't the smartest thing I've ever done. But it felt great. And I guess I have a triumphant smirk on my face, because when I see Waylon in the hallway, he says, "What do you look so happy for? You just have to come back here again tomorrow."

We join the stream of kids heading outside.

"Mac Hardy," I tell him. "He keeps forgetting that he shouldn't mess with me."

Waylon stops and grabs my shoulders. "Kai," he says, "*you* shouldn't mess with *him*."

I bristle. "He's the one who keeps coming at me!" I say.

"Then do a better job of dodging him," Waylon says.

I snort. "What are you so worried about? I can take care of myself."

"I'm sure you can," Waylon says. "But I still want you to keep away from Mac—or any other Hardy."

I wonder if he's somehow heard about my little fight with Mac's dad, even though I only told Lucy. "Fine," I say, just to end the conversation. "The next time I see Mac Hardy, I'll just run away like a little deer."

"Good," he says. "Now do you want to go get ice cream? I can fit you on the back, and Holo on the handlebars."

I look from him to his bike. "You're joking," I say. I hesitate. "Right?"

He laughs. "Of course I'm joking. I'm dangerous, but I'm not insane." Then he steps closer to me, and his voice gets softer. Flirtier. "I can make two trips if you need your brother as a chaperone."

I can't take it when he stands this near to me. I just want to pull him closer. I breathe in his scent of soap and leather.

I don't know how this works.

I don't know how to be a regular girl.

"I have to go," I say abruptly. "Lacey's still in the hospital and Holo and I—we're supposed to help out at the diner." Does it matter that it isn't true? No. I madly motion my brother, who's just coming out of school. *Hurry!*

"Okay," Waylon says, looking disappointed. "I get it."

He walks away, his shoulders hunched.

But he's wrong. He doesn't get it.

I've never felt this way before, and I'm scared.

CHAPTER 47

"LACEY MIGHT GET to come home today," Holo tells me as we walk along the road into town. "This girl in Spanish class told me. Her mom works at the hospital."

"That's great," I say absently. I'm still thinking about Waylon. Being around him makes me feel jittery. Vulnerable.

And if I know anything at all, it's that being vulnerable is dangerous.

"Maybe we should make her a cake," Holo muses. "Do you think she'd like chocolate or vanilla?"

"Maybe you shouldn't have eaten the one she made," I say.

"Probably chocolate," he says, ignoring me.

I'm about to point out that we have no business baking when something big and heavy slams into me from behind. I go sprawling facedown on the road. My teeth smack together on the end of my tongue. My mouth fills with blood as my chin grinds into the asphalt. I can practically hear my skin rip open.

A foot presses down hard on my back.

Holo lands on the ground next to me. His chin splits open, too.

I don't have to see our attackers to know who they are. And I'm going to seriously hurt them—that is, if I can get up.

"Do you like that, freak?" I can hear the smirk in Mac Hardy's voice. "Being down in the dirt like an animal?"

I don't think I can answer. All the air's being pushed out of me. I meet Holo's frightened gaze. It looks like he can't breathe, either. I reach out and touch his arm. Gently. Comfortingly. Just for a second.

Don't worry, it's going to be okay.

Hardy digs his heel in harder. My back cracks.

"I *said*, 'Do you like that?'"

I violently twist my body around and sit up in one fluid motion. Mac Hardy's foot slides off and he stumbles sideways.

"Not really," I gasp. By now I'm on my feet and crouching low, ready. I'll let him make the first move.

But it's Logan who goes for me first. Out of the corner of my eye I see him lunging, fist swinging hard and wide. I dodge him as Holo gets up from the road. Blood streams from his chin.

"You really shouldn't have," I say reproachfully.

"It's rude," Holo agrees, blotting blood with his T-shirt.

Mac and Logan stand shoulder to shoulder now, fists like hammers. Clenched. "Let's go!" Logan says. "Come on, let's go!"

Holo frowns. "Go where?"

Mac sneers.

"I think it means 'let's fight,'" I say.

"Oh, that makes more sense," Holo says.

I bounce on my toes. Holo and I stand loose and ready. We're quicker and lighter and we're not scared.

Sure, they're twice as big as we are. But when it comes down to it, they're just domesticated beasts. Like bulls. And as big as bulls are, they're still prey animals.

Whereas Holo and I are predators.

"Ribs or teeth?" I ask my brother.

"Definitely teeth," he says.

Mac and Logan glance at each other, like *what are these freaks talking about?*

Holo and I smile at them. Then we charge.

Holo lands a punch on the side of Logan's jaw before the kid sees what's coming. A high kick sends my foot crashing into Mac's mouth. Blood gushes from his split lips. He roars in rage and comes at me. I spin away. I aim another kick right between his legs. That bends him in two.

Logan has Holo in a headlock, but my brother's elbowing him in the guts, *bam bam bam*. Then Holo gets his mouth on Logan's arm—and he bites. Logan screams and lets him go, and my brother stands up and sends a fist into Logan's chin. He hooks an arm around Logan's neck and pulls him downward, forcing him to his knees.

Mac's gone purple in the face. He's still got one hand on his crotch.

The Hardys are on the defensive and they know it.

I guess that's why Mac pulls out the gun.

He grins at me as he cocks it. But he's not pointing at me. He's pointing it at my brother.

"There's a couple grand bounty on a wolf these days," he says. "What's the bounty on a teenage freak?"

Holo freezes. Lets go of Logan, who crawls away on his hands and knees.

"Ribs or teeth?" Mac says tauntingly.

Holo says, "Mac, don't."

"*Beg*," Mac says. He swings the gun toward me, then back to my brother.

Instead of cowering, Holo stands up straighter. He says, "You overfed slob, you couldn't hit me in the teeth if you tried."

A flicker of rage crosses Mac's pink face. "I'll take that bet," he says. He sights down the gun's barrel.

Holo's eyes flick over at me. *Help.*

Silent and quick, I reach down. I grab a broken branch from the side of the road and I bring it down with all my strength on Mac's gun hand. He howls and drops the weapon. It goes off with a sharp bang. Logan drops to the ground, hands covering his head.

The gun's lying in the dirt. I lunge for it. So does Mac. But I get there first. I grab it and point it right at his ugly face. "You want us to beg? Let me tell you something, grease stain. *Dogs* beg. Wolves kill."

CHAPTER 48

Dispatch: 911, what is the location of the emergency?

Caller: There's a girl on the side of the road, and she's got a gun!

Dispatch: Can you tell me where you are?

Caller: Just east of the high school. I was driving home when I seen it out of the corner of my eye—

Dispatch: On Lone Pine Avenue?

Caller: Yes, ma'am. She has two boys at gunpoint! Do you think she's going to shoot 'em? I never saw a face like that! Fury in it!

Dispatch: All right, I need you to stay clear of the area.

Caller: I got out of there fast as I could and called you! She ain't goin' to shoot 'em, is she?

Dispatch: Sir, we're sending an officer right now. Can I get your name, please?

Caller: Denny Watson, ma'am. What is the world coming to? A *girl!*

CHAPTER 49

"YOU WON'T DO it," Mac Hardy says.

My finger creeps toward the trigger. *I want to do it.*

"She don't dare," Logan says. But his voice trembles.

Would I dare?

How about just a little graze of the arm? Nothing life-threatening—just a warning. *This is what happens when you keep calling me a freak. When you track me like an animal. When you jump me every chance you get.*

The trigger is cool to the touch. I think Mac would've shot me and Holo if he could've. That means if I shoot him, I'm no better than he is.

I don't care.

I still want to do it.

Mac's eyes bore into mine. Challenging me. Telling me how much we disgust him, no words necessary. He and his brother are never going to leave us alone. Never going to stop telling us that we don't belong in Kokanee Creek, and that wolves don't belong in the Idaho woods.

I hate them.

The world would be a better place without them.

"Kai," my brother warns. "This isn't how it's supposed to go."

I keep my eyes on Mac. Let's see who wins the staring contest when I'm the one with the gun. "I don't know what you're talking about. This is what we call *justice*."

Logan is still on his hands and knees. He's crawling toward his brother.

I move the pistol between Mac and Logan. *Ribs? Teeth? Heart?*

Mac finally blinks. Clears his throat. Says, defiantly, "I know you can't do it."

Oh yes I can.

"You save people, Kai," Holo calls to me. His voice sounds high and scared. "You don't hurt them."

I save the ones who deserve to be saved.

"Go on, you little chickenshit forest bitch," Mac growls. "I'm getting bored."

Logan has gotten all the way behind his brother now. He's using him as a shield. How brave. How brotherly.

My finger presses a little harder on the trigger now.

All it'll take is one tiny squeeze.

And then I hear the siren.

CHAPTER 50

IT PIERCES THE ear like a scream. A flock of crows rise cawing into the air.

The trembling starts in my legs and travels up my body like a wildfire. My arm shakes. The gun wobbles. I can't keep my aim.

My target smiles a slow, cruel smile. "You're dead now," Mac Hardy says. "Game over."

I lower the gun. My shoulders slump. The weight of what I almost did crushes me.

What was I doing? *Was I really about to shoot Mac Hardy?*

I look down at the gun in disgust. Its black metal has a dull, lethal gleam. With my thumb, I flick the safety back on. And then I fling the weapon away as far as I can. It lands with a faint thud somewhere deep in the woods.

"Hey!" Mac yelps. "That's mine!"

"*Fetch*," I snarl.

But Mac's still frozen to the spot. I dig my nails into my palms as the cruiser comes to a screeching halt, spewing up gravel. The chief charges out, his own gun drawn. "Drop your weapons!" he shouts.

Holo flings his hands up. "We don't have any," he cries.

Not anymore we don't.

The chief quickly takes in the scene—me and Holo facing off with the Hardys, Logan slowly stepping out from behind his brother, brushing dirt from his knees. There's no gun in sight. And Holo, at least, looks totally innocent.

Not to mention terrified.

The chief lowers his weapon. "What's going on here?" he demands. "We got a call about a girl with a gun." He turns to me, his expression dark. "Kai? Did you have a *gun*?"

But I'm too overwhelmed to speak. *I was ready to kill Mac Hardy.*

Logan points a finger at me. "She was going to shoot my brother!"

And probably you, too, I think. *Any bullet I would've fired at Mac would've ripped right through him and slammed into you.*

The chief steps closer to me. "Kai," he says, low and fierce, "this is deadly serious. I need you to tell me what happened. I need you to explain yourself."

I try to open my mouth, I really do. But suddenly there are more cars pulling up. People are getting out and they're shouting. A lady with bleached, orangish hair runs right at Mac Hardy with her arms held wide, and then she's crying and hugging him and wailing her head off.

"Mom," he says, snarling, trying to shake her off, "I'm *okay*."

"What did these animals do to you?" she says, grabbing at Logan now. Black lines of mascara run down her cheeks.

Animals—of course.

Like mother, like son.

"Lock 'em up!" someone yells, and another person cheers.

I close my eyes as the shouting gets louder. Pretty soon someone's going to say something about calling the pound. Or the zoo. Or the wildlife exterminators. I know how this goes.

The chief is trying to talk to me, but I can't hear what he's saying.

I'm sorry, but this isn't working, Chief.

We don't belong.

I know it and you know it. The difference is that you can't admit it to yourself.

Then a voice cuts through the noise. A voice I know. A voice that reassures me with its familiar warmth.

"If everyone can just shut the hell up for a second," Waylon yells, "I can tell you exactly what happened."

The shouting stops. I open my eyes and see Waylon standing halfway in the road, fists clenched like he's ready to fight someone, too. His bangs are so long that his face is almost entirely in shadow. I can't read his expression. Can't meet his eyes.

He walks toward the chief, passing a foot from me without glancing my way at all. He shoves his fists into the pockets of his faded jeans and addresses the crowd. "I saw Mac and Logan Hardy start following Kai and Holo after school. *Stalking* them. I know you think those boys are fine, upstanding Kokanee Creek citizens"—Waylon gives a small, sarcastic cough—"but the Hardys have been harassing Kai and Holo since the day they came to town."

"That's bullshit," Mac sneers.

"Be quiet," the chief says to Mac. "Get to the point," he says to Waylon.

Waylon nods. Still doesn't look at me. "Yes, sir," he says, deferentially. "So I followed Mac and Logan, who were following Kai and Holo. And then I saw Mac and Logan come up behind Holo and Kai and knock them to the ground. It was a totally unprovoked attack—Kai and Holo didn't even know what hit them. And when they tried to defend themselves, Mac pulled a gun. He started threatening Holo with it."

"I don't believe it," says orange-haired Mrs. Hardy.

"Well, you're an idiot," Waylon replies calmly. "So Kai took it away from Mac with the help of a giant stick. And then she..." He pauses. Shrugs. "Well, then she took possession of the weapon."

The chief looks over at me. "Is this true?" he asks.

I can't move or speak. *Why is Waylon defending me but acting like I'm invisible?*

"Of course it's true," Waylon says heatedly. "Do you think I'd risk getting my ass stomped every week for telling a lie?" He turns back to the crowd. "You act like Kai and Holo are dangerous! But it's your own kids!" His voice is nearly shaking with rage. "The ones who beat them up—and the ones who stand around laughing while it happens!"

"This is slander," Mrs. Hardy says.

"It's the truth," Waylon says. "Ask Kai and Holo."

Holo comes over to me and grabs my hand. "It's true," he says. "Isn't it, Kai?"

Finally I manage the tiniest millimeter of a nod.

The chief turns to Mrs. Hardy. "Why don't you bring your boys down to the station right now, and we can have a little talk."

She sputters. Looks around at everyone, like one of them might come to their defense. But everyone's quiet now. Waylon's words are sinking in.

I'm still trying to wrap my head around the fact that Waylon saw the whole fight. He saw me with murder in my eyes. And he didn't try to stop me.

I know why.

Because even though he said that we're not dangerous, he doesn't believe it. We have wildness in our blood, and now he's seen what it looks like.

CHAPTER 51

CHESTER WOULD LOVE to toss the Hardy brothers in a cell for a few hours. It'd scare 'em a little, wouldn't it? Plus they could keep Dougie company. Give him an audience for his whiskey-fueled jokes.

But then he'd be late picking up Lacey from the hospital. Plus he's pretty sure Reginald Hardy will punish his sons worse than jail could. Not for attacking Kai and Holo, but for doing such a shitty job of it. For losing the gun. For getting caught.

For being bested by a *girl*.

So after a little talking-to down at the station, he sends Mac and Logan on their way, their mom tearfully trudging behind them. *Don't let me ever catch those boys with a gun outside of hunting season again. You understand me?*

"Hey, Chief," Officer Randall calls as Chester's heading out. "There's a message from an Agent Dunham—"

"Put it in the circular file, Randall," Chester says.

Randall looks at him blankly.

"The *trash can*," Chester says, wishing once again that his second-in-command was just a teensy bit brighter. "If Dunham wants to talk to me, he's going to have to keep calling." He pushes the door open and then turns back. "Course, I may or may not answer."

Some wordless instinct makes him want to keep Dunham as far from Kai and Holo as possible. Maybe it's because he wants to protect them.

Or maybe it's because, deep down, he's pretty sure they've got something to hide.

When Chester arrives at the hospital, Lacey's waiting impatiently in the lobby. She jumps up when she sees him, her dark eyes sparkling with relief. He wraps her in a hard hug and buries his face in her shiny black hair. "I missed you," he whispers.

Lacey's shaky on her feet still, but she's talking a mile a minute. "I swear, I wasn't going to last another second in that room. Do you know how many episodes of *Nailed It!* I watched? Thirty, Chester, *thirty*, and all the while you were doing everything without any help at all. How are the kids? I can't wait to see them! I feel like I've been gone forever."

"It's been three days, babe," he says.

"And Holo's probably grown just as many inches! You don't eat like that unless you're growing like a weed. *Does* he look taller? They've got Levi's on sale at the Feed & Seed. We could get him a new pair this weekend."

Chester shrugs. "Sure, okay, whatever you say."

Smiling excitedly, Lacey tucks her arm into his elbow as they walk to the car, and Chester decides not to tell her about the fight. The gun. The feud with the Hardys that keeps getting worse. For now, he can let her enjoy being released from the hospital, her life miraculously saved by a girl whose past is still a mystery.

He stops at the store to get a bottle of wine, so it's nearing dinnertime when they pull up to the house. Lacey hurries inside, calling for Kai and Holo in an eager singsong. Chester takes an extra minute in the yard, letting the stress of the day fall away. He breathes deep. The air smells clean and fresh, and the meadow's dotted with wildflowers. He feels a smile start to tug at the corners of his mouth. He'll grill those fancy sausages he got the other day, he decides, and Lacey will open the wine and make a salad, and the four of them will sit around the worn kitchen table together. Maybe afterward they'll all watch a movie.

Everyone's home, he thinks. *Tonight is a good night.*

Then Lacey comes out breathless onto the porch. Her face has gone white. Stricken. "Chester," she says, "they're gone."

Gone? What the hell is she talking about?

"Sweetie," he says, "they're probably just out by the creek, catching trout for dinner or something."

Lacey thrusts out her arm. It's still bruised and awful-looking. A folded piece of paper sits in the center of her swollen, bandaged palm. "They're gone," she repeats. "It says so right here. Is there something you aren't telling me? Did something happen?"

He takes the porch steps two at a time. His heartbeat quickens as he reads the note. "Shit," he whispers. He made a mistake: it wasn't the Hardys he needed to talk to after the gun incident. It was Kai and Holo.

Lacey says, "Don't even bother taking off your shoes, Chester Greene. You're going out there, and you're getting them back."

CHAPTER 52

DOWN AT THE station, Chester starts making calls to the informal network of Kokanee Creek good ol' boys who have helped him out before: once to find a couple of teenage campers lost on a hike; once to locate a suspected thief hiding up on Elephant Ridge.

Chester pauses before the last number on his list. It belongs to the best tracker he knows. If anyone can find Kai and Holo, he can. The problem? Reginald Hardy hates Kai and everything she stands for. He wouldn't care if she was lost forever. In fact he'd like it that way.

Randall glances over Chester's shoulder at the list of names. "I wouldn't want to be in the dark woods with *that* prick," he says.

For some reason, Randall's words settle the matter. "You don't have to," he retorts as he dials Hardy's number. "I got other volunteers."

It's near nightfall by the time the small crowd has gathered in front of the station. Somehow Waylon Meloy is there, too, though Chester definitely didn't call him. "You again?" Chester says, annoyed.

Waylon nods and thrusts his chin out, daring Chester to send him back home. Chester almost does it, too, but then he thinks of Kai. Maybe, if the search party finds her—sorry, *when* they find her—she'll be glad to see Waylon's face in the crowd. Maybe then she won't run.

So Chester turns to the rest of the volunteers and greets them all. Says, "I know it's not the best time to search the woods, but if we wait until morning, that's another twelve hours they've got to disappear."

The men—and it's only men; sometimes it still feels like the 1950s in Kokanee Creek—mutter among themselves. Chester knows that most of them probably wish Kai and Holo had never come out of the woods, either. So why are they here to help find them? A chance at a little adventure, maybe, or the prospect of having a new story to tell down at One-Eyed Mike's, the dive bar ten miles south on Route 20. *We chased them dumb feral kids all night long…*

Or maybe it's just because their police chief asked for their help. It doesn't even matter.

"We're going to head up to my place," Chester tells them, "since that's their last known location."

He's about to get into his car when he hears the squeal of tires turning down Main Street. He looks up to see a battered old pickup with only one headlight come to a shaking halt. The door opens and a cloud of cigarette smoke rolls out, followed by Reginald Hardy.

"Let's go find those little animals," he growls.

Hardy's wearing a camouflage vest, a belt festooned with knives and bear spray, and a headlamp. He's got a thermos of coffee in one hand and a rifle in the other.

Jesus, Chester thinks. *He doesn't look like he wants to* find *these kids. He looks like he wants to* hunt *them.*

CHAPTER 53

Chester and Lacey—

I'm sorry, but we have to go.
You tried your best, and so did we. But it didn't work.
Thanks for everything.
We won't forget you.

Kai

I'm done.
Done.
It's not that life in Kokanee Creek feels dangerous—though it does, thanks to those Hardy dirtbags. And it's not that I'm afraid.
I'm just *tired*.
When Holo and I came out of the woods, I thought everything would be better than this. I thought everything would be easier. I thought we could find a place for ourselves.

I know that wolves are territorial and that a wolf entering territory belonging to another pack is likely to be attacked. But I didn't know that humans aren't really much different.

There are too many people who want us gone and not enough who want us to stay. We've got the chief and Lacey and Waylon on our side. And on the other side: pretty much everyone else.

Holo walks behind me, picking his way quietly through the trees. Is he done, too? I don't know. I can't tell what he's thinking, and I'm not going to ask him. He'll follow me wherever I go, because I'm the leader of our pack.

The trees thin as the ground rises. The path gets rockier.

I know I'll miss Waylon. More than I'd like to admit.

I scramble between boulders. The moonlight almost makes them glow. I can hear Holo breathing behind me.

Was this all one giant mistake?

I brush my hand along the rough rock as I pass. My body pulls me in the right direction.

It takes me another two miles of walking to decide: No, I don't think it was a mistake. I tasted sundaes and sweet, fizzy Cokes; I went to high school and I drove a car; I danced with a boy and I saved a woman's life.

Then again, I also spent time in jail, got in fights, and seriously considered cold-blooded murder.

So would I say that overall it was good or bad?

I don't even know.

I just know that it's all over.

CHAPTER 54

CHESTER POINTS TO the break in the trees at the edge of his meadow. "That's where they went in," he says confidently. He wishes he actually *felt* that confident. "There's a deer path nearby that runs east-west for a few miles before turning north. I'm thinking they took that for a while."

"Unless someone's chasin' 'em, animals always take the quickest route to where they're going," Hardy says. "These kids won't be no different." His raspy, know-it-all voice sets Chester's teeth on edge.

"But where *are* they going?" asks Sam Dean. Sam, who lives ten miles outside of town on a struggling farm, is skinny and tanned. Kinda looks like a human version of beef jerky. "Chief? You got any idea?"

"I think I might," Chester says.

Of course, it all depends on believing what Kai and Holo had told him. If he doesn't, he's got nothing. But if he *does*, then there aren't too many places they could be.

"We have to go to where the wolves are," he says.

When he says the word *wolves*, he sees the men's eyes go dark. Their faces get tight and vicious.

They hate wolves.

It doesn't matter if they don't own livestock. Doesn't matter that bad weather kills more sheep than wolves do. That *coyotes* kill more sheep than wolves do. Less than one percent of livestock deaths: on average, that's all wolves can be blamed for.

It just doesn't matter.

"We'll find the kids and shoot the wolves," Sam Dean says.

"No, we won't," Chester says. "We have *one* objective here, and that is finding Kai and Holo."

But they aren't listening to him. Every man goes to his truck and comes back with a gun.

Sam pats his .22, snug in its holster. "You never know what you're going to run into in the woods at night."

"Or who," Hardy adds.

Chester looks each man in the eye in turn. "There will be *no shooting*," he says slowly, "unless you are in imminent danger of being mauled by a wild animal. Do you understand me?"

"Takin' all the fun out of it," Sam's cousin Jimmy says.

"Do you men understand me?" Chester repeats. Louder, so they know he's serious. "Because if you don't, you can go on back home now."

They grumble. Nod.

"Good. All right, let's go."

They fall in line behind him as he heads down the deer trail. Soon the woods are dark. Chester turns on his flashlight. The men walk quietly along the path, sweeping the trees with their own narrow beams of light.

There's no point in calling for Kai and Holo. They've got several hours' head start, and they don't want to be found. Still, it's hard for him not to shout their names. Hard not to plead with them to come back. So Chester just keeps on walking, trusting instinct to help him stay on the right path.

Eventually, around two o'clock in the morning, the search party stops to rest. Chester leans against a tree trunk and closes his eyes.

Wind rustles leaves. Branches crack. A few men snore.

Chester feels exhausted and wide awake at the same time. On edge, too. He has the powerful sense that they don't belong here. That they are intruders in this wild night world.

Far off, he hears the faint howl of a wolf. Then another joins it.

Somewhere in the darkness, two children he has come to love are running away from him.

And part of him wonders if maybe they would be safer if he would just let them go.

CHAPTER 55

"ARE WE THERE yet?" Holo wants to know.

"Dope, you know where we are," I say grumpily. It's dark, I'm tired, and I feel like I've been beaten. *Human world 1, Kai 0.*

"But I'm all turned around," Holo says.

"This is why town life is bad for us. You're forgetting what really matters." Sure, I'm leading us on a weird, twisting way to where we're going—but still.

When we come into a meadow, I point to the starry sky. "Now do you know where you are?"

Holo looks up. Shrugs. "I guess I'll just follow you," he says.

Of course you will, I think. *You always do.*

We cross a stream on a fallen log. Frogs sing; the water burbles. We're getting close.

I hike my backpack farther up my shoulders. It hardly weighs anything. I left Lacey's hand-me-downs behind, and all of the new things she'd bought me, too. The only piece of clothing I brought was the T-shirt I wore when I danced with

Waylon at the Bearclaw Cafe. I couldn't help myself. I imagined that it carried some hint of his touch. His warm, boyish smell.

I brought a journal, too. The copy of *Hamlet* that Ms. Tillman gave me, to remind me of all the things that I don't actually need to know. And my knife to remind me of the things I do.

I also brought the sausages that the chief was going to cook for dinner.

Sorry not sorry.

We pass a stand of blackened stumps, burned in a forest fire before we were born. The new trees are already a little bit taller than we are. We're ten miles from Chester's, fifteen from town. They'll never find us.

But the wolves will.

Dawn's still a ways off when we come to the big pine that has always marked the edge of their territory. *Our* territory. I don't have to call them this time. This time they just come.

They rush at us in an explosion of fur. Jaws snap, tongues loll, tails wag. Bim wiggles and whines. Ben spins in dizzy, happy circles. Harriet comes charging out of the woods, yipping excitedly. When she jumps on Ben's back, he whips around and snaps at her muzzle. It looks like they're trying to maul each other to death, but their tails are wagging like crazy. This is play. This is pure, wild joy. A family reunion.

"Calm down, you guys," Holo says, laughing, but it's useless. There's just too much happiness to be contained. He falls to his knees, and Bim licks his face all over with her giant pink tongue.

Beast is there, too, and her pups, who prance and play under everyone's feet. I throw myself into the middle of them. My pack, my family.

Why did I ever leave?

A light flicks on. A golden square—a small window—illuminates the dark. The wolves and I lift our heads.

More light spills onto the ground as the door to the forest cabin opens.

"Well, well, well," says a voice.

CHAPTER 56

IT'S SEVEN A.M. and the men are going slowly now. They're sore from a night of walking, broken only by an hour of half sleep on hard dirt. Chester is jittery, impatient with their progress. He takes a bite of a protein bar that Lacey must've slipped into his pocket and wills himself not to yell "Hurry up!"

Sam Dean holds out a little thermos of coffee. "Joe?" he says.

"That's kind of you, Sam," Chester says. But considering that he saw Sam make the brew from a packet of instant plus water from a Buffalo River tributary, he declines the offer. "I like sugar in my coffee," he says. "Not giardia."

"I'll take some," Waylon says. He's the only chipper one in the group. "I like to live dangerously. Right, Chief?"

Chester watches as the kid takes a sip, grimaces, and then swallows.

"Delightful," Waylon lies.

Reginald Hardy has taken the search party lead. His narrow, mean eyes sweep the forest floor and the underbrush, looking for signs or tracks. His rifle's slung across his shoulder.

He's bowlegged but surefooted. Chester's grateful to the man, even though he can't stand him.

"There," Reginald says. Stopping suddenly. Sucking on his teeth like they taste good.

"Where?" Chester asks. "What?"

"See that?"

Chester swallows the last bite of his bar and looks where Hardy's pointing. He doesn't see anything but early morning, sun-dappled forest. "No."

Hardy grabs onto a broken branch. Beneath it are a few snapped twigs. "They went this way," he says, and then he starts walking again.

Chester follows him, and everyone else follows Chester. They're no longer walking along an established track. Instead they're trying to find traces of footfalls in vast forests and grassy meadows.

How is this possibly going to work? Chester wonders as they trudge through a stand of old-growth lodgepole pine. *Why am I trusting a man who'd run Kai and Holo out of town on a rail if he could?*

Because he has no other options, that's why.

A mile or two later, Reginald stops at the top of a rise and surveys the land around them. A rocky meadow spreads out below, bending east. A hawk circles high overhead. There's barely a cloud in the sky.

It's a beautiful morning, not that Chester cares.

Then he sees something moving on the far side of the meadow. A dark shape going out of the trees. *Could it be—?* His heart leaps.

Then stops.

It's not Kai. It's a *bear*.

"Freeze," he whispers urgently.

The men come to an instant halt.

All except Sam Dean, who sees the animal and turns to run. Chester reaches out and grabs his arm. Holds him in place with a grip like a vise.

"I said *freeze*," Chester says through clenched teeth. "Running'll trigger a chase response, and you can't outrun a bear."

The bear lifts its great brown head, sniffing the air. No one breathes. Chester's hand's on the pistol at his hip. Hardy brings his rifle into position.

"Well, you know what they say," Hardy says quietly out of the side of his mouth. "You don't gotta outrun the bear. You just gotta outrun whatever assholes you're with."

Chester hears the click of Hardy popping the safety on his Remington.

"Don't shoot, Hardy," Chester says. Grizzlies are a protected species—not animals to be shot on sight.

Unlike wolves.

The bear's heavy head swings in their direction.

"Come and get me," Hardy dares.

The bear makes a huffing sound, almost like a man's cough. It rears up on its hind legs, sensitive nose still sniffing.

"Holy Jesus, he's big," Sam Dean whispers.

The bear drops down to all fours and gives its whole giant body a shake. It stomps the ground with a big front paw. Chester could swear he feels the impact. Sam Dean gives a whimper.

Then the bear makes another coughing sound, turns, and ambles off into the trees. Heading north. Away from them. Away from the track they're following.

Chester feels the breath he's been holding explode out of his lungs.

That was close.

"He woulda made a nice rug," Hardy says, after they're all clear.

Chester gives him a dark look. "Shoulder your weapon and let's go," he says. "Let's get out of its territory as quick as we can."

They move out, making more noise now. If the bear's listening, they want it to know they've got numbers.

"Hey, bear," Waylon calls as he walks. "Hey, bear, we're just passing through, bear! Be cool, bear!"

Sam's jangly and nervous. "Damn," he says to Chester, "I ain't ever seen one so close."

"Hopefully you'll never see one closer," Chester says grimly.

"You got that right."

They cross the meadow. Hardy follows a track that only he can see. The hawk still arcs through the sky above them.

They're almost across the clearing when they hear a crashing sound. It's coming from the trees to the north.

Chester whips around. The bear's charging toward them at full speed. The animal's head is low, its ears are back, and its stride eats the ground. Terror floods Chester's body, paralyzing him. Hardy reaches for his gun but somehow stumbles sideways. Ray Farley screams as he grabs for his bear spray. The bear's thirty feet away, then twenty. Chester's never seen anything so huge in his life.

Ray holds the can out, still screaming, and fires a white cloud into the bear's face. The mist of hot pepper extract sears Chester's eyes. The bear, hit with the full blast, stops and veers away. For a second it looks like it's going to run off into the woods. But then it whirls back, skirting the billows of bear spray. It goes after Sam Dean. A huge hairy paw sends the skinny farmer flying. Then the bear's on top of him. Sam Dean screams and curls into a ball and covers his head and neck with his hands.

Chester's mind is short-circuiting, but he finds that he can move. And he doesn't need to think. He's got his pistol out and he's aiming by instinct.

Crack! The bullet hits the bear's flank.

The bear turns and snaps its jaws in confusion at the wound.

"Go!" Chester shouts at the top of his lungs. "Go!" *Go before someone else shoots to kill!*

The bear runs.

Vanishes.

Jimmy shoots a distress flare into the sky—*Where the hell did he get that?* Chester wonders—and it explodes like a fire-work over their heads. And Chester races over to Sam Dean, who's sobbing and bleeding on the ground.

CHAPTER 57

HOLO AND I wake early. We get up quickly and immediately start walking. We don't speak—because we don't want to make a sound, and because we know where we're going.

In a little while, the trees start to thin. Pines give way to alder and buckthorn. Soon we find ourselves at the edge of a small, hidden meadow. A creek runs along the north edge. Mist curls low through the grasses. I feel different than I have in weeks. I feel light.

Free.

"I'm freaking *starving*," Holo says.

The familiar complaint cuts through my sleepy happiness. "That's why we're out here, isn't it?" I hold up my foraging basket, which I wove last winter from birch branches. "I was thinking a nice mushroom and nettle sauté..."

"With trout," Holo agrees.

"Of course with trout," I say. "But the fish isn't going to catch itself, is it?" Playfully I shove him toward the stream.

Holo rolls his eyes at me before jogging away, calling, "Here, fishy fishy!"

I know that this makes it my job to gather the mushrooms and the nettles. But first I have to soak everything in. First I have to lie down in the clearing, feeling the prickly grass under my back. I prop my head up on a tuft of Idaho fescue and listen to the sounds of birds and wind and water.

It feels so good to be back. This is where I belong.

In the wilderness. The sky for a roof, the sun for a lamp.

But you should've said goodbye.

Yeah, I should have.

I wonder if Waylon Eugene Meloy will miss the crazy wolf girl and her fang-toothed brother.

I wonder if he'll keep speeding, and keep winding up in jail.

I wonder if I'll ever see him again.

"I got one already," Holo calls to me from far away.

"Good for you," I say, but not loud enough for him to hear me.

I roll over and pick myself up. Brush myself off. Pluck a few burrs from my sleeve. Wander over to the patch of nettles that bursts up from the ground in the same spot every spring. I slip on a pair of deerskin gloves to protect my skin from the stinging leaves as I harvest them. Soon I've got a basketful, and then to the green pile I add almost a pound of morels. I'm rooting around for more when Holo comes running up to me, smiling.

He pats the pocket of the cargo pants that Lacey bought him. "Three trout in here," he says proudly.

Sure enough, his pocket is dripping water and possibly fish guts. "I don't think you're supposed to carry fish in your *pants*," I tell him.

He shrugs. "I don't see why not. It's very convenient."

I laugh. Maybe he's right. Who's around to tell us any different?

"Ready?" he says.

I grab my basket and stand up. We stroll back the way we came, careful to take a slightly different route and to step on rocks when we can. This way we don't create an obvious trail to the place where we sleep.

Which is not, in fact, a wolf den.

Don't get me wrong—a wolf den can be pretty comfortable. But not as comfortable as a hand-built cabin nestled in the woods.

Home.

The one that no one knew we had.

As Holo and I approach, a figure steps outside. The woman spreads her arms out and Holo runs to her. They hold each other in a bear hug. She looks up at me with shining eyes. Her face glows with happiness and relief.

"When you weren't in the cabin this morning," she says, "I thought last night was a dream. But you're really here. And you've even brought *breakfast*."

Holo's voice comes out muffled. "We were always going to come back to you, Wendy. And now we're never going to leave."

CHAPTER 58

"TELL ME EVERYTHING," Wendy says, over steaming plates of the food we gathered. Her long brown hair has come loose from its ponytail, and she brushes it away with lean, tanned fingers. "It's been real lonely here without you."

The three of us are sitting around a wobbly handmade table in a small, one-room cabin. Pale spring sunlight shines in the window, illuminating the dried flowers and herbs that hang from the ceiling. The rough walls are covered with ten years' worth of drawings: my wolf portraits, Wendy's sketches of elk and willows, and the crazed scribbles of Holo, aged four.

Suddenly this room seems like the most beautiful one I've ever been in. I didn't realize how much I missed it—and how much I missed Wendy—until now. My heart feels so full it aches. I'm *home*.

"Well?" Wendy prods eagerly.

"Where do I even start?" I say.

"Tell her about the Grizzly," Holo says with his mouth full.

"You saw a grizzly?" Wendy said. "Was it Sheena? Did you

see her cubs?" Wendy has a name for pretty much every animal in the forest.

"Actually, Holo's talking about a grocery store we broke into," I admit.

"And stole from," Holo adds brightly.

Wendy lifts her eyebrows so high they disappear under the bangs she cuts with a pocketknife. "A store's a little different than a campsite," she says. There's a hint of reproach in her voice.

Sometimes, when Holo and I were littler and didn't have the stomach for the blood and stink of gutting a deer, Wendy would let us go "camp hunting." That meant sneaking into people's campsites and helping ourselves to whatever food we could snatch. We were good at it—silent and untrackable. And people always brought so much more than they needed.

"The consequences are different, too," I say wryly.

Wendy's eyes search my face. "What do you mean? Did you get c—"

"It's a long story," I interrupt her.

And it involves a person I need to stop thinking about.

Wendy nods. Spears a piece of trout with her fork. She can tell I don't want to talk about it right now. And she's always let us say and do—and also *not* say, and *not* do—what we want. As long as we keep ourselves safe. That's all she's ever asked of us.

"Are you glad you went?" Her voice is quieter now. Like she wants to give me the chance to pretend I didn't hear.

Holo answers for me. "Yeah, we are. Right, Kai? We had to

find out what was out there! We needed to see the world. Meet other kids. And figure out what regular people were like."

"And Holo needed to learn about light switches," I say dryly.

Wendy laughs. "It's not like you've never seen electricity before, Holo."

"Yeah, but we use candles and run stuff off of car batteries," he points out. "And our TV only ever got one channel."

"I *told* you to build a better antenna," Wendy exclaims. Then she adds, "Even though PBS is the only channel worth watching."

"I don't need to watch *Outdoor Idaho*," Holo says. "My whole *life* is *Outdoor Idaho*."

"But you adored that show."

"Because it was the only show I'd ever seen!"

I smile at their familiar bickering. Holo and Wendy have always loved arguing with each other, and if I don't change the subject, I'll wind up refereeing some ridiculous debate—like about which is cuter, the ground squirrel or the meadow vole—for the rest of the day.

"I promise to tell you everything later," I say to Wendy. "In the meantime, let's just say that we went into the world to see what it was like. And now—well, now we know."

Can I leave it at that forever?

"Honestly, it wasn't the funnest time we ever had," Holo says, his voice serious now.

"Funnest isn't a word," I tell him.

"Doesn't matter if I'm not in school."

The kid has a point.

"You know what was fun, though?" he asks.

"What?" says Wendy.

"We convinced everybody we were raised by wolves."

Wendy stares at him in surprise for a minute. And then she starts to laugh. She laughs so hard that tears run down her narrow, lined face. "And they believed you?" she gasps.

"They couldn't figure out what else to believe," I say. "They're not really in the habit of solving mysteries in Kokanee Creek."

Holo puts his hand out and covers Wendy's with it. "We said it because we wanted to protect you," he says. "Like you've always protected us."

"Thank you," Wendy says. "I'm glad you did that."

Neither Holo nor I mention that the FBI agents somehow know her name. I understand that I need to tell her, but first she needs to know about Ernie.

"Somebody shot Ernie," I say softly. I feel the ache of sadness in my throat.

Wendy's shoulders slump. "I knew he was gone," she says quietly. "But I didn't know what happened to him." She pushes away her plate. "Without Ernie, I'm afraid that Beast has been forced to look for . . . easier prey."

Worry floods me. It even overpowers the sadness. Wendy didn't say *smaller* prey, like rabbits or fawns. She said *easier* prey. Like sheep. Calves. "Do you really think Beast is kill—"

Wendy holds up a hand as a shadow crosses her face.

"What?" I whisper.

She presses a finger to her lips. Listening.

She knows the sounds of these woods. She's been listening to them for nearly forty years.

Her mouth tightens. Somewhere there's a wrong note, and she hears it.

I close my eyes to hear what she did. At first there's nothing. Then: A rustle of leaves. A snap of a branch.

"There's someone outside," I whisper.

Wendy shakes her head. Fear sparks in her eyes. "There's a *lot* of someones."

CHAPTER 59

BEFORE I CAN respond, Wendy grabs the rifle by the door and rushes outside. "Go away," she screams. "Get off my property!" She cocks her rifle and then fires it into the air. The explosion makes my ears ring. Holo half dives under the table.

Shouts erupt outside as I leap from my chair and scramble after Wendy. Sensing my presence behind her, Wendy moves to block my path. I know she's trying to protect me. But I need to find out what's happening. I need to see who's out there. I crane my neck, trying to peer around her—

My mouth falls open.

There's a line of eight men, and they all have guns.

Pointed at us.

"That's my warning shot," Wendy calls to them. "The next one hits someone."

The chief has his gun aimed at Wendy's chest. "*Police*," he says. "You don't want to fire at us."

"Try me," she says.

"Lower your weapon," he says.

"Lower yours first," I shout. I move Wendy out of my way and face the knot of strangers, one of whom is covered in blood and all of whom look pissed.

Relief floods the chief's face when he sees me. "Kai, where's Holo? Are you all right?" the chief calls.

"We're fine," I say. "But we'd be better if we weren't facing a freaking firing squad."

Then Waylon steps out of the shadows. Absurdly, he gives me a friendly little wave. I don't wave back. What is he *doing* here?

This isn't how I wanted to see you again, I think.

"Look," Waylon says calmly, "one of us already got attacked by a bear, so tensions are running a little bit high."

"I guess they saw Sheena," Holo whispers in my ear.

"And she saw them right back," I mutter. Whoever that wounded guy is, he's lucky to be alive.

Waylon, who's the only one without a gun, starts walking toward us. "I don't think anyone here actually wants to shoot anyone, do you?"

Actually I'm pretty sure Reginald Hardy would love to put a bullet through my guts. Finish the job his kid couldn't.

The chief comes forward to stand next to Waylon. "No, they don't," he says. "Disarm, everyone. That is an order from the Kokanee Creek chief of police."

The guns get lowered. Slowly. Reluctantly.

Wendy lowers her rifle, too. But she doesn't let go of it. "Who are you, and what are you doing on my property?"

"With all due respect, ma'am," the chief says, "this is a national forest. It is not your property."

Wendy just stares at him. He stares right back. They have the same steely-eyed gaze.

That's when Thing 1 and Thing 2 come shooting out of nowhere, right into the middle of everyone. They're so involved in their joyful, ferocious game of tag that they're oblivious to the intruders.

Hardy's gun lifts.

You can kill a wolf on sight. You can kill a wolf baby on sight. It's murder. And it's legal.

"No!" I scream.

Beast rockets out of the trees, a black blur with snapping teeth. Those are her children, and she's going to protect them no matter what.

By the time I realize what I'm doing I'm already running, rushing toward Beast, screaming and waving my arms. Trying to protect her, the larger target. Beast pivots sharply away, spooked. A shot rings out. A crater appears in the ground near her tail, a puff of dirt rising above it.

"Kai!" Wendy screams. "Get out of there!"

I don't listen. They're not actually going to risk shooting a girl, are they?

"Go, Beast, run!" I yell. She darts away, but turns back, hesitating. Meanwhile I'm trying to grab the Things, but they dodge me, thinking it's a wonderful game. Thing 1 bites my hand. Thing 2 snarls and dances. They're getting so big—

The chief is hollering, too. I hear another shot.

I duck as the bullet slams into a nearby tree trunk. Hardy's taking aim again. "Come on, you little fuckers," he seethes.

Then suddenly someone steps out in front of him. Someone

has put his body between the end of a rifle and the wolves. And that person is Waylon Eugene Meloy. Loner, speeder, weirdo, heartthrob.

I feel a surge of gratitude so powerful it almost brings me to my knees.

Waylon's voice is strong and smooth. Unruffled, despite everything, just like the day I first met him in jail. "This is not what we came for," he says to Hardy. "We're on the *chief's* mission. You can murder things on your own time."

Hardy's so shocked he doesn't even have a response. The chief hustles over and puts his hand on the rifle barrel. He presses it down so it's pointing at the ground.

"That's enough, Hardy," he says. "You let those wolf babies grow up." Then he says to the rest of the men, "Anyone who fires will be arrested."

Hardy turns away with a vicious curse.

My hand is bleeding. I start to cry. I don't know whether it's from pain or fear or relief. Thing 1 whimpers at my feet. Thing 2 sniffs the air; she catches the scent of my blood and licks her lips.

The chief turns back to Wendy. He's calm but furious. "Now that we're not shooting at each other anymore, who the hell are you, and why do you have my kids?"

CHAPTER 60

"*YOUR* KIDS?" WENDY says.

"Chester, this is Wendy," says Holo. He stands there with his hands on his hips, his pants reeking of fish guts. "Also known as Lupa."

"Lupa," the chief says. "Like the wolf who raised Romulus and Remus, the founders of Rome?"

Wendy nods. "Kai gave me the nickname when she was six. We read a lot of Roman myths back then." She gives a flick of her fingers. And the wolves—Harriet, Ben, Bim, and Beast—materialize from behind rocks and trees. Their hackles are raised. A low growl comes from Beast's throat. Harriet's, too. The Things run and take shelter between their mother's legs.

"You can probably see why Kai called her that," Holo says helpfully.

The men shift nervously. But they don't raise their guns.

Harriet's growl gets louder. She bares gleaming teeth. Takes a warning step toward the group of men. Several of them flinch. Retreat a little ways.

"She doesn't like you because we don't like you," Holo explains. "Well," he adds, "we don't like most of you. We like Chester and Waylon."

"If you like me," Waylon says, "does that mean this terrifying beast won't maul me?"

"Probably," Holo says. "But you never really know."

"Wolves," Wendy says softly, "it's okay."

Harriet lowers her ears and sits down on her haunches. Bim and Ben fade into the trees. Only Beast remains standing, her lips pulled back in a warning grimace.

"You can control them," Waylon says, his voice full of wonder.

"It is not control," Wendy says. "I suggest actions to them, actions which they are free to take—or not. We have an understanding."

"Amazing," says Waylon softly. He looks over at me. "You were telling the truth the whole time."

"Part of it," I manage. I'm clutching my wounded hand. And I'm trembling as the horror of the situation sinks in.

They've found our home. Our *whole lives* we kept ourselves hidden, and now they've found us, and it's my fault.

All of this is because of me.

Grief twists in my stomach like a sickness.

"What's your full name, Wendy?" the chief asks.

Wendy gazes at him with her dark, wise eyes. "Wendy," she says. "Only Wendy."

Just like I am only Kai, and Holo is only Holo. What did we need two names for? For years upon years, we were the only people we knew.

"Are you their mother?"

Wendy hesitates. She looks at us. There's so much love in her eyes that it hurts. I'm dying to know what she's going to say, and she's about to answer when the chief asks a different question. "Wait, let me rephrase that—did you give birth to these children?"

And Wendy shakes her head.

No.

"How long have they been in your care?"

"Thirteen years."

The chief's head drops. "Jesus," he mutters to his feet.

I'm sorry you had to find out this way, I think.

He looks up at Wendy again. His eyes are cold. "Do you have a right to keep them in your care?" he asks. "Are you their legally appointed guardian?"

Conflicting emotions swirl across her thin, weathered face: fear and defiance, terror and love.

"Ma'am?"

Never lie, she always said to us.

We didn't listen to her, did we? We lied to protect her.

But she won't lie to protect herself.

"No," Wendy says quietly.

"I need you to come with me," the chief says.

"What for?"

The chief unclips the handcuffs from his belt. "Turn around, please," he says.

"I don't understand. What is this about? I've done no harm!"

"Chester, don't," Holo cries, but the chief ignores him.

"I don't know who you are, or what you're doing with these

kids. You're under arrest for suspected kidnapping," the chief says.

"She didn't kidnap us," Holo yells.

"Then where did she get you? And where are your real parents?" the chief demands.

The question's like a bullet to the heart. We don't know.

We have never known.

CHAPTER 61

THE CHIEF TAKES another step toward Wendy. And that's when Beast charges.

"No," I scream, as the big alpha female launches herself at his chest. She hits him dead on, all eighty-five pounds of her, and the chief goes flying backward, arms spinning helplessly. He lands hard, flat on his back, with a gasp. Beast stands over him, paws on his shoulders and lips pulled back in a terrifying snarl.

Hardy raises his gun again, a grim smile on his face. There's never been a better reason to kill a wolf.

Wendy yells, "Beast, *go*!"

Beast doesn't listen. So Wendy rushes forward, slamming into her side and knocking the mother wolf off the chief. Then Wendy reaches down to the chief's belt and grabs the pistol. She spins around and points it at Hardy.

"Shoot my wolf and you die," she says.

The two of them stare at each other, eyes full of hatred. The chief scrambles to his feet, white with shock. All the breath's been knocked out of him, but he moves quicker than anyone's expecting. He grabs Wendy's right arm and twists it hard behind her back. She gives a cry of pain and drops the gun to the ground.

"*Do not move*," he says viciously, even as Wendy's spinning around to face him.

"Wendy!" I scream. "Do what he says!"

She looks up at me, and I see all the fight drain out of her eyes. Her shoulders slump. Her arms hang loose at her sides. She's surrendered.

Hardy snorts and spits a wad of phlegm into the dirt.

The chief's voice shakes as he puts the cuffs around Wendy's thin wrists. "You're under arrest for suspicion of kidnapping, for trespassing, for maintaining an illegal structure on National Forest System lands, and for threatening the life of an officer of the law."

"Wendy didn't make Beast attack!" I cry. "You don't have to arrest her!"

Holo runs to me and buries his face in my neck. I can feel his tears, hot against my skin. "Don't let him," he gasps. "He can't."

The chief ignores my words. Ignores Holo's tears. He says, "Kai, I need you to tell us the fastest way back to town."

What? Does he honestly think I'm going to help him put the woman who raised me into a jail cell? A roaring fills my ears. It's getting louder by the second. It drowns out whatever the chief is trying to say to me next.

I shake my head to clear the noise. *I didn't know despair could have a sound.*

Then I see that Holo's covering his ears.

And that the branches on the trees are swaying. Dirt and leaves go flying into the air, pulled by a powerful updraft. The men duck down, covering their heads. Wendy's hair is a tangled cloud around her face.

A giant black helicopter passes low and deafening overhead. It skims the top of the thrashing pines, heading west. Then it lands in the meadow a hundred yards away.

"Run!" Wendy screams.

CHAPTER 62

HOLO DOESN'T THINK—HE obeys.

It's instinct. Self-preservation. *If you can't fight, flee.*

He knows Kai's running, too. If they get separated, they'll find each other again. They know the woods better than anyone. And they always stick together.

Pretty soon he hears footsteps, quick and light behind him. *There she is*, he thinks. Knowing her, she'll probably pass him any minute. Laugh at him as she leaves him in the dust.

I'm going as fast as I can, Kai. We just have to get away.

Brambles scrape his legs. Branches whip his face. He doesn't feel them. He doesn't feel anything but the need for escape. He has to go where the wolves went. To the higher ground. Higher's always better.

He sprints through a forest obstacle course, dodging thickets, scrambling over fallen trees. His legs burn with fatigue. He can't hear his sister's footsteps anymore, not over the hard, rasping sound of his breath. He just has to trust that she's there. Or maybe she's split off to give their pursuers two targets. It doesn't matter. They'll meet later on top of the ridge. They knew how to hide where no one can find them. They'll wait there until it's safe. And when it is, they'll rescue Wendy. They can do anything, as long as they're together.

He hears thrashing in the brush behind him.

Kai! She's getting closer. He slows, just a little, so she can catch up. So she can race by him, smiling.

Crash! Something slams into him from behind. Pain shoots through his whole body like fire.

It isn't until he's flat on the ground, with a panting, two-hundred-pound body cursing and pinning him down, that Holo realizes his mistake. It was never Kai behind him.

It was a man.

An enemy.

An FBI agent.

CHAPTER 63

AGENT ROLLINS, RED in the face and gasping for breath, drags my brother out of the woods in handcuffs. He's got mud on his knees and his suit's in tatters. But he has a triumphant sneer on his face.

My brother looks so small all of a sudden. Broken. Terrified. A gash on his cheek drips bright blood onto his T-shirt.

"Oh, Holo," I cry, "why'd you run?"

When he turns to me, his eyes are full of anguish. "Why didn't you?"

The question hits me hard. *Why didn't I?*

When the helicopter landed, Wendy was screaming, my brother had vanished, and everything was chaos. And in that moment, Waylon had reached for my hand. Squeezed my fingers tight between his. Held me there.

First I froze. *Tonic immobility.*

And then—though suddenly I could move again—I *stayed*.

I can't explain it. I can't justify it. But I couldn't pull my hand away from his.

"I thought you were behind me," Holo says. His voice breaks. He looks like he's about to cry.

"They just would've caught her, too, you know," Waylon says quietly.

Holo's sorrow turns to anger faster than a blink. "As fast as Kai runs?" he practically spits. "No way."

"Well, I *didn't* run, and it's too late now!" I snap.

Guilt makes my words come out with sharp edges. I've betrayed my brother. I've betrayed Wendy. The wolves have scattered, the forest is crawling with men with guns, and I'm the only member of my family not in handcuffs.

I never should have left the woods in the first place.

Agent Rollins says to my brother, "Didn't anyone ever teach you that running from the law is a bad idea? A person could get hurt that way."

Holo bares his fangs at him. "I didn't know who the hell was behind me; I was just obeying my *mother*."

He's never called her that before. Neither of us has.

Does your sister take care of you, Holo? The social worker's question still haunts me. Because I knew I hadn't. But Wendy always had, for as long as I could remember.

And now she can't.

Holo tries to get closer to her, but Rollins holds him back.

"Let Holo go!" Wendy shrieks. She stumbles forward, trying to reach him, too, but the chief pushes her down.

"Sit," he says fiercely. "You're in enough trouble already."

"She didn't do anything wrong!" I yell.

"That's where *you're* wrong, Kai," the chief says. "This woman's broken a lot of laws. And she's dangerous."

"Well, so am I! Remember how I took down your deputy in the Grizzly Grocery?"

"You spent a few days in jail for it," the chief says grimly. "And if you don't calm down, I'll have you cuffed, too."

The gray-haired FBI agent, Dunham, says, "I think everybody should cool their tempers. No reason to make this unfriendly."

"Screw you," I say. "What're you even doing here? Can't you see the chief's perfectly capable of arresting us?"

"Watch it, Teen Wolf," he warns.

So much for keeping things friendly.

Agent Rollins says, "The chief might've put the handcuffs on, but he knows our badge trumps his."

The chief reflexively looks at his ragtag bunch of fake deputies. Compares it to the two suits with the waiting helicopter. He clearly can't dispute what Dunham says. "Are you going to walk off with my suspect?" he asks the older agent.

Dunham gives a weird little smile. He says, "We're going to *fly*, Chief. Wendy and I have a lot of catching up to do."

Wendy and I both look at him in surprise.

"How do you know my name?" Wendy asks.

But apparently that isn't information Dunham feels like giving out right now. He says, "Kai, Holo, Wendy—let's go."

"We've been looking for them all night," the chief yells. "You can't just take them!"

"I can," Dunham says. "And you're going to watch me."

I shake my head, remembering the way that black death trap buzzed over the trees. "No way. No way are we getting in that thing."

"Unfortunately, you're wrong," Dunham says matter-of-factly. He strides over to me and the next thing I know, my hands are cuffed behind my back.

"What the hell? Am I under arrest?"

"Not necessarily," he says. "Right now it's just a safety precaution." He gives my shoulder two quick pats. Like I'm a dog. "But you never know."

"If we don't give you the opportunity to resist, everything's going to go a lot smoother," Rollins says to me. Then he turns to the chief. "We'll see you back at the station. In what, five hours or so? Enjoy your walk."

"You asshole," the chief says helplessly.

"Move out," Rollins barks, and then he gives me a little shove.

I curse at him. But then I start walking.

The propellers start with a roar as we approach. Dust blasts my face, and the wind whips my hair into my cheeks so hard it stings. I duck down. Dunham nudges me forward again and then Rollins grabs me by the waist and lifts me into the helicopter. Dunham handles Holo and Wendy. Holo is pale with fear and fury. Wendy's face is frozen in dread.

What the hell is going on? I want to yell.

But she won't know the answer. And the FBI agents aren't going to tell me.

With a horrifying shudder, the helicopter takes off. The pilot banks left and I go leaning toward Holo. Then the helicopter straightens and lifts. Every bone in my body's rattling. We turn again—I lean again.

It's a million times worse than a car ride. It's the worst thing

I've ever felt, and I once pierced my own eyelid with a stolen fish hook.

I think I'm going to throw up.

"I don't feel good," I shout.

The agents pretend they can't hear me. Or maybe this death machine's so loud that they really can't.

The next wave of nausea builds on top of the first. My stomach twists. My eyes start to water.

I'm definitely *going to throw up.*

My throat clenches.

I can feel the bile rising up. It's hot and it stings.

And I remember one of Wendy's rules of the forest: *Waste nothing. Use everything you have.*

I can definitely do that.

I scoot as close as I can to Agent Dunham. I smile tearily at his smug, tanned face. And then I lean down and barf all over his gleaming black shoes.

CHAPTER 64

JUST ABOUT EVERY resident of Kokanee Creek turns up to watch us get pulled out of the helicopter and escorted into the police station. They stand with their arms crossed, heads nodding, like we've confirmed their worst suspicions about us again. *I've done nothing wrong!* I want to yell.

Actually, scratch that—I want to flip them off for making all their shitty assumptions. Unfortunately, I'm still in handcuffs.

Inside the station, Officer Randall immediately starts sucking up to the FBI guys, asking if they want coffee, saying how sorry he is that the chief never got back to them when they called, blah blah blah. Meanwhile, Pearl wants to know where the chief is, because Lacey's been calling the station all morning. Dougie pokes his head in the front door. "Mind if I come in for a nap?"

Agent Rollins interrupts the general chaos. "I need access to your interrogation room, Officer," he says sharply. "And my colleague needs a roll of paper towels and a bathroom."

Randall points toward the jail cells. "Ya'll are welcome to chat back there," he suggests. "We use the interview room as a supply closet. But I think there's some folding chairs in the hall there, so help yourself."

"Are you kidding me?" Agent Rollins says, then mutters something about rural rednecks and small-town police budgets.

"I assume your station has running water at least," Dunham says frostily.

"Oh sure," says Randall. "Bathroom's down the hall. Looks like you got something on your shoes, huh?"

Dunham stalks by him, shoulders stiff with annoyance.

Holo looks at me and giggles. "Nice one," he whispers.

Rollins says, "Let's go, kids."

So that's how Wendy, Holo, and I wind up in the same cell Holo and I slept in back in April, sitting on cold metal chairs with handcuffs cutting into our wrists. When Dunham comes in, shoes clean again, he sits down on my old thin, stained mattress. Rollins follows him but remains standing. Dunham folds his hands over his crossed leg and says to Wendy, "You don't know how long I've been waiting for this."

Waiting for what? I think. *And am I crazy to think that he sounds* relieved?

Wendy must be wondering the same thing, because she says, "I don't know what you're talking about. I don't know what you want from me, or why you've brought us here, or—"

"I'd like to take your handcuffs off now," Dunham says, interrupting her, "if you're ready for that. It'll make this a lot more pleasant." He turns to me and Holo. "I'm pretty sure Wendy's going to cooperate," he says. "But can I trust you?"

Holo nods. I shrug. *I don't know—can you?*

"They'll be *fine*," Wendy insists. "They shouldn't have been treated like criminals in the first place!"

"I hear they have some delinquent tendencies, though," Dunham says, smirking like this is all some kind of joke. Then he swivels his head around and calls, "Officer Randall, can we get some water back here? Or that coffee you were talking about?"

I have *no idea* what's going on. At first it seemed like we were being arrested, and now it sounds like we're all going to have a coffee date. When Dunham unlocks our handcuffs, I rub my wrists where the metal bit into my skin. Thinking, *When is any of this going to make sense?*

Dougie comes strolling into the cell area. "Who're *you*?" he wheezes to the agents. He gives them a drunken appraisal. "Nice suits. Who died? Not me, I hope." He places a hand on his chest, makes a dramatic, dying face. "I can feel my very heartbeat fading. Here's to all the Jack I was still hopin' to drink—may I meet you again, upstairs or downstairs, wherever I be sent—"

"Get out of here, boozer," Rollins says.

"That's enough, Dougie." Randall hurries over and takes the town drunk by the arm. "Now's not the time," he says, steering Dougie toward the front door. "Go sleep it off in the park; the weather's fine." He calls over his shoulder, "Coffee'll be ready in a minute."

"But I didn't even get to pet the little animals," Dougie whines loudly. He turns around and winks at me.

I bare my teeth at him. Holo snarls.

Dunham finishes freeing up Wendy. Then he sits back down on the mattress and gazes at her face like he can't believe what he's seeing. He says, "Wendy Marsden, I have been looking for you for thirty-five years."

CHAPTER 65

WENDY *WHO*? I think. She only has one name. Same with me and my brother. Same with the wolves and the bears and everyone else.

Wendy looks at the agent in confusion.

Agent Dunham says, "The name doesn't ring a bell?"

"I've never heard it before."

"Huh. All right," Dunham says. "That's okay." He rubs his grizzled chin. "So you've lived in those woods since—"

"Since always," Wendy says. "As long as I can remember."

"But you weren't always alone, were you?"

"I had Kai and Holo." She glances over at me. Her voice sounds strong, but her eyes have become darting and afraid.

"Before that," the agent says. "When you were younger. When you were a child. Were you alone then?"

Wendy shakes her head. "I lived with my father. He was a woodsman."

"A woodsman?" Rollins repeats. "Is that a lumberjack or something?"

Wendy ignores him. "He'd been a professor, but he'd been fired when I was a baby. 'They didn't support my research,' he told me. I didn't know what that meant, or what he researched, but I didn't ask. Father didn't like it when I asked questions. He wanted me to listen. To absorb. To obey."

This is more than Wendy has ever told us about her past. And there's something about the way she talks about her father that sends a cold, strange shiver up my spine.

"So he educated you, out there in the forest?" Dunham prods.

"Of course. He knew everything about everything, it seemed like. I tried to take it all in. History, poetry, water catchment, trapping skills. I could forage for mushrooms before I could read." She smiles proudly. Defiantly. "I learned to skin and gut a deer and recite Wordsworth and Keats. Father taught me about the Roman Empire and the ancient civilizations of Mesoamerica, and he taught me how to catch fish with my bare hands."

"Did you ever leave the woods?" Dunham asks.

"We never left the woods, and I never knew any other children. We spent our days keeping ourselves alive and our nights reading books."

"Was it a good childhood?" Dunham wants to know.

Wendy laughs nervously. "I have nothing to compare it to. But whether I liked it or not back then wasn't even something I could consider. It would not have been...permitted." She presses her lips together in a thin line. It's obvious she wants them to stop asking her questions. But they won't—not yet.

"What happened to your father?" Rollins asks.

Wendy doesn't answer right away. When she does, her voice comes out flat and emotionless. "He died."

"How old were you?"

"We never celebrated birthdays. But I'd guess I was probably a year or two younger than Holo."

"How did he die?"

Wendy twists her hands in her lap. "I don't know. He didn't come home from his hunt one night. The next day I went looking for him. I found his body by the stream where we fished, halfway into the water. Part of his leg was gone. But I think that happened after he died. There wasn't enough blood for that to be what killed him."

The words are bone-chilling. But Wendy recounts the memory as calmly as she might recall the weather.

"So what did you do then?" Dunham asks.

Wendy takes a deep breath. "He was a big man, too big to move. I had no choice. I left him where he was. The scavengers took what they wanted, and then I buried what was left. It wasn't much by then."

"Lovely," Rollins mutters.

"Then it was just me and a .270 Winchester bolt-action rifle," Wendy goes on. "And everything Father had taught me. I barely survived the winter."

"Why didn't you try to find help?" Holo blurts.

Wendy looks at him like this is a strange question. "Father had told me all about other people and how dangerous they were. He said that the world was corrupt and evil, that the only good people in the world were the two of us. Keeping to the forest, taking only what we needed, living like animals.

Living like an animal was a good thing, you understand. It was honorable. It meant that you took only what you needed, you raised your young to the best of your ability, and you trusted the earth to provide what you needed."

"You make it sound mighty poetic," Dunham says.

"It was what it was." Wendy bows her head. "Like I said, I didn't know anything different."

"Then what happened?" Dunham presses.

"I was all alone for years—how many, I don't even know. Until one day I found a young, injured wolf." She smiles at me and Holo. "That was Beast's grandmother, and she was the first friend I ever had." Then she folds her arms across her chest and says, "But that's enough for now. I can't talk anymore. I need to rest."

Dunham leans forward and lowers his voice. "You can rest soon. But first I think it's time for me to tell you what I know about your life," he says.

Wendy looks up at him, startled. "But I don't *know* you. I've never seen you before. How do y—"

"That man wasn't your father, Wendy," Dunham interrupts. "He was your *kidnapper*. He stole you from your parents' yard when you were three years old, and he took you into the woods. From that day until the moment he died, he kept you hidden from everything you knew and everyone who loved you."

A black hole seems to open in my stomach. Wendy was *kidnapped*? *Stolen*? I can't believe it. I see the way the news hits Wendy—not quickly, like a blow, but like a weight slowly pressing down, harder and harder, until it threatens to crush her.

"That isn't true," she gasps. "It can't be."

"You don't know how long I've been looking for you," Dunham says. "I wasn't the only one, either. For years it seemed like the whole world was looking for little Wendy. They could never find you. And then, eventually, they gave up. They forgot about you." He stands up again. Crosses his arms across his barrel chest. "But not me," he says. "*I never did.*"

CHAPTER 66

MY HEARTBEAT POUNDS like a drum in my ears. *The woman who raised us is a lost child, too.*

Wendy's gripping the sides of her metal chair and trembling. Her head starts shaking back and forth, faster and faster. "No," she says, "no no no." She looks like she's about to have a fit.

"Wendy," I say, moving toward her. "Wendy, can you hear me? Wendy, it's okay."

But she can't answer me, because she's starting to hyperventilate. Dunham looks worried; Rollins watches her like this is just another normal Thursday morning. When Officer Randall shows up with the coffee, he tries to offer her some, but she's shuddering so hard she knocks it right out of his hand. The cup goes spinning into the corner. A puddle spreads slowly across the floor.

I've never seen Wendy like this—never seen her so helpless—and it terrifies me. It tears my heart in two. I try to put my arms around her but Dunham stops me. Pulls me back.

"Give her space," he says. "Let her work through this."

"You did this to her!" I yell.

I know this isn't really true, but I have to blame *someone* for the way she's crumbling before my eyes. Didn't he stop to consider how this information would affect her? Did he honestly think she'd take this earth-shattering revelation in stride?

Randall says, "Should I call Dr. Meyer?"

No, not that old piece of driftwood!

"There's nothing life-threatening about a panic attack," Rollins says condescendingly.

Before anyone can stop him, Holo slips off his chair and curls up around Wendy's feet—the way Beast sometimes would. The alpha female could always tell when we were sad or hurt, and she understood how to comfort us. Because we were *family*.

My throat tightens and my eyes start to sting. Suddenly I can't breathe through my nose.

"You're lying to me," Wendy gasps.

"No, that's what *he* did," Dunham says. "Every single day of your life."

CHAPTER 67

I START TO cry again. Twice in one day! Holo looks up at me, like *Do you need me on* your *feet now?* I shake my head. Draw in ragged breaths as the tears slide down my cheeks.

Poor Wendy. She knows her real, full name. She knows that the man she thought was her father was a criminal. And now she realizes that somewhere out there are people who missed her—*mourned* her—for over three decades.

Everything Wendy ever believed in was wrong. It's like losing two whole lives at once. No wonder she's panicking.

I make a decision that very instant: if there's a truth about my past—and of course there is—I don't want to know it. Ever.

Holo's hand reaches out and closes softly around my ankle. He's crying now, too.

Randall comes into the cell with a wad of toilet paper in his hand. "Sorry," he says. "This is all we got."

Rollins grabs the wad and thrusts it toward my face. I take a few crumpled sheets and wipe my eyes. Holo does the same.

Wolves grieve, but they don't shed tears. Humans are the only animals who do that.

For the record, crying doesn't make me feel better.

Eventually Wendy's breathing slows. She's not hyperventilating anymore. Instead she's starting to moan. Softly, but like she might never stop.

I blow my nose. Holo uncurls himself from around Wendy's ankles and sits up, sniffling.

Dunham says, "Well, Kai—Holo—I know this is pretty overwhelming. But it's necessary. It's like I told Chief Greene. 'The FBI never forgets a missing child.' We found Wendy. And now we've found you."

My breath catches in my throat. "Does that mean that someone wanted you to find us?" I ask. *Someone like...our family? Our real mother?*

Dunham's face falls a little. "Honestly, no. I'm sorry. We found you because we were looking for Wendy. But just because no one's reported you two missing doesn't mean that you aren't." He leans forward. "I want to talk about where you came from. What do you remember, Kai? What can you tell me? Is there anyone who might be looking for you? Missing you?"

I shake my head. "I don't remember anything," I say. "As far as I can tell, the only ones missing us now are the wolves."

CHAPTER 68

"I KNOW HOW we got to the woods."

Holo surprises himself by saying this.

He doesn't really want to talk to these big, official men, but obviously Wendy can't. All she can do right now is moan. And he can tell by the look of alarm in his sister's eyes that she hates everything about the subject.

"Please tell us," Dunham says graciously.

Holo nods. He keeps his body pressed close against Wendy's shins. Reassuring her. Animals like to be close to one another. They take comfort in physical presence.

He thinks back to what Wendy used to tell them every night before they went to sleep. A bedtime story, told in a warm cabin by the light of a flickering candle. And then he starts to tell the tale.

"Once upon a time, there was a man and a woman who had two children, a boy and a girl. They lived in the forest, far from anyone, and they hunted and fished for their food," he says. "But one year, the winter was so long and dark that they ran out of things to eat. The snow fell and fell, and then it fell some more. The fish froze in the river, and even the wild animals were starving.

"So the man and the woman led the children deeper into the forest. They built them a fire, and they told them to stay there. 'We will find food,' they said, 'and then we'll come back for you.' The boy and the girl waited for many hours. The fire burned out, and night fell. No one came for them. The children huddled together for warmth.

"And then the girl saw a flickering through the trees. At first she thought it was fire, and she almost cried for joy. But it wasn't fire. They were being watched—by golden eyes, and tawny eyes, and eyes the color of flames.

"'Who's there?' the boy asked his sister. 'Wolves,' whispered the girl. And she began to cry because she knew that the wolves, too, were starving, and hunger knows no mercy.

"Slowly the animals came out from behind the trees. They crept toward the children, silent as death. The boy and the girl held each other, too frightened to move. The wolves came closer and closer. They sniffed the cold fire, and they sniffed the children's warm skin. The children closed their eyes, because they were going to be eaten.

"But then the wolves lay down beside them. They kept the children warm with their fur and their breath all night along. And in the morning, they led them to their new home." Holo looks up at the FBI agents. "What I mean is," he says, "they led us to Wendy."

For a long time no one says anything. Even Wendy's utterly silent.

Holo is confused. Hadn't he told them exactly what they wanted?

Then he hears his sister start to laugh. Quietly at first, and then louder. Pretty soon she's almost cackling.

"Oh, Holo, you dope," she says. "That is a goddamn *fairy tale*!"

"What?" he says, not understanding.

"It's 'Hansel and Gretel' meets 'Little Red Riding Hood,'" she says. "It's not freaking *true*; it was a bedtime story! Wendy, tell him!"

Wendy, of course, doesn't say anything. Embarrassment hotter than fire floods Holo's cheeks. His sister is right. For as long as he can remember, he's believed a lie.

"So where did we come from?" he asks his sister.

"Don't ask me," Kai says. "And if you ever find out, don't tell me, either."

CHAPTER 69

LOOK, I USED to believe the fairy tale, too. We'd heard it so many times. It was as familiar to us as air. As the sun. As the wild green woods themselves.

But one day I found myself thinking: *Really? That's really how it went down? With the winter and the wolves?*

Because I knew that on a winter night, the cold is truly lethal. And to a starving wolf, anything is prey.

But I never asked Wendy. And I told myself that it didn't matter where we came from; it only mattered where we'd ended up. We lived with Wendy, and we loved her; she loved us fiercely and protectively back. And wasn't that a lot more than some people could say about their real parents?

"It's time, Wendy," Agent Dunham says. "Tell the children what you know."

Wendy closes her eyes. Moans again. When she finally speaks, her voice sounds so small. "I found them in the woods. They were utterly alone."

Holo reaches for my hand. "See?" he whispers.

"And?" Rollins says. "Go on."

"It was winter, wasn't it?" Holo asks stubbornly.

Wendy shakes her head. "It was early fall. The days were still warm, but the nights were getting colder and longer. I'd gone out to look for elderberries in the foothills. I was a couple of miles from my cabin when I saw a tiny shoe sticking out from underneath a bush. I couldn't believe it. There'd never been *anyone* in this remote part of the forest—especially not a child. I honestly thought the shoe had fallen out of an airplane or something. So I went over to pick it up. And that's when I realized that it was still attached to a foot." Wendy's voice cracks, and she begins to cry again. "They were huddled together in the bush. They were all alone and so, so tiny. They didn't have coats. Their lips were blue. They were on the brink of death."

That's us *she's talking about.* I feel sort of queasy.

"What do you estimate was the age of the children when you found them?" Agent Dunham asks.

Wendy sniffles and wipes her eyes. "Maybe two and five. Somewhere around there. I mean—Holo had on a diaper. A filthy diaper."

"And what did you do after you found the children?" Dunham asks.

"I told you, they were nearly dead. I yelled for help. I screamed at the top of my lungs. I thought their parents must be nearby. But no one answered. There was no one, *anywhere*, in that whole huge forest. No one but me and those poor little lost babies." She breaks down again. She's crying so hard you'd think we'd actually died.

"And so what did you do?" Rollins asks.

When her sobs subside, Wendy says, "I carried them back to my cabin." She tenderly brushes Holo's hair back from his forehead. "I wrapped them in blankets. I bandaged their cuts and I fed them good food and I nursed them back to health. They were beautiful children. I was so happy I found them. They were a gift from the forest. It was just like my father said—" She stops and gives her head a hard shake. "It was just like I'd been taught: 'nature will provide.'"

Dunham rubs his grizzled chin again, looking puzzled. "And it never occurred to you to come out of the woods—to seek actual medical care for these children? To find the people they'd been separated from? The people they belonged to?"

But Wendy just stares straight ahead, like she can see straight back into the past. She doesn't seem to hear him. "I taught them the ways of the forest. Taught them to watch and listen, and to hunt and gather. I taught them how to read and write, too. I taught them everything I know, and they're smarter than any of you. Smarter than all of you put together. I saved their lives! And I raised them up like they were my own children." A sob catches in her throat. "They *are* my children. I found them, and I saved them. They're mine."

"You saved them, yes," Dunham agrees. "No one's going to argue with you about that. But you know as well as I do that these kids weren't yours to keep."

Wendy opens her mouth to protest, but I cut her off. "She isn't going to say anything more," I say. "Not without a lawyer."

Dunham looks at me in surprise. Rollins scowls.

"But I—" Wendy begins.

"You aren't going to say anything more," I repeat.

Wendy crumples even smaller. "I'm sorry," she whispers.

What's she sorry about? Saving us from dying of cold and starvation? For telling us a fairy tale instead of what really happened? I can't see even why it matters—not when the truth will just be duller and uglier than the lie.

CHAPTER 70

DUNHAM WANTS WENDY out of the cell now. He says it's time to try to locate and contact members of her family.

"My...real parents?" Wendy whispers.

Dunham's voice goes soft and sympathetic as he tells us that Wendy's parents died two years ago—her dad of cancer, her mom of a stroke. "Before that, I talked to them every month," he assures Wendy. "Every month for all those years. *They* never forgot you. And they never gave up hope."

I can tell by the way Wendy's eyes dart around, looking at the exits, that she isn't ready for this. That all she wants to do is disappear. She did it once, and she can do it again. If she vanishes into the woods, no one but the wolves will be able to find her again.

But she can't run away now, not unless she's going to do it alone. Because we're still in the jail cell. Even though it's not locked, we can't leave. Randall says we have to wait for Ms. Pettibon to come.

I overheard Pearl calling her on Rollins's orders. He said

that Holo and I had been "unofficial guests" of the chief too long. When Pearl protested—"They all like it just fine," she said—he snapped at her. "We need to keep constant track of these kids while their case is under investigation. Since Chief Greene is apparently incapable of doing that, Kai and Holo need to be in state-approved care."

I don't know what state-approved care means, but I don't like the sound of it.

An hour passes. Then another.

"Chester will come back soon and let us out," Holo says. He's sticking his finger into a hole in his T-shirt and slowly making it bigger. "He'll take care of everything."

Holo is so damn trusting. Me, I'm just pissed at the chief for following us. For bringing a dozen armed men with him. For trying to arrest Wendy, who was only trying to protect us.

But he's probably the only one who's really on our side.

"Excuse me," says a bright, grating voice. Ms. Pettibon is sliding past Rollins and into our cell. "I'm here to see . . ."—her lips almost curl when she says this—"*them*."

She has the same red hair, the same fake-flower perfume, the same bullshit, lipsticked smile. I can feel the growl rising in my throat, but I push it back down.

Rollins says, "They're all yours," and goes back to picking paint off the cell bars with his fingernail.

"Well," Ms. Pettibon chirps to me and Holo, "you're not acting like wild animals, so obviously you've made some behavioral improvements since we last met."

Holo looks over at me, like *Should I bite her? Because I can totally do that.*

As much as I'd enjoy seeing him sink his fangs into her shoulder, it'd do more harm than good. I shake my head no.

"But, unfortunately, despite these improvements," she goes on, "there are clearly still issues with conduct, discipline, and attitude. If this weren't the case, then you wouldn't have been brought here in handcuffs, no?"

Her tone's so condescending it makes me want to scream. On second thought, maybe Holo *should* bite her. I'm considering giving him the A-okay when Wendy bursts into the cell, having left Agent Dunham pecking away at Randall's computer.

"Who are you?" she demands.

Ms. Pettibon starts to hold out a plump manicured hand. When she sees Wendy's scarred, dusty one, she changes her mind. Smiles falsely. There's a slash of pink lipstick on her teeth.

"Arlene Pettibon, Child and Family Services."

"What are you doing here?" Wendy demands.

Ms. Pettibon stiffens. "CFS intervenes when it is determined that a dangerous family condition is present. You see, when children are not being properly cared for, we step in to provide a stab—"

"Kai and Holo don't need you to take care of them," Wendy says. "That's my job."

Now Ms. Pettibon's lips make a bright-pink frown. "Really? Then how do you explain the fact that they ran away from you, and shortly thereafter they were arrested for shoplifting and vandalism?" she asks. "And then they were nearly expelled from school, which I can see you knew nothing about. This doesn't paint a very good picture of your caretaking, ma'am, to say nothing of the fact that you have no claim to these children. And while Officer Greene and Lacey Hernandez have temporarily harbored them, they are not licensed caregivers or foster parents. As such, Kai and Holo will go into official foster care, where they can be in a supportive environment with other kids like them."

What the hell?

"There aren't any kids like us, lady," I snap, "and if you haven't figured that out by now, then you're even dumber than I thought you were."

"Kai," Wendy says sharply. "Don't."

Ms. Pettibon ignores this exchange completely. "There are two different houses with openings," she goes on. She beams like she's about to give us really good news. "One will take the girl, and one will take the boy."

CHAPTER 71

HOLO AND I look at each other in horror.

Wendy leans forward like she's getting ready to fight. "You can't do that."

"Of course I can. The family that's willing to take Holo is in Archer," Ms. Pettibon goes on. "That's just fifteen minutes south. They have a big yard and several other boys. He can probably continue on at Kokanee Creek High School. Kai, on the other hand, will need to go to Blackfoot, which is about an hour southwest— *YEEOUCH!*" Ms. Pettibon's eyes go wide as she claps her hand over her shoulder. Enraged, she turns on Holo. "You little beast!"

My brother, who has just *bitten* her, is struggling to hold back laughter. "I didn't even break the skin!"

Ms. Pettibon obviously doesn't find this funny. "What is *wrong* with you?"

"Oh, lots of things," Holo says. "Do you want to hear the list?"

I can't believe it—except that I can. What would I do without my brilliant, insane brother? I suck in my cheeks so I'm not smiling, too. "Ms. Pettibon, I don't think your foster families are going to want kids who bite," I say. "There'd be, you know, safety concerns." I gnash my teeth at her. Make like I'm about to chomp her, too.

Ms. Pettibon gets to her feet. "I'm going to speak to my supervisor about this. In the meantime, you should stay in jail! *All* of you!" Then she stomps down the hall, passing the chief, who's just come in the front door.

"That boy's dangerous," she shouts. "A psychopath, most likely—"

"What are you talking about?" the chief asks. He looks exhausted and dirty and pissed.

But Ms. Pettibon just blows past him, shoving Randall out of the way as she stomps outside.

"Follow her," I yell to the chief. "Tell her we aren't any of her business!"

He clearly doesn't understand what's going on, but he hears the urgency in my voice. He spins around and follows her outside. A few minutes later he's back, shaking his head.

"You should've kept your teeth to yourself, Holo," he scolds. "She was talking about juvie."

"What's juvie?" Holo asks.

"Let's hope you never find out."

"What'd she say?" I demand. "Is she sending us away?"

"She's extremely angry. She wants you out of Kokanee Creek."

"But she can't—"

"She can do a lot," the chief says grimly. "But I've held her off for now."

"So are you going to let us out? Let us go back home?"

"To that cabin on government land? That's what you're talking about?" The chief's still struggling with the fact that we grew up lost in the wilderness and yet somehow only a handful of miles from town.

"Yes," Holo and I say at the same time.

"You know I can't do that."

"So where are we supposed to go?" I demand. "That's the only home we've ever known, and you're taking it from us!"

"It never belonged to us," Wendy whispers.

"But we didn't know that!" I remind her.

She shrugs. "Does it matter?"

"If you won't let us go back," I say urgently, "then we all have to come stay with you. I'll move in with Holo. Wendy can have my room. We can't be sent away. Chief, she's the only mother we remember. The only mother we know."

"But you ran away from her," he says. He sounds confused. Exasperated. Tired.

"Just for a little while! Then we went back, remember? Please, you can't separate us."

The chief leans against the bars of our cell as he considers this. He doesn't look thrilled about bringing Wendy to his house. Maybe it's because the whole situation is wild and totally overwhelming, or maybe it's because a couple of hours ago, they almost shot each other.

Probably it's both.

"You know what Lacey would say," I press. "*Mi casa es su casa.*"

"Please," Holo begs. "Wendy doesn't have anywhere to go now. Neither do we—unless you let us stay."

The chief sighs. He swings the cell door wide open and then turns around and starts to walk away from us. "Fine," he calls. "You can all stay for now. Until whatever happens next."

Holo grins happily. "What's going to happen next?"

Wendy just looks down at the floor. I think she's crying again.

"I don't know," I say. "But we're going to face it together."

CHAPTER 72

THE CRAZY THING is that I go back to school the next day as if everything's totally normal. As if our whole world hadn't been taken away from us by a posse of dudes with guns and a couple of uptight FBI agents.

At the door of room 112, Ms. Tillman greets me with a smile. "How's your brother doing?" she asks. "I miss having him in class."

Hmmm, let's see. He spent more time in jail, he's lost his childhood home, and he's probably going to be put in foster care.

"He's fine," I say. Why upset her when she can't do anything about it?

Waylon comes in just as the bell rings and flops down next to me. "That scene in the woods was crazy," he whispers. He scoots his desk a few inches closer. "When they put you in that chopper, I was afraid I was never going to see you again."

"Pretty soon you might not," I say grimly. Bartsville. Where the hell is Bartsville?

"What did the FBI want with—"

"Waylon Meloy," Ms. Tillman warns. "Please close your mouth, open your notebook, and start working."

"Sorry, Ms. T," Waylon grumbles.

He starts dutifully scribbling. I assume he's working on the figurative language essays we're supposed to be writing, but a few seconds later, a note lands on my desk.

Remember when I stopped that guy from shooting you? Want to go to the dance with me?

P.S. "Yes" is the correct answer to both of these questions.

I get the same feeling in my stomach that I used to get when I jumped off of high river banks in the summer. A queasy giddiness. A thrilling panic.

Of course I remember how he stepped in between me and a gun. And how he kept me from running away.

I remember every moment I've spent with him, ever since that day I saw his slow, teasing smile for the first time.

But underneath his messy cursive, I write: *I thought the dance already happened.*

He scribbles back. *I got the date wrong. So...what do you say?*

I don't want to say no, but I'm scared to say yes.

Then another piece of paper lands on my desk.

It says: *Well?*

I ignore it. A few moments later, another note skitters across my page.

Well???!!!

I can't help smiling. I look over at him and shrug. He rolls his eyes. Gives up on me for the rest of the period.

But when the bell rings, he leaps up and says, "Okay, now I'm demanding an answer."

I'm nervous and grinning as I slip into the hall. I don't know why I can't just say yes. Or no. Or *anything*.

Even though his class is in the other direction, Waylon hurries along beside me. "Do you want me to beg?" he says. "Because I will totally beg."

And then he falls on his knees in the hallway. My cheeks flush hot as fire. He's going to make a scene when all I want is to be as invisible as possible. Which—let's be real—has never been even *close* to invisible.

I start to walk away from him. But he follows me, still on his knees. "Kai, wait!"

I turn around. "You're making a fool of yourself!"

"You know me well enough by now to know that I don't care. You and me," he says, "are iconoclasts."

"I always thought of myself more as an outcast."

Waylon shakes his head. "You can't be cast out of anything that you never truly tried to get into," he says. "Look at you. You were always too interesting for this school."

Well, I might not be here much longer.

"Get up," I say. "Please."

"Say yes."

"Will you get up?"

He nods.

"Fine. I'll go to the dance with you. For ten minutes."

When he stands up, his smile's so big and bright I can hardly bear to look at it. "I'll pick you up at seven," he says. Then he blows me a kiss and runs off to class.

CHAPTER 73

"WHAT'RE YOU DOING?" Wendy has wandered into the room I now share with Holo to find me half-dressed, up to my shins in a pile of Lacey's clothing.

"I'm going to a dance," I say grimly, yanking off a checked top I'd hoped would be fine but instead made me look like I was wearing a kitchen tablecloth. "And I'm supposed to look nice or something."

Wendy sits down on the bed and tucks her bare feet under her. Her hair is clean and braided; she smells like Ivory soap.

Lacey, especially, has welcomed her in like a sister. She and the chief give Wendy lots of space; they happily eat her foraged salads; they don't ask any prying questions about her past. And I know Wendy's trying to settle in, too. But she's so shy and skittish that sometimes she bolts from a room the minute someone else walks into it.

It's like living with a deer, Lacey had whispered.

"A dance," Wendy repeats thoughtfully. "Are you going with a boy?"

"A guy," I correct her. "Yes. His name is Waylon."

"How strange."

"His name?" Personally I think Holo is a weirder name than Waylon—not that I'd tell her that.

"No, just the idea of going to a dance." Her eyes get a curious, faraway look in them. "With a boy."

Guy, I think but don't say. I pick up another top and hold it up to my chest. Pink is not my color. Red's even worse.

"I can't even imagine what that would be like."

It strikes me like a slap across the face. Wendy's never had a crush on anyone. Never held hands. Never had a first kiss.

Of course, I'm iffy on those things myself. But I'm only seventeen. Ish. Wendy's over twice my age.

"Where did you meet him?" Wendy asks.

"Jail."

Wendy looks startled.

I slip a black dress over my head. "He's not a criminal. He was just riding a motorcycle too fast."

"That looks pretty on you," she says. Apparently she's not worried about Waylon's checkered past.

I smooth the front of the dress. "It's too short," I say. I've tried on six tops and five dresses and I've hated them all. I bend down and grab the jeans and sweatshirt I was wearing before. They'll have to do.

"Why did you go?" Wendy blurts. "I mean—why did you leave the woods?"

I freeze. Why did I? I still can't really explain it.

I take a deep breath. There are way too many words and feelings, and I don't know how to sort them all out. So I pick the simplest explanation. The one that's the truth, if not *all* of it. "I wanted to know what it was like out here," I say softly. "Didn't you? I mean—how did you spend all those years alone?"

Wendy plucks at a stray thread on my bedspread. "I thought about leaving sometimes. But then I'd say to myself, 'Just one more day. Tomorrow you can go into the human world. But for today, stay here.' And the next day would come, and I would find myself saying the same thing. 'Just one more day.' And so the years passed. And I kept staying." She looks up at me. "Leaving wasn't a choice I could make, I guess."

But I made it for you, didn't I? I brought the men, and they dragged you out of the forest.

And suddenly I feel the sting of tears. "I'm sorry," I say. "For leaving. For leading those people to our house. For ruining everything."

"It's not your fault," Wendy says quietly.

But we both know that it is.

Wendy starts to say something else, but then I hear Holo calling from downstairs. "Kai! Hurry up! Your date's here!"

I wipe my eyes. "He's not my *date*," I yell back. "He's my *friend*."

"Whatever!"

I turn to Wendy. "I'm sorry. I have to go. Do I look like a normal teenager?" I ask.

She laughs—a small, sad little chuckle. "How would I know?" Then she reaches up and pats my cheek. "You look beautiful. Have fun," she says. "And come back and tell me all about it."

I kiss the top of her head. "See you later."

I go downstairs to find Waylon waiting for me on the

porch. I feel so shy I can barely say hello. But he doesn't seem to notice.

"I was here once already," he says, rolling his eyes. "Half an hour ago. I was on the motorcycle, though, and Lacey told me to turn right back around and get a vehicle that wouldn't kill us both." He hooks a thumb behind him, gesturing to a low black car. "So I had to borrow my mom's ancient Saab."

I squint at it. "Where's the roof?"

"It fell off on the way over," Waylon says.

"What? How?" I exclaim.

Waylon starts to laugh. "It's called a convertible, Kai," he says. "It's supposed to be that way. Now hurry up and get in."

CHAPTER 74

THE CAR'S SO low to the ground that Waylon could probably park it underneath Chester's pickup.

"So this is *less* dangerous?" I say doubtfully as I sink into the passenger seat. "It looks like it'll barely go ten miles without falling apart."

"You could be right," Waylon admits. "Luckily school is only four miles from here." He gets in behind the wheel and then cocks his head and looks at me.

"What?" I ask. His frank gaze makes me self-conscious.

"Usually people dress up a little for a school dance," he says. "See?" He points to his shirt and smiles teasingly. "This is called a button-down, Kai. It's different than a regular T-shirt. And by different, I mean nicer."

"Sorry," I say, flushing a little. "My wardrobe is...limited." I don't tell him that I tried on a dozen outfits. How I put my hair up, then down, then up again. How, in the end, it felt like trying to look nice and failing seemed worse than deciding not to give a shit in the first place.

"Well, it doesn't matter anyway," Waylon says, turning the key. The car sputters to life. "You're more beautiful than any-one at that school. You could wear a garbage bag and you'd still look better than everyone else. You could put sticks in your hair. You could smear mud all over your fa—"

"Okay, I get it," I say. "Thank you."

The wind blows my hair into my face as we drive beneath the trees. Waylon reaches into the seat pocket and then holds up a plastic rectangle.

"And *this*, my feral friend, is what's called a cassette tape." He sticks it into a slot in the dashboard. "The singer you're about to hear is Waylon Jennings."

A deep mournful voice comes out of the car doors. *Mama, don't let your babies grow up to be cowboys...*

"Were you named for him?"

"I tell people I was. But Waylon was just my grandpa's name."

When Waylon pulls into the school parking lot, the ner-vousness I'd been feeling becomes a heavy ball of dread. I basically *hate* this place. Why'd I let him convince me to come here when I didn't absolutely have to?

Waylon hurries around the front of the car, opens my door, and says, "Just remember, all you have to do is this." And then he does the wild, idiotic dance he did in Lacey's cafe, kick-ing out his legs and swinging his arms and tossing his head around like a maniac.

I laugh. "You look like you're being electrocuted."

"Thank you." He holds out his arm. "Ready?"

I'm *not* ready, but I tuck my hand into the crook of his

elbow anyway and try not to think too much about how warm his skin feels beneath his nice button-down.

The dance is being held in the cafeteria, which has been decorated with strands of Christmas lights and blue and white streamers. Bouquets of blue and white balloons dot each table, and the floor's covered with paper confetti.

The dance floor's in the middle of the room and it's already crowded. It's hard to make out the other students' faces in the dim, colored light—not that I ever bothered to learn their names—but they're all doing versions of the stupid-looking dance Waylon demonstrated in the parking lot. The girls are in tight dresses or belly-baring tops. The guys look like they didn't even change after school. A few teacher chaperones lean against the walls, looking at their phones.

"Let's do what we came here for!" Waylon practically has to shout over the music. "You like this song?"

I shrug. I've never heard it before. It's got a thumping bass line that's making everyone just sort of bounce up and down... I guess I can do that.

"Sure," I yell. "Yes."

Waylon puts his hands on my shoulders and steers me into the crowd. Then he spins me around so I'm facing him, and he grabs my hands and starts jumping. "Pretend you're on a pogo stick," he yells.

"A *what*?"

He laughs and shakes his head. "Never mind!"

I start jumping up and down with him. I feel dumb at first, but after a minute or two it starts to get fun. It feels good to let out so much energy—to fling my head around and swivel my hips, to try to match my body to the rhythm of the song. When everyone starts pumping their hands in the air, I copy them. Waylon's laughing and so am I.

"I'm doing it!" I yell.

"You're amazing!" he yells back.

I'm not amazing, I'm ridiculous, but who cares?

Then the track shifts, and the music slows down. Waylon grins and holds out his arms. "May I have this dance, m'lady?" he says, giving me a mock bow.

I hesitate. I remember the last time we slow-danced, how I shoved my nose into his neck the way Beast used to nuzzle Ernie, which had confused Waylon and horrified me.

"Well?" Waylon says. "Cuz if you don't want to, I'll go ask Mr. Chive to dance with me." He inclines his head toward the gym teacher, who's goofily swaying on the far side of the cafeteria.

"I dare you," I say.

He shakes his head. "Don't do that. Just dance with me."

You can do this, Kai. All you have to do is keep your nose out of his neck.

"Fine." I step into the circle of Waylon's arms. They tighten around me. I suck in my breath as I lean into him. Pressing myself close. My heart's beating so hard I think he must be able to feel it against his ribs. We sway back and forth, turning in slow circles. All around us, other couples spin, their bodies tight against each other.

I close my eyes. Breathe in Waylon's warm scent. Let the music guide my feet. For once I'm not thinking. Not worrying. I'm just being *alive*.

The next thing I know, I'm on the ground, and Mac Hardy's standing over me, his face twisted in anger and hate.

"Dogs aren't allowed at dances," he says.

Behind him, Waylon struggles to free himself from Logan Hardy's grip. We were *ambushed*! I start to get up, but Mac kicks my feet out from under me and I fall to my side. The other kids back away.

"Fight," someone says softly. "*Fight.*"

Logan sneers, "Can't you get up?"

I push myself up halfway on my hands. Then I falter. Grimace. Shake my head.

A killdeer will fake a broken wing to draw predators away from its nest.

A seventeen-year-old outcast will fake an injured leg to draw a predator closer.

Mac edges nearer. "Ooooh, does the pooch have an owie?"

No, but you will.

I spring up from the ground and launch myself toward him. He doesn't have time to react before my fist connects with his nose. Even over the sound of the music, I hear it crack as the force of the blow travels up my hand to my shoulder, hard as the recoil of a gun.

Mac's hands fly to his face. He staggers sideways. Blood pours through his fingers. Logan lets go of Waylon and charges at me, screaming.

I consider punching him, too. But I don't want the janitors to have to clean up too much blood.

So I reach for Waylon's hand, and we run.

CHAPTER 75

WE JUMP INTO the convertible—leapfrogging over the doors instead of opening them—and peel out of the parking lot. The tires squeal as Waylon takes the turn way too fast.

"That dance sucked anyway," I shout over the screaming engine.

Waylon throws back his head and laughs. "I know! Why'd we go?"

"Because you said we should!"

Waylon glances in the rearview mirror to make sure no one's following us. When he doesn't see any headlights, he downshifts. The engine stops sounding like it's shrieking in pain.

"Everybody needs to go to a high school dance at least once," he tells me. "It should be a requirement for graduation, like biology."

"What's so important about jumping around in the dark with a bunch of people you don't like?" I rub my knuckles. They hurt where I smashed them into Mac's nose.

"Well, I hope there was at least one person there you like," Waylon says pointedly.

"Okay, yes, there was one." I glance over at him. "I mean, I think Mr. Chive is an underrated teacher—"

Waylon laughs. "You're the worst," he says.

He turns down an unfamiliar road. Trees loom tall on either side of us.

"No, high school dances are the worst," I say.

"Only when someone attacks you on the dance floor," he says. "Normally the worst thing you can say about them is that they're boring, or that the DJ sucked. But a high school dance is a rite of passage. Like learning to drive. Or drinking your first beer. Or having your first kiss."

So far I have done none of these things. I wonder if he knows that. "How about killing your first deer?" I ask.

Waylon shoots me a sideways look. "I probably wouldn't have put that on the list."

"What about gutting your first fish? Giving yourself your first stitches with a needle and thread?"

"Your rites of passage involve too much blood!" Waylon shakes his head, laughing.

"What's so funny?"

"Well, when I first met you, I said I was probably too dangerous for you."

"And now you're ready to admit that you were wrong."

"Considering the damage I've seen you do to people twice your size, uh, yeah." He shrugs one shoulder. "But, you know, live and learn."

After a little while he turns off the road and comes to a stop

285

in front of a faded red building with bright neon signs hanging in the windows. BUDWEISER. COORS LIGHT. BBQ. OPEN.

He holds out his hand to me. "Ready?" he says.

"For what?"

Waylon doesn't answer. He just grins and pulls me inside.

The narrow room's even dimmer than the high school dance. The air smells old, somehow, or maybe stale. Like wood and dust. Also like yeast and smoke and . . .

Waylon nudges me in the arm. "Stop wolf-sniffing," he whispers. "It's just the smell of a dive bar."

I'm glad it's too dark in here for him to see me blushing.

"What'll you have?" he says. "Beer? Jack and Coke?"

I blink at him. "I have no idea."

He playfully pats my cheek, like I'm a little kid. "Find us a seat. I'll be right back."

I sit down at a sticky wooden table in the corner. Waylon comes back with two tall beers in frosted glasses and sets one down in front of me. "Now, pick that up—yes, with the handle, just like that," he says, "and now clink your glass against mine. Cheers!"

"Cheers," I repeat. "Um, I know I'm not an expert on the human world, but aren't there rules against drinking beer at our age?"

Waylon shrugs. "I try not to let the rules apply to me," he says. "I find them constricting. So, how does that rite of passage taste?"

I take a sip and try not to make a face. But Waylon sips his slowly, like he actually enjoys it.

"First taste of beer: check," I say gamely.

He keeps his eyes on me as he smiles that heartthrob smile of his. My stomach gives a queasy, thrilling lurch, and a shivery sensation zings up and down my spine. As he grabs my free hand with his and puts my fingers to his lips, I find myself hoping that there's at least one more rite of passage we can check off tonight.

CHAPTER 76

MY HEAD FEELS fuzzy and I'm a little off-balance as we leave the bar.

"The second beer tasted better than the first," I say to Waylon, giggling.

"It went down better, too," he says. He puts his hand lightly in the small of my back and leans in close. "Which is why I'm cutting you off," he whispers playfully. "We can't have you dancing on the tables."

"As if," I scoff, although for some reason the idea doesn't sound nearly as shocking to me as it should.

"I'm going to miss that place when I'm gone," he says as the door swings shut behind us.

I stumble a little on the uneven pavement. "What do you mean, when you're gone?"

"I got a scholarship to the University of Idaho. Hey, don't look so shocked!"

Is *shocked* the word? Or would *hurt* be better? Waylon

never said anything to me about leaving. "But I never saw you doing any work!" I cry.

"I have a slacker reputation to keep up," he says. "I do all my assignments at home."

"And you get good grades?" I should probably stop sounding so incredulous, but I can't help it.

"I'd probably be valedictorian if I didn't always skip PE."

"Wow," I say faintly. My head reels. College—what a nice, normal, human thing to do. What an impossible idea for someone like me. "I guess you have secrets, too," I say.

"Maybe I do," he says. "But I'll tell you any of them, Kai. All you have to do is ask."

Heat rises to my cheeks as we get into the car. Does he really think it's that simple? Anything I really want to know, I'd be too shy to ask.

Do you get goosebumps when my fingers graze your skin? Do you lie in your bed at night and think about kissing me?

Waylon starts the engine. Says, "You don't want to go home yet, do you?"

He forgets that I don't have a home anymore. "I don't want to go back to the chief's," I correct him.

"Good," he says. "Because there's more we have to accomplish."

CHAPTER 77

KOKANEE CREEK'S TINY downtown is quiet now, its old-fashioned streetlights lit, and moths dancing in their glow.

"Maybe we should get another beer," I say. "There's a bar just down the street from the jail."

Waylon snorts. "The bartender there knows exactly how old I am, and unlike the good folks at Ruby's Roadhouse, he *cares*." He pulls into a parking lot behind Kokanee Creek Elementary School. "Anyway, we've already checked first beer off the list. But what about all those super classic childhood things you haven't done? Like swinging on a swing or sliding down a slide?"

"Are those things prerequisites for drinking beer?" I ask. "I really hope you didn't just screw up my human education!"

Waylon laughs, and the sound seems to ripple down my spine. "They're not prerequisites for anything. They're just fun. Come on."

I sink into the rubber seat and wrap my hands around the chains. The swings are designed for people *much* smaller than we are.

"Lean back," Waylon says, "and then you'll pump your legs like this—see?"

I watch him arcing smoothly back and forth. *Okay, Kai, little kids can do this. So can you.* It's awkward at first, but I get the hang of it eventually. I rise up to the black sky, and then I fall down to earth. Rise up, fall back down, rise. I start laughing, and Waylon does too.

"Isn't it great?" he says.

I don't know, is *it?* My stomach feels like it's doing somersaults. I may or may not feel like barfing. After another minute I scuff my feet and come to a stop. "I can't tell if I love it or hate it," I admit.

"Slide next, then?" he says, grinning.

I look at his face, beautiful and shadowed in the darkness. I don't really care about another children's toy. I want to be close to him. I want him to whisper into my neck again. I want—

"Or," Waylon says, "we can try this." He's holding up a lighter and a funny-looking cigarette. He sees my blank look. "It's a joint," he explains. "Which I also borrowed from my mom, along with the car. But she doesn't know that part."

I look around the empty playground like I'm expecting the chief to pop out from behind a tree or something. "I hope *this* isn't on your list of 'classic childhood things,'" I say.

"No, you did so well on the swings that you skipped a bunch of grades."

"Is it a good idea?" I ask.

"Depends on who you ask," Waylon says. He lights the joint and inhales. The exhale comes several seconds later. "According to me, yes, it is." He holds the joint out to me.

I take it. The end is smoldering, and the smell is vaguely skunky. "I guess it's another rite of passage, huh?"

He nods. "Totally. And if we'd done this before the dance, maybe you wouldn't have smashed Mac's nose into his brains."

"You think I shouldn't have done that?"

When under attack, an animal uses all its strength to defend itself.

Rival wolves will fight to the death.

"On the contrary, I think you should do it daily. Mac's personality has nowhere to go but up."

A thin line of smoke from the joint spirals upward, and a reckless feeling surges inside me. I know I'll be suspended from school for hitting Mac. I've lost my home. I don't know what the future holds, so I might as well stop asking questions. Stop worrying and *live*.

I put the joint to my lips. Waylon lights the end again, and I inhale. Immediately I cough a white burning cloud right out of my mouth.

"Agh," I gasp. "It hurts!"

"Take a little at a time. Hold it in. Then let it out. Like this." Waylon demonstrates again.

I'm nervous as I take it back from him. I feel stupid and innocent.

"You don't have to if you don't want to," he says.

"Yeah, I *know*," I practically growl. "Just...give me a minute."

I put my mouth right where his lips were. I inhale, and the end grows more red. The paper crackles. The smoke stings my throat, but I don't let myself cough. I take it deep into my lungs and hold it there for as long as I can before exhaling.

I look at Waylon. "Did I do it right? I don't feel anything." I start coughing.

He hands me a water bottle. "Give it a minute."

I take a sip, then drain the rest of it in giant gulps.

"How about now?" Waylon says a little bit later.

I think about this. I cock my head, and the world seems to slowly tip sideways. I slide off the swing and walk very deliberately—it seems to take more effort than usual—over to the grass. Suddenly it becomes extremely important for me to lie on the ground. I let my knees go soft. I melt into the cool grass. There's barely any moon, so the stars above me seem especially bright.

Waylon comes to lie down beside me. "How're you doing?" he asks.

I blink. My eyelids are heavy. *Blinking is weird,* I think. *And eyeballs are weird. They're wet spheres sitting inside two holes in your face. Which is really gross if you think about it.*

"Hello?" he says.

"What?" I say.

"I asked you how you were doing."

I giggle. "Sorry. I forgot." Between the question and my answer a black hole had opened up. A black hole where I was thinking about . . .

What was I thinking about? I can't remember.

I've never felt the grass against my back like this. Never felt how delicately the wind can ruffle my hair. I actually don't need to think at all. What I need is to scoot closer to Waylon, until the whole side of me is pressed against the whole long, warm side of him. I listen to the sound of his slow, steady breath.

My hand finds his in the darkness. Our fingers intertwine. *Just kiss me*, I think.

Waylon rolls to his side so he's facing me. With his other hand he traces the line of my cheekbone down to my lips. My skin melts under his touch.

He says softly, "Would it be all right if I ki—"

I don't let him finish. I'm already grabbing him and pulling him toward me. Our lips meet in a hot, desperate crush, and the world starts spinning for real now. I didn't even know how much I wanted this. Needed this.

His hands are in my hair and mine are sliding up the smooth skin of his back. He says, "Kai," and his voice comes out ragged. I give his neck a little nip and he sighs, smiling, and then he bends down and kisses me again and again and again.

CHAPTER 78

WENDY SHAKES ME from sleep before the sun's even up. Groggily I roll over. My head hurts and my mouth feels like it's full of cotton. I'm still in the clothes that I wore to the dance. I can still taste Waylon on my lips.

"Kai, get up," she says. "We have to go."

"Go where?" I'm so tired that I don't even care.

Holo yells, "Put on your shoes!"

The urgency in his voice jolts me fully awake. I clumsily do what he says, and then Wendy throws me a sweatshirt and pushes me toward the stairs. She's not even trying to keep quiet, and the chief stumbles out into the hallway, yawning. "What's going on?" he says, blinking.

Wendy says, "We're going to save our family."

"What?" the chief says.

I go, "What?" Neither of us has any idea what's going on.

Then I hear that now-familiar roaring sound, that mechanical thunder that comes from the sky. My bones start to vibrate. The whole damn cottage starts to rattle.

Chester's eyes widen. "What the hell?" he says. He runs to the window in time to see the FBI helicopter landing in his front yard.

"Come on," Wendy says to me and my brother.

The three of us are already on the porch when Agent Dunham opens the door to the helicopter and yells what seems like "Let's go!"

Not again, I think. *I don't want to throw up this early*, but Wendy drags me toward the terrifying machine. I just have to trust her that she knows what she's doing. Whatever our mission is, it's urgent and we have to go.

My stomach's twisting already.

"At least we're not handcuffed this time!" Holo shouts.

Yeah, sure, that's one *bright spot.*

After Dunham checks to make sure we're strapped in, he gives a thumbs-up to the pilot. Then comes that awful, lurching moment when we lift into the sky. I feel like I left my guts behind as we rise above the meadow and swing over the dark trees. The sun's just beginning to come up. It lights the clouds with rays of gold.

Wendy scans the sky with worried eyes.

"What are you looking for?" I yell over the sound of a motor, but she doesn't hear me. She's too focused on staring out the window.

The pilot heads east, toward where the trees thin and the open grasslands begin. The sky's getting lighter by the second. I've never seen the world from this height—I guess I was too busy barfing last time—and it's crazy. I can see 360 degrees around me. Everything looks totally different, but I know where we are. All of this is our territory. All of this is the wolves' territory.

I feel dizzy and my head pounds. *Keep it together, Kai.*

Luckily my stomach's empty. If I'd eaten any breakfast, it'd be in a puddle on the floor by now.

We fly low and slow, making giant circles, until Wendy points, jabbing a finger at the window. She knocks Agent Dunham on the shoulder, gesturing to him. In the air, a few hundred yards off, we can see the flashing lights of another helicopter.

"There they are," she yells.

There who *are? What the hell?*

I look at Wendy in confusion. She shoves a pair of binoculars at me. Along the side of the helicopter, where there should be a door, there's an open space. And in that open space is Reginald Hardy, holding an assault rifle.

Suddenly I understand, and I nearly convulse with horror.

He's flying out to hunt Bim and Ben and Harriet, to kill Beast and her babies.

He's going to murder my family.

CHAPTER 79

AGENT DUNHAM SAYS something to the pilot, who nods and accelerates. Pretty soon we're coming up alongside the other helicopter. Then we stop, hovering barely fifty feet away from it.

Below us is a broad flat valley cut through by the river. I scan the ground frantically. I don't want to see anything moving down there.

Please, Beast, stay hidden. Keep your babies close.

Our pilot's attempting to radio the other helicopter while Dunham's trying to get Hardy's attention. Hardy glances our way, spits, and then leans farther out, looking for the same wolves we are.

If Hardy kills another wolf I love, I swear I'll rip Dunham's gun from his waistband and murder him.

"What's that down there?" Holo shouts in my ear.

I look where he's pointing. Squint. We're flying low enough that I can see what it is without binoculars: a dead sheep, bloody and half-eaten in the scrub brush.

But there shouldn't be a sheep carcass here! The ranches are miles off, way over on the other side of the ridge. Wolves wouldn't kill a sheep and drag it all this way—they *couldn't*. I don't understand.

Wendy taps me on the knee. "It's bait!" she cries.

Oh God, I think. *Of course.*

The other helicopter suddenly descends.

"Stay with him," Wendy screams to the pilot.

We go swooping down, way too fast. My stomach flies up into my throat and lodges there. I can't breathe. Holo grabs my hand.

"What's happening? Are we crashing?" he yells.

I shake my head. I don't think so. But I swear I'd be fine with crashing if it meant I could get out of this awful thing. We're barely forty feet off the ground now. The other helicopter levels out and so do we. Hardy's leaning halfway out, head swiveling, gun clutched tight.

Two dark shapes come rocketing out of the brush.

"Harriet!" Holo screams. "Ben!"

I don't see the rest of the pack, but I know they're nearby, drawn by the carcass that Hardy must've somehow left for them.

There's no good cover here. Nowhere to hide.

All any predators can do now is *run*.

I see another gray shape—then three more. Beast is nipping at the heels of her babies, urging them on, driving them away from these black monsters in the sky.

The pups have grown bigger, but they're not big or strong enough yet. They won't be able to keep up. And Beast won't leave them.

Reginald Hardy looks over our way and smiles, and I know exactly what he's thinking. He's going to want to chase them for a while. Herd them. Get them good and scared and tired, so they're easier to hit.

After all, riding in a helicopter's fun.

And bullets aren't free, so he wants to make them count.

The helicopter follows the wolves, and so do we. Hardy tries to line up a shot. I can see a red laser sweeping across the ground. For a moment, the dot tracks Beast's spine. The wolf swerves to the side, almost as if she can feel it. The red dot goes wide, then swings back.

"Get in front of them!" I scream. "Block his shot!"

Dunham gestures to the pilot. *Do it.*

We shoot forward and drop down even lower, putting ourselves between the other helicopter and the racing wolves.

Our pilot's yelling something into his radio. Holo's white with terror.

"Stay in the way," Dunham shouts.

My chest is tight with panic. Tears are streaming down my brother's face. The pack is running in a line, but they could splinter any minute. And we can't block Hardy's line of fire if the wolves run in different directions.

Dunham pushes his way to the back of the helicopter and slides the door open. The wind comes rushing in so strong it takes my breath away. Dunham grabs on tight to a strap and leans out toward the other helicopter. With his free hand he holds up his badge. "Back down!" he yells, as if they could hear him over the thunder of the engine. "You can't do this!"

The wolves are crossing a stream now, leaping and splashing.

Harriet's in the lead, and though Beast is the fastest, she's bringing up the rear, keeping her babies in front of her. The water's full and high from the spring rains, and one of the pups goes under. I scream. Shove my knuckles against my teeth in terror. Taste blood.

After an unbearable minute, the small dark head reappears downstream. Beast is desperately trying to keep the other struggling pup above the water. Bim circles back and runs close to the drowning pup. He stands on the far bank, yipping frantically. The pup, swimming with all its strength, makes it a few feet closer to shore. Bim lunges, grabs it by the front leg, and pulls it to the bank. The pup doesn't even stop to shake himself off—he just keeps running.

There's nothing but range grasses and juniper ahead of them.

They're racing as fast as they can.

Dunham's screaming his head off. Waving his badge. Finally he brings out his gun.

Hardy sees it and ducks back into the helicopter. And I guess the pilot must've seen it too, because he suddenly lifts the helicopter into the air. It hovers above us, fighting gravity. Then it turns. Flies away.

Wendy folds over, her head in her hands. Holo looks at me in shock.

I jab Dunham in his broad shoulder. I yell, "Now we need to *land*."

CHAPTER 80

THE PILOT BRINGS the helicopter down with a jolt on a flat patch of dusty ground. The rotors slowly wind to a stop. I climb out of the helicopter into the middle of nowhere. My legs are shaking. My stomach's in knots. I'm still trying to wrap my head around what just happened.

Holo jumps down to the dirt beside me. Wendy follows, and then Dunham emerges from the cockpit. The sun's all the way up now, but it's still cold. The wolves are long gone.

"This way," Wendy says, cocking her head, and starts to set off in the direction they went.

Dunham tries to come with us, but Wendy says, "Please. Stay here."

He looks like he wants to protest.

"We won't find them if you come with us," she says.

Dunham's shoulders drop. He nods. Turns back to the helicopter.

"Thank you," she calls after him, and he lifts his hand in a wave without looking back.

The three of us break into a trot.

"What was that all about?" I ask. "The helicopters, Hardy, everything!"

Wendy lopes along, as surefooted as a wolf. It's going to be hard to keep up with her. "Lacey overheard Hardy at the diner. He said he'd found a pilot who'd help him hunt wolves."

"You can do that?" I gasp.

"Yes and no," Wendy says. "Hardy can't *legally* kill a wolf from a helicopter, but who's going to stop him?"

"We did!" Holo says proudly.

We run another two hundred yards before Wendy answers.

"Thanks to Agent Dunham, we did," she says.

I push up my sleeves. It turns out that it's *not* cold, not if you're chasing after wolves. "How'd you get that jerk to do it?"

"Dunham's got a good heart," Wendy says.

"Could've fooled me," I say.

Wendy smiles grimly. "I think he feels sorry for me. I was the lost child. For decades. And that haunts him. Anyway, he's a good man, Kai."

I grunt. I'm going to need more proof.

Wendy slows down, then stops. She bends down to examine the ground. I try to catch my breath in this short pause.

"We're on the right track," she says, straightening.

So we start up again, slow and steady. If we have to, we'll go all day.

"If Hardy had illegally shot any wolves today," Wendy goes on, "he probably wouldn't have faced any consequences. For all I know, he'd get a bounty for their heads."

I'll never understand how someone could kill an animal so

wild and beautiful. And how someone else could pay them to do it. "One wolf is worth a million Hardys," I pant.

Holo sweeps his arm across the whole vista. The distant, snowcapped mountains look a million miles away. "There's enough room for all of us," he insists. "Wolves *and* people."

"Unfortunately that's not how most folks see it," Wendy says.

I know she's right, but it's another thing I'll never understand: how humans think that they're the only animal that matters.

We keep on going, not talking anymore. The minutes and the miles pass. Finally Wendy stops as we near the edge of the forested foothills. She's not out of breath in the slightest. She gives me the briefest, smallest of smiles. Then she lifts her chin and opens her mouth. A haunting, lonely howl rises from her throat, starting quietly and then building in strength. The sound is familiar and strange at the same time—part of language I know but somehow barely understand.

Holo and I join in. Goosebumps rise on my skin as we howl in harmony.

In the distance, I hear a faint answering call. Then another. Holo turns to me, eyes shining.

"They heard us," he says.

We sit down and wait. It feels like forever until I hear them, padding their way back to us. And I start sobbing the minute they come into view, tails wagging, tongues lolling. They're alive. They're *safe*.

Harriet crashes into Holo. Bim covers Wendy's face in kisses. The pups skitter around, biting everyone, and Ben circles us, yipping greetings. I approach Beast, who's standing nervously off to the side.

I sink to my knees in front of her. She steps toward me. Blinks. Whines.

I remember when I was younger, I would look deep into her golden eyes, and I could swear she understood everything about me. She loved me and made no judgments about me; I was in her pack, and that was all that mattered.

A human rarely looks at another human like that.

"I love you," I whisper.

Beast whines and her ears pitch forward. I reach out and touch her ruff. She smells like grass, like blood, like warm wet fur.

Wendy turns to me. Her face, like mine, is streaked with tears. "They have to go now," she says in a choked voice. "They have to go far away."

"How are you going to tell them that?" I ask. Knives of grief pierce my throat.

Wendy doesn't answer. I suppose she doesn't know how to explain it. But I know her bond with the wolves is deep— as deep as her bond is with us. She's known them since they were born. She knew their mothers and their fathers and their sisters and their brothers. There is a language, somewhere between human and wolf, that they alone speak.

Wendy flicks her hand and the wolves gather around her. She crouches down among them. Holo and I watch as their tails stop wagging. They hold themselves at complete attention. Listening. Understanding.

Finally Wendy stands. She gives three harsh claps that echo through the silent morning. "Go," she screams. "Go!"

There's just a single, tiny moment of hesitation. And then the wolves turn as one, slipping away into the brush like shadows.

Vanishing. Forever.

And I howl my sadness to the sky.

CHAPTER 81

I'M LEANING CLOSE to the bathroom mirror, trying to put on lipstick. Lacey told me I should look nice, so that's what I'm doing, even though I don't understand why looking nice involves painting my lips a different color. I also put on mascara, which makes my eyes look extra big. A little scared, too—or maybe that's just how they'd look anyway.

"Kai, we have to go!" Lacey calls. "We can't be late."

I quickly finish swiping the red across my lips and then run down the steps two at a time. Holo, who's waiting by the door, gives me a startled look.

"Did you put on makeup?" he asks.

"Yes."

"In the pitch dark?" he says. "With your left hand?" Then he cracks up.

I snarl at him. How am I supposed to be good at it? I've never done it before. I grab a Kleenex on my way out and wipe everything off. *At least my hair's brushed*, I think.

I'm also wearing a skirt for the first time in my life, plus a pair of Lacey's clogs. Holo's got on a button-down shirt and a tie Lacey must've tied for him. It looks like it's strangling him.

"You're beautiful children," she'd told us. "But you have to show them that you're *civilized*."

"Even if we're not," Holo had muttered.

Now, Lacey and the chief wear nervous expressions as we drive. Wendy sits in the back with us, dressed in Lacey's clothes and twisting her hands together in worry. I feel sick— from being in the car, as usual, but also from fear. We're headed to the county courthouse, where our future's going to be decided by a bunch of strangers.

Holo whines softly as he stares out the window.

"Hush," I tell him. "You have to remember to act human."

Even if it's too late for it to matter.

"Chester," Lacey says, "you missed the street."

The chief curses under his breath. Pulls a U-turn, makes a left, and then comes to a stop in front of a two-story brick building with white columns and an American flag hanging limply over the double front doors.

"I don't want to be here, either," Lacey says to us. "But everything's going to be fine, I just know it."

I hope she's right.

There are at least twenty people gathered on the sidewalk, sipping takeout coffee and chattering. They go silent when we climb out of the car. Their eyes follow me and my brother as we walk up the steps to the county courthouse.

Funny how people who never even bothered to *pretend* to care about me or Holo are suddenly so fascinated about what's going to happen to us now.

I can feel the growl building in my throat. But I don't let it out, because I'm trying to act civilized.

The courtroom where our fates are going to be decided is small, bright, and freezing cold. A man with a buzz cut and a weird, patchy mustache sits at a table on the left, making notes on a big pad of yellow paper.

"The state's lawyer," Lacey whispers. "Ellis Howells. People say he's such a you-know-what, his own mother doesn't like him."

"What's a you-know-what?" Holo asks.

"Just be quiet," I hiss.

The five of us sit down at the other table across the room. A few minutes later, a really pale, really tall man joins us. This is John Adkins, the lawyer for our side. He's someone the chief knows from high school, who came all the way from Boise to help us out.

"Good morning, everyone," he says with a reassuring smile. "Don't worry, we're going to get this settled real quick."

"From your lips to the good Lord's ears," Lacey says, nodding and crossing herself. But she smiles a little. She seems so sure that it's all going to work out.

Behind us, the spectators' benches fill up until people are practically sitting on one another's laps. What are they hoping to see? Me and Holo growling at the judge? I for one am not going to give them that satisfaction.

Then, just like on the TV shows Lacey likes, we rise for the Honorable Sue Bevins. Judge Bevins is short and seemingly round under a giant black robe. She gives an appraising glance around the room, nods, and then turns to Howells. "Good morning," she says curtly. "Mr. Howells, if you are ready to begin, you may make your opening statement."

Howells doesn't waste a single second. He says, "Your Honor, I've been a lawyer for thirty years, and I've never seen a case as strange as this one."

Gee, thanks. I've never seen a mustache *as strange as—*

Suddenly Howells is right in front of us, gesturing at us like we're Exhibit A of Courtroom Weirdness. "It sounds like a story," he says. "A *fairy tale*. A woman finds a little boy and a little girl lost in the woods. They are tiny. They are alone. And they are perhaps only minutes away from freezing to death. So she takes them home. She gives them food, and she warms them by the fire. She saves their lives. And that is the fairy tale part, Your Honor. But then the story gets darker. It concerns what this woman does—or *doesn't* do—next. Instead of making any effort to find their parents, or to alert the proper authorities, this woman decides to *keep* these children, and to raise them herself. Which she does, in utter solitude, for approximately twelve years."

The people in the room make little noises of shock. They look excited, too—like this case is going to be a lot better than TV. Way in the back I see Mrs. Hardy, with her bright orange hair and her small, mean eyes. The rest of the family's nowhere to be seen, but Mrs. Hardy keeps sending me quick, furious looks, like it's *my* fault that her husband got fined for illegal hunting.

Fine, maybe it is, considering I'm the one who told Chester all about it. But I won't pretend I'm sorry.

Howells stands taller, clearly relishing the audience reaction.

His voice grows bolder. "But then, just this spring, Kai and Holo *escaped*—"

"Objection," John Adkins says.

The judge raises an eyebrow. "Sustained."

Howells isn't fazed. "Your Honor, Kai and Holo 'left Wendy's care' in April. Immediately upon their arrival in Kokanee Creek, they burgled and vandalized a store. They threatened an employee. The police were called, and they were taken to jail. After spending the night there, Kai and Holo were taken in by the chief of police, Chester Greene, and his partner, Lacey Hernandez. The couple enrolled the children in the local high school, where they got into numerous altercations with other students. During this time, the woman who raised the children, Wendy Marsden"—and here he points to her, a sneer on his face—"made no effort to find or contact them."

There's more murmuring among the spectators. A woman with blond braids glares at Wendy, like *How could you? You monster!* I wish Holo would bite her. I wish he would bite everyone in the courtroom.

"Now, no one is on trial here today," Howells says smarmily. "Though certainly there is much evidence of wrongdoing by the concerned parties. We are here because of these two lost children. Their fate—their entire *future*—is up to us. It is our solemn duty to do right by them." He pauses to let that sink in.

The spectators nod. As if they have any idea what's best for us! As if they even *care*.

"It is our opinion," says Howells, "that doing right by Kai and Holo means making them wards of the state of Idaho."

CHAPTER 82

MY WHOLE BODY goes rigid. My brain even seems to shut down. I struggle to focus as Howells calls Principal Simon to the stand. She says something about our "incredible intelligence, matched only by an equally incredible belligerence" and says we need much more supervision and support than we're getting—I catch *that* much. Then there's Arlene Pettibon, talking about Holo's violent tendencies, and Mrs. Hardy wiping away tears about how we bullied her two giant sons.

None of it is true, and none of it is fair.

Holo is gripping both Lacey's and Wendy's hands, looking whiter than snow. The chief just looks furious.

John Adkins's cross-examinations don't help, either. Ms. Pettibon and Mrs. Hardy keep insisting that we're wild. Not just uncivilized—*dangerous*.

"Don't worry," Adkins says as we break for lunch. "You have to think about a court case like a basketball game. You're down in the first half, but you come back in the second."

"We'd better," the chief says darkly.

Arlene Pettibon passes by him. "Lovely day, isn't it, Chief Greene," she trills.

Why can't he arrest her for her stupid, simpering smile? I can't stand Arlene Pettibon, and I can't stand being in this courthouse any longer. Mumbling "I'll be back" to Wendy, I practically run outside, where the sun's shining and the birds are chirping and it looks like any other stupid beautiful spring morning.

I want to kick something and scream at someone. Instead I collapse down onto a bench and dig my fists into my eye sockets.

All of this is my fault.

"Hey you," says a low, gentle voice.

I look up, blinking and squinting against the sun. It's Waylon Eugene Meloy, wearing a pair of new Levi's and a sport coat that looks like it's been kept in a trunk for forty years.

I try to unclench my fists. "Came to watch the show, huh?" I ask flatly.

"I came to see you," he says. "You haven't been in school."

I nod. Shrug. I hadn't gone back to Kokanee Creek High School after the dance. I couldn't see any reason to.

"I guess I wasn't feeling much like a Cougar," I say.

Waylon sits down on the bench next to me. "That's because you're really more of a wolf," he says, taking my hand. He brings my fingers to his lips and kisses them.

A sob I can't let out lodges painfully in my throat. Waylon doesn't know what happened with Beast and her family. *My* family. Waylon doesn't understand what's at stake for all of us.

I can't be the one to tell him.

Oh, Beast—Bim—Ben—Harriet—I miss you.

Why didn't we follow you? Why didn't we run when we had the chance?

I know the answer to that, of course: Because we trusted the chief when he said that everything was going to be okay.

Waylon digs the scuffed toe of his boot into the sidewalk. "School's not nearly as fun without you," he says.

I push thoughts of Beast and her pups from my mind. Fake a small, wry smile. "Are you having trouble finding someone to pass annoying notes to in ELA?"

Waylon nods. "Yes. It's very depressing. But on the bright side, I'm pleased to report that, thanks to you, Mac Hardy has two extremely black eyes."

"Good." I wish I'd knocked his eyeballs right out of his head.

Waylon kisses my fingers again and desire fills me—desire mixed with fear and grief. I pull my hand away.

"I'm sorry," I whisper. "It's too much."

"You're smart enough you could go straight to college. You know that, right?" Waylon says, with a sudden urgency in his voice. "You could take a test. Get your GED this summer. You could go to the University of Idaho, too."

"Uh-huh," I say, as if this is a possibility, which it isn't. I don't even know if I would want it to be. Right now I don't know anything at all.

Waylon says, "You don't mean that, I can tell."

I twist the silver bracelet that Lacey fastened onto my wrist this morning. "Who's to say what'll happen? It feels like ever since I came out of the woods, everything in my entire life has been a surprise." I look up at him. I feel suddenly shy. "Especially meeting you."

Waylon grins. "Yeah, well, I certainly didn't expect to meet a feral hottie with a bunch of canid siblings—"

I put my finger over his lips to shush him. I know he's just trying to lighten the mood, but I realize that I have something serious to say to him. "Shut up and listen," I say. "Because right now I need to thank you."

He looks at me quizzically. "What for?"

"Thank you for being so reckless that you ended up in jail that day. Thanks for saying hi to me. And for being such a weirdo that you don't mind hanging out with other weirdos."

"Well, honestly, I—"

"I said shut up," I tell him. "I'm not done yet. Thank you for terrifying me on your motorcycle and for teaching me how to dance so badly. Thank you for my rites of passage." I take a deep breath. It's hard to say all this, but it feels good to do it. "Remember back when we were in jail, you said that being your friend might just change my life?"

"Yes, and—"

"What part of shut up do you not understand? You were right, though. It did change my life. So thank you, Waylon Eugene Meloy, for being my friend, and for being funny and gorgeous and maybe just a little bit dangerous—"

Then Waylon's hands are on my cheeks and his warm, soft lips are against my own. We kiss for a long time. And when he pulls away, he looks like someone is ripping the heart right out of his chest.

"I just want more time with you," he says. "You can't let them take you away."

"I won't," I say.

Being with him makes me believe it.

CHAPTER 83

AFTER LUNCH, ELLIS Howells calls Chester Greene to the stand.

The chief moves stiffly to the front of the room, obviously uncomfortable in his new suit and tie. He sits down and clears his throat, looking at Howells like he'd rather fight him in the street than answer his questions in a courtroom.

"We attempted to identify and locate Kai and Holo's family," the chief testifies. "But they do not remember their parents, and there were no reports of missing children matching Kai and Holo's descriptions. They don't know their last name, and if they have birth certificates, no one knows where they are." He looks over toward our table and his eyes meet mine before flicking away again. "Kai and Holo might not *officially* exist."

Howells paces the floor in front of the judge. "But what made you think you should take them home with you? What is it about these two children that causes the adults they encounter to lay spurious claims to them?"

"What does *spurious* mean?" Holo whispers.

"Shhh," I hiss.

"It means false," Lacey tells him. "I swear, if that you-know-what keeps talking, I'm going to—"

"Objection, Your Honor," John Adkins blurts. "Conjecture."

"Sustained."

"What you need to know," the chief says stiffly, "is that I became a police officer because I wanted to help people, and because I wanted to serve my community. I've always done what I thought was right and best. So when those two children came running out of the woods, wild and scared, what seemed best to me was to take care of them. You can't do that in a jail. So I let them into my home. I told myself I could teach them about life among...well, among other humans." He glances over at Holo and me again, and his expression softens. "Though I'm pretty sure they taught me more than I taught them."

"That's very poetic," Howells says. "What I ask the court to remember is that you, Chief Greene, did not maintain contact with the proper authorities, including Ms. Pettibon. You did not go through official channels when you took those children into your home."

"I didn't know if they were lost, or if they were runaways, or if they were abandoned on purpose! All I know is that they were *cared for.* Kai and Holo were loved by Wendy, and they were loved by us."

Howells practically sneers at this. "Love doesn't negate *laws*," he says. "You talk as if Kai and Holo were stray kittens you could take home with you! But we don't play finders keepers with human children."

"I'm well aware of that fact," the chief says. "But I was working on their case. I have been all along. But as far as I could
tell, they had nowhere else to go."

"Right. Until you discovered Wendy. And the whole entire
past that Kai and Holo had lied about." When the chief doesn't
say anything, Howells presses him. "You learned that these
two adolescents had been lying about where they lived."

The chief sighs. "Yes."

"But Kai and Holo still did not reveal their true identities."

The chief throws up his hands. "Because they don't know
them!" he cries. "Look," he goes on, "say a girl runs away from
home and she winds up on the streets. She meets a boy out
there. They grow up together, sleeping rough in Seattle or
Boise. Eventually they have a couple of kids themselves. They
do this all on their own. They live their lives off the grid and
under the radar. And so when they go missing in the woods,
no one notices that they're gone. No one knows to look for the
two little kids they left behind, whether on purpose or not.
Thank God that Wendy was living out there in the national
forest. Otherwise a hunter or a hiker would have stumbled
across two tiny, frozen corpses."

I swear I hear a stifled sob from the back of the room.
*Wow, does someone actually feel sorry for the kids they called
animals—freaks?*

"That's quite a story, Chief Greene," Howells says.

"You got a better theory?" the chief challenges. "The point
is, the story I just told has a happy ending—that is, if you
and the state of Idaho will stay out of it. Kai and Holo have
people who love them and will take care of them until we can

find their next of kin. And Wendy Marsden, who was lost for decades, has been found."

Howells smiles smugly. "And you are of the opinion that Wendy should continue to raise Kai and Holo?"

The chief hesitates. Lacey goes tense.

"Yes," the chief finally says. His voice is emotionless. "I am of that opinion."

Lacey's shoulders slump down. She reaches for my hand and squeezes it. "I knew I couldn't keep you," she whispers. "But I wanted to."

CHAPTER 84

FINALLY HOWELLS RESTS his case, and our lawyer, John Adkins, calls his first witness. He and the chief had agreed that Wendy was too fragile to testify—she's shaking even now, and tears keep trickling down her cheeks—so Nancy Bankowski, our guardian ad litem, walks to the stand instead. She's our court-appointed legal advocate—and, unlike Ellis Howells, she knows us (at least a little) and cares about what we want. She visited us at the chief's last week, and asked us all kinds of questions about Wendy and the wolves.

As Judge Bevins listens, nodding now and again, Nancy explains how we've been cared for by Wendy for all of our conscious lives, and that Wendy has provided a loving and stable home. "Considering that the authorities have been unable to locate actual blood relatives," Nancy says, "there is no one better suited to care for Kai and Holo than Wendy." She turns to Howells and adds, "And even if a relative *could* be found, I still believe these children should be allowed to stay with the woman who raised them."

"Please elaborate," Adkins says. He knows she's making a good case. That the judge is really listening.

"Barring neglect or abuse, our goal is always to keep kids with their parents. Since Kai and Holo don't know who their parents are, they should be with the person they know and love. Wendy loved them, fed them, homeschooled them, and taught them the skills to survive. For all intents and purposes, she is their mother."

Howells is scribbling madly on his yellow notepad. When it's his turn to cross-examine, his questions sound more like accusations. "One of the skills Wendy Marsden taught Kai and Holo was thievery, is that right?"

Nancy blinks at him. "I don't know what you're talking about."

"We have reports of campground thefts that date back *years*. Not valuable things, like camp stoves or flashy tents. But food. Batteries. Aspirin."

Holo and I share a quick, worried glance.

"The sorts of things people living in the woods might need."

"You have no proof that Kai and Holo had anything to do with those thefts," Nancy says.

Howells paces, back and forth, back and forth. "Circumstantial evidence is still *evidence*," he says. "But let's move on. Another of the guardian's duties is to ensure that a child has proper medical and dental care. Did Wendy ever take these children to a medical professional?"

"I can't be certain," Nancy says.

She knows full well we never went to a doctor, barring that old windbag the chief brought into our jail cell. But Nancy doesn't want to give Howells anything he can use against Wendy.

"What about a child's emotional growth? Is raising children in utter isolation a healthy parenting strategy?"

Nancy crosses her arms across her chest. "Holo and Kai seem very well-adjusted."

"And would you say that robbing a store and getting into fights at school is a sign of being well-adjusted?"

"I'd say that there were extenuating circumstances," Nancy says.

Howells smirks at her. "And what might those be?"

Nancy looks back in defiance. "I've got plenty of opinions," she says. "But why don't you ask the two of them?"

CHAPTER 85

I DIDN'T REALIZE how terrifying it would be to take the stand—to face a roomful of glaring strangers and try to say what I wanted to say. Mrs. Hardy's shooting daggers at me with her eyes. The lady with the blond braids just stares, her mouth hanging open like she can't wait for me to do something crazy. When I have to swear that I'm going to tell the truth and nothing but the truth, I can barely get my words out.

The judge says gently, "I think you've been through a lot lately, Kai, and I don't see the need for you to be examined and cross-examined and put through that particular wringer." She even gives me a little smile. "So I just want to talk to you for a minute."

Her kindness brings a lump to my throat. Any minute now my eyes'll start their waterworks.

I swear, once all this is over I'm not going to cry for another seventeen years.

"Holo and I just want to be with Wendy," I say. "Lacey and the chief have been amazing to us, but Wendy is our mother.

It doesn't matter who gave birth to us. Whoever she is, she's been gone for twelve years. If she's alive—and I don't think she is—she's a stranger to us."

"I understand your desire to stay with Wendy Marsden. But what about the fact that you have no home now?"

Yes, that's definitely a problem. "We'll build another one," I say.

"Not on public land, I hope."

"No."

Not where you can find it, anyway.

"Has Wendy made any efforts to find new housing?"

"It's only been ten days since that armed posse came to our house."

"I'll take that as a no," Judge Bevins says, looking down at me over the top of her glasses.

I feel like her sympathies are changing. She doesn't like Howells any more than we do, but that doesn't matter. In the eyes of the court, Wendy hasn't behaved like a proper mother.

The tears I kept from falling in front of Waylon spill out of my eyes, down my cheeks, and onto my stupid, uncomfortable blouse.

"You have to understand," I say, my voice breaking. "The three of us never had that much, and now we've lost it all. The house—the wolves—the life that we made. All we have left is each other." I look out to the room and meet Waylon's gaze, and then I look to Lacey and the chief. "And a few people who care about us. The rest of the world doesn't want us. It doesn't understand us." Then I narrow my eyes at Howells. At the people from Kokanee Creek who've come to watch our fates be decided by strangers. "It thinks we belong in a cage."

Holo's face is buried in Wendy's shoulder. She's crying, and I know he is, too.

"We aren't dangerous," I say pleadingly. "We're not troubled. And we're not wild animals. We're just people who live a different life than you do. People who care about different things, like trees and deer and wide-open spaces, and who don't care about air conditioning or fast food restaurants or high school or any of the shit you all think is important!" Judge Bevins raises one silver eyebrow. "I'm sorry, Your Honor," I say quickly. "I meant to say 'stuff.'"

She nods. "Thank you, Kai," she says. "You're a well-spoken young lady. Most of the time." And then she smiles at me as if she likes me.

And I tell myself that everything's going to be all right.

CHAPTER 86

AN HOUR AFTER the lawyers make their closing statements, Judge Bevins strides back into the courtroom. Her expression is impossible to read. She sits down and carefully spreads her black robe around her. It's like she's trying to take as much time as possible while the whole room holds its breath. Except for Holo, who sniffs at the air like he might be able to *smell* what she's thinking.

I'm gripping Wendy's hand with my left hand and Holo's with my right; Holo's also squeezing Lacey's fingers so tight that his knuckles are bloodless.

Judge Bevins leans forward and speaks into the microphone. "This is one of the more difficult decisions I've had to make," she says slowly. "One must weigh the integrity of the family unit against the integrity of its actions. The matter of love versus the matter of the law." The microphone squawks, and Judge Bevins jumps a little. Frowns. "Children belong with their parents, whenever this is possible. But what if there are no parents to be found? No relatives?" She pauses. Folds

327

her hands together in front of her chest. "Then they must become the wards of the state until a permanent home can be found for them."

"No!" I scream before anyone can shush me. "You can't do this!"

"Kai," Adkins says. "Be quiet."

"In some circumstances," the judge goes on, "the court could see fit to let minors reside with the woman who has been caring for them. But considering how habitually and unrepentantly Wendy Marsden broke the law—and seems to have encouraged the minors in her care to do the same— we cannot in good conscience allow her to raise two more offenders."

Beside me, Wendy and Lacey are sobbing. The chief's face is red and furious. But the judge isn't done.

"And considering Kai and Holo's record of misdemeanors and altercations, we believe it is best for them to take up residence at the Brookside Juvenile Facility."

Shock and fury keep my tears at bay. I stand up and shout, "Who are you to say what's best for us? You don't know anything about us!"

Everyone in the courtroom audience is suddenly talking at the same time. Are they glad we're going? Do they think that justice has been served? I don't know and I don't care.

"You can't make us go!" I scream.

Judge Bevins slams the gavel. "Quiet!" she yells. "I have rendered my decision."

I turn to my brother. Terror twists his face. "*Run*," I say.

He does what I tell him. Just like he always has, because I'm the alpha. We jump up from our chairs and race toward the exit. Wendy cries out. The chief's calling my name. I think Lacey already fainted.

I'm sorry—but we have to save ourselves.

CHAPTER 87

I EXPLODE ONTO the sidewalk and sprint across the street. A car honks, swerves, screeches to a halt. "Hey!" the driver calls. "Watch out!"

Holo catches up to me. His arms and legs pump. His breath's already coming hard. So's mine. We're not as fast as we used to be.

"Where are we going?" he pants.

"The woods!"

There's a stand of trees about a mile off. I don't know what's on the other side of it, but I'm praying for more trees, a forest that goes on forever. A forest we can get lost in.

I can hear people shouting behind us, calling for us to stop, but their voices are growing fainter. Maybe we're not as fast as we used to be, but we're still faster than everyone else.

We cut down an alleyway behind a grocery store. Dodge forklifts and a delivery truck behind the hardware store. Skid around the corner and come out across the street from a city park.

So close to safety.

Holo's fading, though.

"Come on!" I shout. "Keep up with me!"

He digs deep, finds another burst of speed. We race into the park, passing a little duck pond and a handful of people throwing balls for their dogs. One of the dogs comes after us, thinking this is a game. He nips at Holo's heels until I take off my bracelet and throw it at him. It hits him on the nose and he veers off with a yip.

"Nice one," Holo gasps.

I'm breathing too hard to answer. My thighs are on fire. But I can see on the other side of the park there's the highway, and then the trees. We're almost there. Just a few hundred more yards.

Holo stumbles. I yank at his sleeve, *come on, come on!*

Police sirens sound in the distance. It doesn't matter. They're too far away. And they can't drive into a forest.

We come to the edge of the highway and pause. I bend over, trying to catch my breath while I wait for a break in the cars. Holo puts his hands on his knees, too. His face is almost purple.

"Five-minute mile, I bet," he says. His chest is heaving.

"Don't gloat yet," I manage. I straighten up. "Wait till we're hiding. We can cross right after this red truck passes us."

But the red truck doesn't pass us. It slows. The window rolls down.

"Shit, Holo, *go!*" I scream.

We race across the road, nearly getting hit again. Behind us I can hear the truck's engine rev, and the next thing I know it comes flying down the berm on the forest side of the highway. It passes us on the dirt and spins out right in front of us, blocking our way. Out of the driver's window pokes the barrel of a gun. Then Hardy's narrow, mean face.

"You two animals better stay right where you are," he sneers.

Holo and I look at each other. Do we dare?

I nod, ever so slightly. *We dare.*

At the exact same time we launch ourselves in opposite directions, Holo around the front of the truck, me around the back. We only have that little field to cross and then we'll vanish into the trees.

A bullet smashes into the ground near my feet. Holo screams in fear. Just a little bit more—

Then something huge hits me from behind. Pain explodes in my shoulder as I land hard on the ground. The next thing I know, my hands are being roughly yanked behind my back and I feel the cold click of handcuffs around my wrists.

"Citizen's arrest," Hardy growls.

Mac has Holo in a headlock. Holo's howling and snapping his teeth.

A police van comes bumping over the ground, kicking up clouds of dust. It lurches to a halt and out come three cops.

"We'll take it from here," the biggest one says.

As he stalks toward us, I'm yelling for the chief—for Wendy, for Waylon—but none of them can hear me. Holo and I are yanked up and shoved into the back of the van. Holo gnashes his teeth and cries, and I scream my rage as loud as I can.

But no one comes to save us.

No one will. No one can.

Our story ends like it started—with a chase, a fight, and then handcuffs.

A cage.

EPILOGUE

CHAPTER 88

CHESTER'S EATING LUNCH at the KC Diner when he gets the call. He doesn't finish his burger and he doesn't pay his bill. He just runs out the door. He hears Lacey calling after him, but there's no time to explain. He'll text her later. Right now he just has to *go*.

He sprints down the street to the station, grabs his keys, and throws himself into the car. The map on his phone says it's a forty-eight-minute drive.

Chester bets God fifty bucks he can make it in thirty-five.

But the voice in his head is wondering what the rush is. *Isn't it already too late?* the voice asks.

Chester just ignores it. A man can't always be logical. Sometimes the irrational heart takes over. And the heart says, *Get there as fast as you can*.

Chester takes the back way out of town. Pulling onto the highway, he hits ninety-five miles an hour, then a hundred. Sirens blaring, lights flashing. The cars ahead of him seem to melt out of his way as they pull over to the side of the road. If he weren't so upset it might be thrilling. It's not every day he has an excuse to drive as fast as his old cruiser will go.

Then again, it's not every day he gets news as bad as this.

Thirty-two minutes later, he arrives at his destination, a cinder-block sprawl in the middle of nowhere, with a chain-link yard under a cloudy white sky. The director of the facility is there in the lobby waiting for him, his hands clasped at his waist and a concerned expression on his face. "I'm so sorry," Roy Washburn says. "We really didn't see this coming."

Chester tightens his fists in anger. Says, "You're a *locked facility*."

The director turns pink. "Yes, we are. But we can't always control for human error—or human ingenuity."

"So which was it?" Chester demands. "Did one of you people fuck up, or did those kids trick you?"

"We are currently investigating," says Washburn.

Chester sinks down into one of the hard lobby chairs. A cyclone of emotions swirls inside him, the greatest of which are fury at Brookside and fear for Kai and Holo.

Where have they gone? Will they be okay?

"How did it happen?" he asks.

Washburn wipes his brow with a yellowing handkerchief. "As I said, the matter is under investigation. What we do know is that they escaped during their shift on road cleanup crew."

"Road cleanup crew?" Chester repeats, incredulous. "That's what convicts in state custody do!"

"We find that giving our residents responsibilities improves their behavior and their spirits."

"And how did you find Kai and Holo's spirits?" Chester

practically spits. "Because the last time I saw them they were pretty damn unhappy here."

Barring the sheen of sweat on his brow, Washburn is unruffled. "They were starting to make a few friends. But they did still have a tendency to growl at the staff."

"I wonder why," Chester says sarcastically.

"They had a visitor just yesterday," Washburn goes on. "A kid on a motorcycle. I can't remember his name."

"Waylon Meloy," Chester says. Thinking, *If he had anything to do with this, I'm going to throw him into jail so hard he'll bounce.*

"Take me to their rooms," Chester says. "I want to see if there's anything—"

"Of course," Washburn says. "Follow me."

But even as he does, Chester knows he won't find anything. Kai and Holo are way too smart. They aren't going to leave any tracks.

CHAPTER 89

CHESTER RINGS DUNHAM on Sunday morning. They're not friends, not by a long shot, but Chester's come to realize that they're on the same side. They both want the best for Wendy and those kids.

Not that they've been able to get it. Dunham finally located a couple of Marsdens down in Florida, but he hadn't been able to convince Wendy to talk to them. Meanwhile Chester had spent the last three months visiting his favorite wolf kids in juvie.

When Dunham picks up, Chester says, "Kai and Holo ran."

"What?"

"I can't locate Wendy, either. The number I had for her has been disconnected."

Dunham's working out of Pocatello now, a couple of hours south. He makes a low noise in his throat. Almost sounds like a wolf growl. Then he says, "Runaways aren't an FBI matter."

"I know that," Chester says. "That's why I called you on your day off."

"Shit," Dunham sighs.

He shows up in Kokanee Creek three hours later, wearing a pair of hiking boots and carrying a nylon daypack. The men take Chester's truck up the logging road as far as they can into the hills, and then they start walking. Chester marked the trees on the hike out the last time, so big chalk X's lead them toward the cabin. Chester carries a pack with water and Lacey's homemade trail mix. They ford a couple of creeks. Scramble up embankments. Duck under fallen trees.

"You didn't tell me it'd take this long," Dunham grumbles.

"You should've brought your bird," Chester says. "I never got to ride in it."

Dunham grunts. "They don't give me the keys."

Chester freezes. Says, "Shhh."

Ahead of them, barely visible through the trees, is a big buck. He stands there, head lifted, listening.

Chester's heart pounds. The stag stares at them for a long time, regal as a king. "Not gonna hurt you," Chester whispers.

In the quiet he can hear Dunham's hard breathing. His own, too. They've been hiking for nearly six miles now and they're sweating and exhausted. Generations ago, their ancestors might've belonged in woods like these, but the two of them don't. They belong behind desks. Beneath artificial lights. Their food wrapped in plastic and heated in a microwave.

It's a shame, Chester thinks, *what we've done to ourselves. What we've done to just about everything we touch.*

The deer swivels its head. A second later, it turns and bounds away.

"Wow," Dunham says softly. "That was something."

Then they keep walking. After another few miles, the trees thin out a little. The creek cuts back west. And Chester can see the cabin in the distance. His heart starts pounding.

The door's open.

He drops his pack and runs.

CHAPTER 90

THEY'RE NOT HERE.

Chester realizes it with a sickening twist in his stomach. A film of gray dust covers everything. There's a nest of field mice in the corner of a pillow. His lip curls at the sight of those pink, blind, wriggling babies.

On the seat of a handmade chair he finds a folded slip of paper. *To Chief Greene*, it says.

Chester opens it and reads, blinking away tears.

I wish I didn't have to write this. I wish your last visit to Brookside wasn't the last time I'd ever see you and Lacey.

When you live alone in the woods, there's no one to meet—but there's no one to say goodbye to, either. I don't know what's better. What's easier.

I learned a lot, living in your world. Though sometimes I think that what I learned most is how much I don't know and don't understand.

Like: why is a cow's life worth more than a wolf's?

What is it about land that makes you all want to put a fence around it?

Why is a phone more interesting than a bird?

Why did people treat us so badly?

I guess I'll wonder about those kinds of things for a while.

But here's what I know. I know there's no such thing as a bad wolf, but you sure as hell can't say that about your fellow man. Doesn't that bum you out a little?

It's true that nature doesn't care about me, but she doesn't care about anyone. She just is. And we do our best to live by her rules.

I'll miss Lacey's beautiful voice and your fake-grumpy smile. I'll miss watching TV with you in the living room, even though all your shows were terrible. I'll miss the little yellow room under the eaves that took in a girl from the woods.

You and Lacey would make great parents. I know, because I overheard it, that she wanted to keep us. But you understand that we could never be yours. We—me, Holo, and Wendy—belong only to ourselves.

We'll always be lost children.

We're going far away, but sometimes, in the middle of a moonlit night, you might just hear us howl.

Love,
Kai

P.S. I never once called you anything but "the chief." I'm sorry, Chester.
P.P.S. We'll miss you. Always.

Chester folds up the note and sticks it into his pocket. He roughly wipes at his eyes.

"You okay?" Dunham asks.

"Does it look like it?" Chester says gruffly.

Dunham claps him on the shoulder. Says, "I'm sorry, brother. But you know, if you need to track them down, I might know a guy who doesn't forget and who doesn't give up." He points his thumbs toward his own chest.

Chester smiles grimly. "To get the FBI involved would mean accusing Wendy Marsden of kidnapping."

"It would," Dunham says. "I guess it just depends on how much you want them back. Or maybe you think they're better off out there, wherever they are."

Chester takes a final glance around the cabin. Dusty as it is, it's cozy. Welcoming. It feels like a home.

"I think this would've been a nice place to grow up," Chester says.

And that settles it. They start walking the long way back to town.

CHAPTER 91

I WAKE JUST as the sun is peeking over the mountains. For a few minutes I don't move except to snuggle deeper into my sleeping bag. Beside me, Holo snores softly. On the other side of him, Wendy breathes slow and steady.

Even at this elevation, it's cozy in our lean-to. But then again, it's still summer. Soon we'll have to think more seriously about how to keep ourselves warm and fed. But for now we're enjoying the long, warm days and the cool, star-filled nights.

I stretch my arms, wiggle my fingers and toes, and then I get up to get the fire going. A silvery mist hangs over the lake. Every once in a while I hear the splash of a jumping fish.

Aka *breakfast*.

We have actual fishing poles now. Lightweight sleeping bags, too, water filters, headlamps, first aid kits, and even a tiny propane camp stove. It's useful gear, but it's also a disguise: We look like backpackers instead of runaways.

During the three hellish months Holo and I spent in

Brookside, Wendy worked as a gardener in Ashton, getting paid under the table and saving every penny she made. Small-town squirrels made for easy hunting, she said, and people never locked up their henhouses.

By the time we escaped, Wendy had more money than any of us had ever seen. Between that and a few visits to unattended campsites (sorry, not sorry), we fully outfitted ourselves for adventure.

And by adventure, of course, I mean spending the rest of our lives on the run.

I know it didn't have to be this way. I know that every single messed-up thing that happened to us was my fault. If I hadn't coaxed Holo out of the woods, we'd still be in that little cabin, with ourselves and the wolves for company.

But we also would have never known what it was like to make a friend, or fly over the treetops. We would have never tasted a milkshake. I would have never had my first kiss.

So was it all a big mistake?

I don't know the answer to that question right now, and I'm not sure I ever will. What I do know is that the sun is getting higher in the sky, and my stomach is growling, and there is my human family to feed—and my wolf family to find.

Ahh-wooooooo!!

JAMES PATTERSON
THE WORLD'S #1 BESTSELLING WRITER

ABOUT THE AUTHORS

James Patterson is the most popular storyteller of our time. He is the creator of unforgettable characters and series, including Alex Cross, the Women's Murder Club, Jane Smith, and Maximum Ride, and of breathtaking true stories about the Kennedys, John Lennon, and Tiger Woods, as well as our military heroes, police officers, and ER nurses. Patterson has coauthored #1 bestselling novels with Bill Clinton and Dolly Parton, and collaborated most recently with Michael Crichton on the blockbuster *Eruption*. He has told the story of his own life in *James Patterson by James Patterson*, and received an Edgar Award, ten Emmy Awards, the Literarian Award from the National Book Foundation, and the National Humanities Medal.

Emily Raymond worked with James Patterson on *First Love* and *The Lost*, and is the ghostwriter of six young adult novels, one of which was a #1 *New York Times* bestseller. She lives with her family in Portland, Oregon.

JAMES
PATTERSON
RECOMMENDS

JAMES
PATTERSON
& ANDREW BOURELLE

THE WORLD'S #1 BEST-SELLING WRITER

TEXAS
★
RANGER

OFFICER RORY YATES COMES HOME—TO A MURDER CHARGE

TEXAS RANGER

So many of my detectives are dark and gritty and deal with crimes in some of our grimmest cities. That's why I'm thrilled to bring you Detective Rory Yates, my most honorable detective yet.

As a Texas Ranger, he has a code that he lives and works by. But when he comes home for a much-needed break, he walks into a crime scene where the victim is none other than his ex-wife—and he's the prime suspect. Yates has to risk everything in order to clear his name, and he dives into the inferno of the most twisted mind I've ever created. Can his code bring him back out alive?

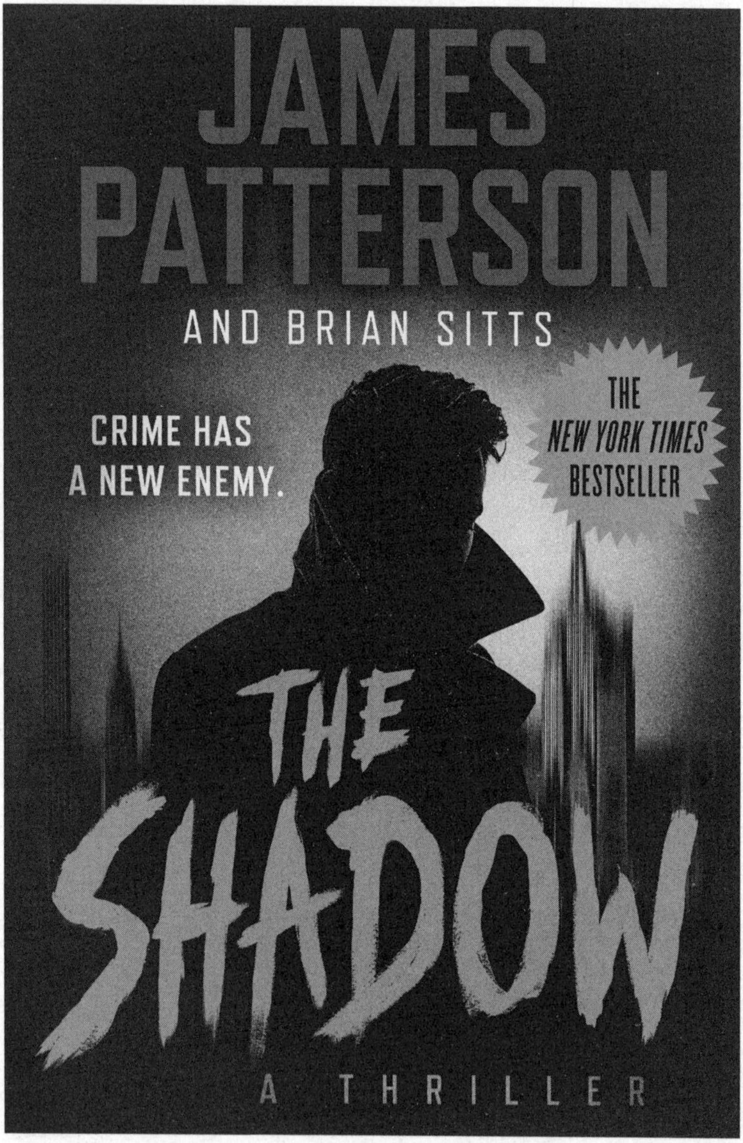
JAMES PATTERSON
AND BRIAN SITTS
CRIME HAS A NEW ENEMY.
THE NEW YORK TIMES BESTSELLER
THE SHADOW
A THRILLER

THE SHADOW

Only two people know that 1930s society man Lamont Cranston has a secret identity as the Shadow, a crusader for justice—well, make that three if you include me, and it is my great honor to reimagine his story. But the other two are his greatest love, Margo Lane, and his fiercest enemy, Shiwan Khan. When Khan ambushes the couple, they must risk everything for the slimmest chance of survival...in the future.

A century and a half later, Lamont awakens in a world both unknown and disturbingly familiar. Most disturbing, Khan's power continues to be felt over the city and its people. No one in this new world understands the dangers of stopping him better than Lamont Cranston. And only the Shadow knows that he's the one person who might succeed before more innocent lives are lost.

JAMES PATTERSON

1ST
TIME IN
PRINT

THE MIDWIFE MURDERS

and RICHARD DiLALLO

THE MIDWIFE MURDERS

I can't imagine a worse crime than one done against a child. But when two kidnappings and a vicious stabbing happen on senior midwife Lucy's watch in a university hospital in Manhattan, her focus abruptly changes. Something has to be done, and she's fearless enough to try.

Rumors begin to swirl, with blame falling on everyone from the Russian mafia to an underground adoption network. Fierce single mom Lucy teams up with a skeptical NYPD detective, but I've given her a case where the truth is far more twisted than Lucy could ever have imagined.

From the Creator of the #1 Bestselling Women's Murder Club

JAMES PATTERSON

2 SISTERS

DETECTIVE AGENCY

FIRST TIME IN PRINT

& CANDICE FOX

2 SISTERS DETECTIVE AGENCY

Discovering secrets about your own family has a way of changing your life...for better or for worse. Attorney Rhonda Bird learns that her estranged father had stopped being an accountant and opened up a private detective agency—and that she has a teenage half sister named Baby.

When Baby brings in a client to the detective agency, the two sisters become entangled in a dangerous case involving a group of young adults who break laws for fun, their psychopath ringleader, and an ex-assassin who decides to hunt them down for revenge.

For a complete list of books by

JAMES PATTERSON

VISIT
JamesPatterson.com

 Follow James Patterson on Facebook
@JamesPatterson

 Follow James Patterson on X
𝕏 **@JP_Books**

 Follow James Patterson on Instagram
@jamespattersonbooks